PRAISE FOR

PAWS FOR MURDER

"Welcome to Merryville, Minnesota, and Izzy McHale's Trendy Tails Pet Boutique. Not only will you find the cleverly designed pet togs hard to resist—you'll soon be yearning for more adventures with Izzy; her best friend, Rena; and pet pals, Packer and Jinx. Annie Knox has created a warm, funny, flawed but completely endearing sleuth in Izzy McHale, and I'm already panting for the next book in the series."

—Miranda James, *New York Times* bestselling author of the Cat in the Stacks mysteries

"Five paws up! Annie Knox dazzles with four-legged friends, fashion, and foul play. *Paws for Murder* is tailor-made for the pet and mystery lover."

—Melissa Bourbon, author of *A Killing Notion*

"Everything you could hope for in a good cozy. . . . I spent the duration of the tale dying to know what happens next yet simultaneously wanting to savor every word. The story is swiftly paced, the plot is tightly woven, and the mystery's a real head-scratcher."

—*Crimespree Magazine*

"A witty whodunit, *Paws for Murder* marks a strong debut, one that fans of corpses and canines, felonies and felines, will lap up."   —*Richmond Times-Dispatch*

continued . . .

"This was a fast-paced, action-filled drama that once I started I could not put down. . . . With a lovable yet quirky cast of characters, witty and engaging dialogue, and a feel-good atmosphere, this book is full of tailor-made charm."   —Dru's Book Musings

"The characters you will meet in this book are strong, vibrant ones and you will find yourself there in Merryville, helping to solve the case! This was such a fantastic read! I couldn't put it down. Annie is great at her craft and you can see it in this book!"
                                                              —Shelley's Book Case

"The mystery weaved through the entire book [keeps] readers guessing until the end . . . [a] great start to a fun series!"   —Socrates' Book Reviews

"A charming read and an enchanting start to a rich new series."   —Thoughts in Progress

"If you are a fan of cozies, you will definitely like this one. Animal lover? This is for you. Like both and you're in for a treat. *Paws for Murder* by Annie Knox is delightful, with loads of images to brighten each page."
                                                              —BookLoons

ALSO AVAILABLE BY ANNIE KNOX

The Pet Boutique Mystery Series

Paws for Murder

Groomed for Murder

A PET
BOUTIQUE MYSTERY

Annie Knox

AN OBSIDIAN MYSTERY

OBSIDIAN
Published by the Penguin Group
Penguin Group (USA) LLC, 375 Hudson Street,
New York, New York 10014

USA | Canada | UK | Ireland | Australia | New Zealand | India | South Africa | China
penguin.com
A Penguin Random House Company

First published by Obsidian, an imprint of New American Library,
a division of Penguin Group (USA) LLC

First Printing, September 2014

ISBN 978-0-451-24112-2

Printed in the United States of America
10 9 8 7 6 5 4 3 2 1

PUBLISHER'S NOTE
This is a work of fiction. Names, characters, places, and incidents either are the
product of the author's imagination or are used fictitiously, and any resem-
blance to actual persons, living or dead, business establishments, events, or
locales is entirely coincidental.
    The recipes contained in this book are to be followed exactly as written.
The publisher is not responsible for your specific health or allergy needs that
may require medical supervision. The publisher is not responsible for any ad-
verse reactions to the recipes contained in this book.

For my personal constituency,
Elizabeth and Bethany

Acknowledgments

As always, much credit goes to my steadfast agent, Kim Lionetti. She has spent more than her fair share of time holding my hand, nudging me forward, and looking out for my interests. My dear friend Melissa Bourbon Ramirez is a constant source of support and inspiration, but she was particularly helpful in bringing this book to fruition. Thank you, Misa! And I would be remiss if I did not thank my husband for every book I write. He makes it all possible. Love you, baby. Finally, a very special thank-you to Elizabeth Bistrow, creator of Merryville and rockin' editor. I promise I'll take good care of Izzy, Packer, Jinx, and the rest of the gang.

CHAPTER
One

"What do you think of the meatball?" Ingrid Whitfield handed Harvey Nyquist a tiny paper plate bearing a single bite-sized meatball, speared with a toothpick and resting in a small pool of creamy brown gravy.

Harvey shoved his well-used handkerchief into his pocket and reached up from his seat on my sofa, careful not to shift my dog, Packer, who was snoring loudly in his lap. As he grasped the plate in his liver-spotted hand, I detected a faint tremor, and he grabbed at the toothpick with the sort of lunging movement of a person whose fine motor skills are deteriorating.

He chewed the meatball thoughtfully. "Good," he said. Packer snorted softly and raised his head, his doggy dreams distracted by the rich scent of meat.

"Good? Don't you think the nutmeg's a little strong?"

"Maybe."

Ingrid heaved a long-suffering sigh. "Well, do you want them as is, or do you want less nutmeg?"

"Ya, sure." He rubbed the end of the toothpick in the leftover gravy and sucked it off, his eyes closed and a contented smile gracing his face. Packer whined and licked his chops. Harvey held out the plate for him to clean, and Packer looked up at Harvey like he was the king of dogs. My little four-legged traitor.

"'Ya, sure'? What kind of answer is that? Pain-in-the-ass old coot," Ingrid muttered, but there was no heat to her complaint, and she gave Harvey's shoulder a flirtatious little shove before she returned to my galley kitchen. No doubt about it, brusque and brash old Ingrid had a soft spot, and its name was Harvey Nyquist.

When the couple had first arrived in Merryville, I couldn't figure out why Ingrid was so smitten with Harvey. They'd been high school sweethearts, torn apart by his family's decision to send him to military school, and before Ingrid had flown off to join him in Boca Raton, I'd seen pictures of the lithe, handsome man he had been. Ingrid had rhapsodized about the love notes he would write to her and the numerous times he had serenaded her in front of God and everyone.

But Harvey Nyquist sixty-some years after the serenading stopped? The man didn't say boo, he had some sort of chronic sinus problem that produced earsplitting sneezes on a regular basis, and he looked like someone had stuffed a madras sack with sunburned potatoes.

When I met Harvey, I decided Ingrid's determination to live happily ever after with him was driven by nothing more than the memory of a love long ago.

But during the week since their arrival, I'd watched Harvey as he watched Ingrid bustling about my apartment, rearranging my knickknacks, finding hidden deposits of dust to clean away, and cursing about the little details of their upcoming nuptials. He looked at her as though she were his last mooring to this earth, all the light in his face reflected from her vitality. He didn't just love Ingrid. He needed her. And having someone need you is a powerful aphrodisiac.

"Well?" I asked, pointing at the meatball-filled tinfoil take-out box on my counter.

"I guess they'll do," Ingrid groused.

Ollie Forde, who'd made literally hundreds of thousands of Norwegian meatballs for the residents of Merryville over the years, would be delighted to learn that his spherical masterpieces would "do."

"That's good," I said, struggling to hide my frustration. "The wedding is tomorrow, after all, and we should probably finalize the details today."

As if to punctuate my pronouncement, Harvey whooped and sneezed. I heard Packer whimper from the bluster of it all, and Jinx—perched on the passthrough between my kitchen and dining nook—swished her tail in annoyance.

In truth, we should have finalized the details the day

Ingrid and Harvey rolled into town, with absolutely no advance notice, and declared they were going to get married in Merryville within the week.

Ingrid had decided at the last minute that she wanted to get married in her hometown of Merryville instead of at the Cherub Chapel of Bliss on the Las Vegas Strip. More specifically, she and Harvey were getting married in my store, Trendy Tails, the space Ingrid had called home. Trendy Tails occupied the first floor of 801 Maple, a house Ingrid had owned for decades. The second floor had been Ingrid's apartment, and I still lived in the third-floor apartment. Ingrid and Harvey's announcement had turned the entire house on its head.

The wedding plans got off to a rocky start when Ingrid had discovered that the tenant I'd found for her apartment was still in residence, so she and Harvey would have to bunk with me. "There goes the nooky," she'd complained.

They'd only gone downhill from there. Soon she was chafing under the froufrou influence of my mom and Aunt Dolly. If Ingrid had had her way, she would have dressed in her best plaid shirt, signed the paperwork, and been married in ten minutes. But Mom and Aunt Dolly had managed to find her a feminine skirt suit with a peplum to give Ingrid some curves, had ordered a huge bouquet of lilacs, and had even stitched a deep purple lace-edged pillow to one of Packer's harnesses so he could serve as a canine ring-bearer. "It's just me and Harvey," she'd muttered, "not the damn royal wedding."

Yesterday, we'd hit a new snag. Ingrid, who was

usually perfectly happy with a bowl of canned soup and some soda crackers, suddenly became hypercritical about all the food options we had (which were scarce, given our short timeline). "Not as good as mine," she'd griped about every single dish we proffered. For someone who claimed not to want a fussy wedding, she had become quite a demanding bride.

Now she looked at me with narrowed eyes. "You know I love you, Isabel McHale, but I don't appreciate the sarcasm. Ollie Forde makes a good meatball, but you have to admit the man can be a little heavy-handed with the nutmeg. We'll have the wedding tomorrow with or without meatballs, but I'm not paying through the nose for a plate of crapola."

I narrowed my eyes right back. "You know I love you, Ingrid Whitfield, but you've become an irascible old biddy."

Ingrid's frown melted away, and she threw back her head in laughter. "'Become'? I've been an irascible old biddy since the day my mother birthed me. That's precisely why you love me."

I snickered. "True enough. But you know what they say about too much of a good thing."

"Well, if it wasn't for that interloper on the second floor . . ."

"Hey. No fair. You asked me to rent out the apartment, and when Daniel asked for an extra couple of weeks, I had no idea his stay would interfere with your wedding. You weren't due back for another month. A little notice would have helped," I added pointedly.

Ingrid plucked another meatball from the small tray. "So what's up with this Daniel Colona guy?" she asked before popping the morsel in her mouth.

"Honestly? I don't really know. He pretty much keeps to himself. He comes down to the shop pretty regularly to buy Rena's treats for his Weimaraner, Daisy May, but he doesn't talk about himself much at all."

"You said he's a writer?"

From the other room, Harvey sneezed again. I waited until he was done trumpeting into his hankie before answering.

"That's what he said when he called about the apartment, but he's never given so much as a hint about what he's writing."

"I can't believe the crew around here hasn't figured out all his deepest secrets by now. You and your friends are pretty nibby."

"Oh, believe me, it's not for lack of trying. We've had some long conversations about Mr. Colona over dinners, drinks, card games—you name it. I think he's a novelist, maybe a J. D. Salinger kind of guy, and he's hiding out while some sort of sex scandal blows over."

"Really? Why do you say that?"

"I don't know. He's got these dark, haunted eyes and long black hair. He could play Heathcliff in a remake of *Wuthering Heights* if he grew just a few more inches. He's got to have a troubled past and a broken love story."

"You get all that from his hair? I think you're being overly romantic."

"That's what Rena says." My best friend and business partner had been teasing me mercilessly about having a crush on my tenant . . . which I definitely did not. I had a couple of light crushes going, but neither of them were on Daniel Colona.

A week after Harvey and Ingrid's wedding, Trendy Tails was playing host to a doggy wedding . . . pupptials, if you will. The dogs in question were Hetty Tucker's retired greyhound, Romeo, and Louise Collins's pudgy beagle, Pearl. Hetty and Louise had always been close, so they hadn't been difficult to work with. But their sons . . .

Neither Hetty nor Louise could drive, so each depended on her son to get her to our planning sessions. Sean Tucker and Jack Collins were night and day. Sean was intellectual, reserved, a true romantic. In a past life he might have written lots of poetry about sheep or painted women frolicking through the woods in diaphanous gowns. Jack Collins was a cop. A man's man. In a past life, he was a cop. At our meetings, the two men danced around each other like alley cats with their backs up, hissing and spitting at each other at every opportunity. They were different, sure, but I'm not sure where the animosity came from. I honestly didn't know what to do with either one of them. But I definitely thought they were both pretty cute.

"Anyway," I continued, "Rena thinks he's a retired crime boss who's writing a tell-all book. She says that once you get past his polished shoes and perfectly pressed dress shirts, he looks a little rough around the edges, like maybe he's broken a few knees in his time.

Meanwhile, Lucy and Xander both think he's an investigative journalist doing an exposé on . . . well, they don't exactly know what he plans to expose. And of course Sean and Dru, the practical members of our little gang, think we're all crazy and we ought to let the man have his privacy."

"Sean and Dru are probably right." Ingrid leaned forward and called into the living room. "Don't you think so, Harvey?"

"Ya, sure."

Ingrid chuckled. "It's nice to be right all the time," she said.

"I know we shouldn't be such busybodies, but honestly, our speculation is perfectly tame compared to Aunt Dolly. She's come up with far more harebrained theories than the rest of us. She's completely obsessed with the man."

"Your aunt Dolly is a nut job," Ingrid huffed.

I shrugged. "Yeah, well, she's our nut job. She fancies herself quite the sleuth after the hubbub last Halloween."

Last fall, my friends and I found ourselves in the middle of a murder investigation, trying to keep Rena from being hauled to the hoosegow. Ever since we'd sussed out the killer, Aunt Dolly had taken to watching and taking notes on true crime shows. She'd even suggested she might try to get her private investigator's license.

"She's dragging me right behind her, straight to the loony bin," Ingrid complained. "All this stuff with the wedding: favors and veils and nonsense."

I gave Ingrid a sidelong glance. "Come on. I know you're not a girly girl, but you must be enjoying all the attention just a little."

Ingrid grinned at me around a gravy-stained toothpick. "Maybe just a little," she said with a wink.

Lord, help me, I thought. *Between Ingrid blowing hot and cold, Dolly blowing plain old crazy, and Harvey endlessly blowing his nose, this wedding might be the death of me.*

That afternoon, I set to work making favors for the wedding, listening to Rena humming out of tune while she worked on cookies for Ingrid and Harvey's reception. I sucked in a big lungful of vanilla-and-sugar-scented air.

At the tinkling of the bell above our doorway, I looked up to find Aunt Dolly using her rear end to bump open Trendy Tails' door. She managed to maneuver herself into the shop with her arms filled with boxes of white tissue wedding decorations. Thankfully, I'd already ordered decorations for Pearl and Romeo's doggy wedding. We could give the decorations a dress rehearsal, using them to perk up Trendy Tails for Ingrid and Harvey.

"How's the blushing bride today?" Dolly asked, her voice brimming with high spirits and good cheer.

I set down the last little packet of Jordan almonds, bundled neatly in a circle of white tulle, and raised a finger to my lips. "She's upstairs," I mouthed.

"Gotcha," Dolly mouthed back.

I stretched my back and answered her in a voice that

wouldn't carry up to my apartment on the third floor, where Ingrid Whitfield had gone to sulk. "Take your pick," I said. "Irritable, grumpy, annoyed, occasionally hostile. She's spent a lot of time storming up and down the stairs muttering that she and Harvey should have just gone to Vegas like they originally planned. At one point she bellowed at Harvey that they should call off all this 'stuff and nonsense' and just keep on living in sin."

Rena sauntered out of the kitchen to join us during my explanation. "We've been having a great time," she deadpanned. "Maybe we should get Ingrid on that show about bridezillas. I bet she'd be their first post-menopausal bride."

Dolly snorted a laugh as she carefully lowered her load onto the giant red worktable in what used to be the dining room of the gingerbread Victorian house. She shoved aside the tangle of ribbons and fabric swatches that littered the table, the detritus of my early morning efforts to create "cat's pajamas." The unfinished results hung on a wooden cat-shaped form I'd had specially made by a carpenter in Bemidji. Eventually, I would try the jammies on Jinx, but she was too feisty to serve as a model during development.

"I guess we shouldn't be surprised," Dolly whispered. "Ingrid's always been a pill, and a bride must be an awkward hat for her to wear."

Dolly made a good point. Our octogenarian friend would pick corduroy over cashmere any day of the week.

Still, I thought Ingrid's irritability went deeper than

that. She seemed uncharacteristically vulnerable. I had a sneaking suspicion why.

Ingrid had spent most of her adult life running the Merryville Gift Haus in the space now occupied by my store, Trendy Tails. She'd supported me in starting up the business right before she left for Boca, but it must still have been difficult to come back and see no trace of her own well-loved shop left. What's more, the second-floor apartment in which Ingrid had lived for over four decades was now occupied by a stranger, a renter she'd never even met. It's hard to deal with the fact that life in your hometown could continue on without you.

"Well," Rena said, "one way or the other it will be over tomorrow."

"That sounds ominous," Dolly said with a shiver.

Rena laughed. "You haven't seen ominous until you've seen the thundercloud that gathered over Ingrid when she found out Jane Porter was bringing a plus one to the wedding."

"Oh, she's just being ridiculous. I mean, it's not like Jane's marrying Knute Hammer," Dolly huffed. "They just gad about town together."

Rena started pulling rolls of crepe-paper and tissue-paper wedding bells from the box Dolly had brought. "Why would she care about Jane's love life, even if Jane *was* going to tie the knot with Knute?"

Dolly hummed thoughtfully. "I think the whole reason Ingrid invited Jane was that she had a vision of Jane curled in a puddle of misery while she walked down the aisle with Harvey. Jane having a date takes some of the fun out of it."

"Geesh," I muttered, fanning out a honeycomb bell and slipping the plastic clips in place to hold it open. "Ingrid's always been brusque, but I've never known her to be mean-spirited. Other than a few sour grapes over a canasta hand, what does she have against Jane anyway?"

"You don't know?" Dolly gasped.

Rena's eyes lit from within as she leaned in for a good dish. "No, we don't. . . . Spill it."

Dolly hummed nervously, studying the ceiling as though she could pinpoint Ingrid's precise location there. "Well," she finally whispered, "Jane and Arnold Whitfield dated in high school, when Harvey and Ingrid were together. Everyone thought Jane and Arnold would get married and Harvey and Ingrid would live their own happily ever after. But then Jane moved to Chicago to do some TV work, commercial bits, and such. Harvey got sent to military school, and things just sort of happened the way they happened. . . . Next thing you know, Arnold and Ingrid were engaged.

"Then back, oh, thirty-some years ago now, when Arnold was still alive, Ingrid spent a few months up in Duluth looking after her sister who'd broken a hip. When she got back, she and Arnold had a big blowup, and he ended up spending a month or so with his brother in St. Paul. When he came home, he brought Ingrid a fancy new dishwasher. I don't think either one of them ever told a soul about that fight, but we all knew. And we all knew its cause: Jane and Arnold had, uh . . . well . . ."

Rena squealed. "Oh no, they didn't! Arnold Whitfield and Jane Porter had a fling?"

"Hush," Dolly urged, glancing up at the ceiling again.

"Man," I whispered, "Jane picked the wrong woman to betray, didn't she?"

"You bet she did," Dolly continued. "Ingrid seemed to forgive Arnold, but she never forgave Jane. What's more, without so much as a word she made sure everyone in Merryville remembered that Jane's morals were a little loose. I know Ingrid never hung her head in shame over the affair, but this . . . Well, this was her big chance to beat out Jane in the love game once and for all."

I slipped a ribbon through the grommets on the tops of three of the honeycomb tissue bells, making a little cluster to hang from the chandelier in the front room. "Wow. I never would have guessed. I can't imagine Ingrid putting up with a tomcatting husband. I guess everyone has secrets."

Dolly finished nestling the bundles of Jordan almonds in a lace-lined basket. "That they do, my dear. That they do. Don't you ever forget it."

CHAPTER
Two

Everyone who was anyone turned out for Ingrid and Harvey's wedding. My sisters and parents were there, graciously standing near the back to allow other guests a better view. I counted every member of the Methodist Ladies' Auxiliary. The *Merryville Gazette* had even sent a reporter to cover the event for what passed as our society page. I admit, I was delighted to see Ama Olmstead taking photos of the array of goodies laid out on the cherry red folk art table that dominated Rena's barkery, while her husband, Steve, stood back and patiently held her bags—so many bags it looked like she was ready to go on the lam. Not only was she chronicling the nuptials, but she was providing Trendy Tails with a little free publicity. I admired the way they worked, tiny Danish Ama having merely to give her strapping Norwegian husband a glance before he handed her a lens or some other sort of camera paraphernalia.

Ken West emerged from the kitchen, a tray of his savory hors d'oeuvres in his hands. Ken had come to Merryville from Madison to open a high-end seafood restaurant, the Blue Atlantic, but when it went out of business, he stuck around doing catering jobs. He'd recently secured backing—thanks to a little blackmail—from Hal Olson to open a new restaurant, this one with a more realistic steak-and-chops menu. He'd recently begun the process of revamping the building that once housed the Grateful Grape—just across the back alley from me—into his new concern, Red, White & Bleu. The conceit was to pair just the right wine with locally sourced beef, pork, venison, and fish. I'd even heard a rumor that he was bringing in a sommelier from his days in Madison to help with the pairings.

I admit I was a little disappointed about Ken opening Red, White & Bleu. As smug and unpleasant as I found Ken to be, he really did a nice job with catering, and I imagined that the restaurant would take up too much of his time for him to continue with these little jobs.

A small mob of no-nonsense Merryville men—all over fifty—crowded around Ken to grab his mini-chicken-potpies and beef skewers, along with a few of Ollie Forde's Norwegian meatballs. I noticed the widowed contingent of the Methodist Ladies' Auxiliary staring at the men with predatory eyes, looking for a weak one to cull from the herd.

Even the much-maligned Jane Porter had shown up, hanging on the arm of Knute Hammer. Knute Hammer was the minister at the Hope of Christ Lutheran

Church. Though he was slight of frame, he towered over the gently rounded, petite Jane Porter—a birch tree giving shelter to a plump squirrel. All things considered, it was hard to imagine that Arnold, the man who'd loved strapping, forthright Ingrid, would find much of interest in Jane's Cupid's-bow mouth and coy, lash-batting gaze.

Still, the past was what it was, and according to Dolly, Ingrid's bitterness had never mellowed. I just hoped the two women wouldn't come to blows during the reception.

It really was a true Merryville event. The only person glaringly missing was Hal Olson, Merryville's most outspoken mayoral candidate. I was a little surprised, because Hal always had a new deal in the works, something that needed the shaking of hands and the slapping of backs, and with the election coming up in just a month, glad-handing the denizens of Merryville was all the more important. Missing an opportunity to hobnob like this seemed out of character.

His wife, Pris, was in attendance, though. She stood right in the thick of the action, but most of the guests carefully avoided her eyes. Half the town was terrified of Pris's tongue, as sharp and precise as a surgeon's scalpel. Pris didn't seem to be bothered by the absence of her husband or her lack of conversational partners. Still, everyone with eyes could see the Hal-shaped hole at Pris's side and could guess that there must be tension between the two. I, however, knew the depths of their marital discord. This was not an isolated incident but part of a long trend of Pris and Hal avoiding each other whenever possible. A few months earlier, in a rare moment of camaraderie, Pris had confessed her desire to ditch Hal and the financial bonds that kept them tethered.

Don't get me wrong. Pris and I were not friends. In fact, Pris and I were archrivals in the Merryville pet care industry, though our businesses seemed to drive us into each other's paths more than they kept us apart. In such a small town, you couldn't do much without collaborating with people you barely tolerated. Take, for instance, the upcoming doggy wedding between Pearl Collins and Romeo Tucker. While I was dressing the duo and providing the site for the wedding, and my friend and partner, Rena, was catering the event for the animal guests, Prissy's Pretty Pets was helping with decor and with grooming the pups before their walk down the aisle.

Trying to be a gracious hostess, I sidled up to Pris. "How's it going?"

Pris flashed her beauty-queen smile. "Izzy! Don't you have just the worst feeling of déjà vu?"

"What do you mean?" Pris's smile rarely boded well for me.

"Well, it was only, what, six months ago that we were standing right here in Trendy Tails, the room packed with guests, Ken West in the kitchen providing delicious nibbles just like today. And look how that turned out."

That night had ended with a dead body.

I chuckled uncomfortably. "I think that was a once-in-a-lifetime sort of thing."

Pris just smiled.

"The room looks lovely," she said.

"Thanks." Given the short notice, we'd done a fine job with the decorations. I'd spent the morning clearing away all the merchandise on the floor and draping the glass case beneath the cash register with a swag of deep purple velvet. White tissue paper and tulle twined around the handrail of the staircase leading down from the second floor. We'd scattered the room with milk glass bowls of mixed nuts and the all-important wedding mints: little pastel pillows that melted on your tongue. While many of the guests would stand, we'd placed a handful of chairs at the front of the room for Ingrid's contemporaries and their shaky knees. All in all, Aunt Dolly, Rena, and I had transformed Trendy Tails into a chapel of love that rivaled any in Vegas. All we were missing was the Elvis.

"What's up with those two?" Pris asked. "They look like they're ready to take it outside."

She lifted her glass of punch in the direction of the chairs. Hetty Tucker and Louise Collins were sitting side by side, chattering and giggling like a couple of teenagers. They were flanked by their sons, Sean and Jack, who were glaring at each other over their mothers' snowy permanent waves.

"You got me," I muttered. "They've been like that for weeks. Every time we meet to talk about Romeo and Pearl's pupptials, I feel like I need to send them to separate corners."

"Well, in my experience, men only get their dander up like that over one thing: women. I'd lay odds that those boys are in a tiff over some female's affection."

Pris had probably been the subject of many male rivalries, so she would know. Sean was newly single, and we'd been renewing a friendship from our high school days . . . a friendship I secretly hoped might blossom into something more. But Sean hadn't shown any signs of reciprocating my affection, and I hadn't heard of Jack having a girlfriend since high school. Maybe it *was* a woman. Or maybe they'd had a run-in on the grade school softball field and had never let it go. Who could tell? After my fiancé of many years had left me high and dry, I'd given up trying to figure out the male mind.

I saw Rena waving at me from across the room. I made my excuses to Pris, and wound my way through the guests toward the kitchen door.

"Are we ready?" I asked.

"I think so," Rena replied with a weary sigh. "Dolly just texted down that Ingrid was dressed and ready to go, Harvey's been standing by that makeshift altar for the last thirty minutes, and I caught the reverend checking his watch."

"Great. I'll get everyone in order, and you can send Dolly a text telling her to send Ingrid down the front stairs, and then she can hurry down the back stairs and not miss a thing."

I grabbed my hand-tied bouquet of lilacs off the red country table, made my way to the altar—an arch of lavender and white balloons—and beckoned to Reverend Wilson. As he took his place between Harvey and me, a wave of whispers rippled out through the room, leaving silence in their wake. Someone coughed, the sound like a shot in the quiet room.

Somewhere behind me, Rena pushed PLAY on an MP3 player, and the sweet notes of Pachelbel's Canon in D filled the air.

After a few moments of tense anticipation—during which I harbored the fleeting fear that Ingrid had escaped down the back stairs and fled into the twilight—her taupe pumps appeared between the balusters of the staircase. Everyone sighed softly as the bride made her way down the last of the stairs. She wore a periwinkle suit with a flirty little peplum and carried a cascading bouquet of frothy lilacs. A blusher-length veil covered her face, a gift from Dolly, who had worn the same veil when she married. The outfit was out of character for Ingrid, but I could tell by the tilt of her chin and the faint smile playing across her rose-painted lips that she felt beautiful.

I scooched out of the way so she and Harvey could stand squarely before the minister. Rena cut off the music, and Reverend Wilson began the service, his resonant voice holding us all rapt.

By the time Rena sent Packer scampering across the store, the ring pillow balanced precariously on his back, there wasn't a dry eye in the house. Except, of course, for Ingrid. She looked vaguely embarrassed by the tears pouring down Harvey's weathered cheeks. I was right there with him, choking back unexpected sobs of joy for my friend and mentor.

I'll be honest—while most of the tears I shed were for Ingrid and Harvey, a few were for myself. I didn't love Dr. Casey Alter anymore—he'd made sure of that when he ran away to New York with a perky little nutritionist—but I still felt as though some part of life had passed me by. I didn't miss the groom a bit, but I did miss the wedding I'd been planning, the prospect of being a bride.

"Do you, Harvey, take Ingrid to be your wife? To have and to hold, in sickness and in health, for richer or for poorer, as long as you both shall live?"

"I do," Harvey sighed, his voice trembling with raw emotion.

"And do you, Ingrid, take Harvey to be your husband? To have and to hold, in sickness and in health, for richer or for poorer, as long as you both shall live?"

"I—"

Ingrid stopped short, midaffirmation. The sharp noise that had startled her into silence still echoed through the room. My first thought was that our coughing guest was at it again, but before I could consider that thought further, the room was filled with a thumping that grew louder with each report.

Hetty Tucker was the first to utter a gasping scream, but she was quickly followed by other guests as something heavy tumbled down the stairs behind Reverend Wilson.

It came to a stop in a heap at the bottom of the stairs, and it didn't take long to see the hand extended, fingers curled in a gesture of supplication, to make out the outline of a hip beneath the black mass, and to realize that the crumpled object at the foot of the stairs was a person.

I was closest, and I reached the injured person's side first. I looked down to see a sweep of inky black hair partially hiding the unmistakable strong, square jawline of our second-floor renter, Daniel Colona. I also saw blood. So much blood that Daniel Colona had to be dead.

Behind me, I heard someone speaking frantically to a 911 operator, begging for police and an ambulance to come to Trendy Tails. I glanced over my shoulder to find a shaken Ama Olmstead, panting softly from her sprint through the partygoers to the front of the pack, fumbling with the bags hanging off her shoulder and clicking off pictures with trembling fingers, likely capturing the most significant story of her career.

As I leaned down to check for a pulse, a flash of movement caught my eye and stopped me in my tracks. I glanced up the stairs. There, on the landing, stood my aunt Dolly, a gun in her hand and a look of horror on her face.

Before I could recover, Jack Collins nudged me out of the way and knelt to check Daniel's pulse. I saw him look up the stairs in Dolly's direction. He then caught my eyes, and gently shook his head.

Sure enough, Daniel was dead, and my aunt couldn't have looked more guilty if she'd worn a sweater with the word "murderer" embroidered across the chest.

I glanced around the room at the sea of wide eyes and dropped jaws. From across the room of shocked partygoers, Pris Olson caught my gaze, lifted one eyebrow, and raised a glass of punch in a silent toast.

Right then I knew one thing for certain: I was never throwing another party again.

I led Jack through the first-floor kitchen, just as Ken West was walking in from the alley.

"Where are you coming from?" Jack snapped.

"A smoke," Ken snapped back. "Perfectly legal, Officer." The last word rolled out in a snide drawl, an equally snide smile gracing his face.

"Did you see anything, Ken? Anyone else come out the back door?" Jack's urgency must have pushed through Ken's usual contrariness. He straightened up, on alert.

"See anything? No, what happened?"

"Daniel Colona is dead, and it looks like he was shot in the upstairs apartment. Did you see anyone going through your kitchen?"

Ken shot me a look of pure amazement. He'd been there for my last murder party.

"I didn't see a thing. I, uh, went out to have a smoke with Steve Olmstead."

"So he can vouch you were outside the whole time?"

"Well, no, I guess not. He came in before I did. But I didn't have any reason to kill Daniel Colona." He shook his head. "Wow. I can't believe this is happening again."

"Did you see anyone leave through the back door?" Jack was growing impatient. I knew he wanted to get upstairs, but he had to ask these questions while the answers were fresh in Ken's mind. Ingrid had been the only one to use the front stairs, which meant the killer must have used the back.

"No."

Just that: "No."

"But . . ." Jack prodded.

"I, uh, wasn't right by the door the whole time." Jack's eyes narrowed and his lips thinned. Ken held up his hands. "Nothing shady, I swear. I just took a little walk down the alley. Stretched my legs."

Jack was done dillydallying. But I tucked Ken's comments away for further consideration. Assuming Dolly was innocent—and loyalty prevented me from assuming anything else—either the murderer was still in the building (heaven forbid), the killer had managed to sneak out back and through the alley without alerting Ken (which would be tough given that all the shops on either side of the alley had motion-sensor lights), or Ken West was, himself, the killer. Ken was a bit of a sleaze at the best of times, but his answers to Jack's questions seemed especially cagey.

Weird.

Jack led the way up the back stairs, and through the open door to Daniel's apartment. I called softly to Dolly as we made our way through the half-light.

She turned slowly, eyes glazed, hands trembling. With incredible care, Jack removed the gun from her hand and set it on an entertainment center out of Dolly's reach, as though she might lunge for the weapon and start taking potshots at Jack and me.

"I'm sorry about this, Ms. Johnston," he said as he gently raised her hands above her head and began to pat her down. He paused when he reached the pocket of the daring kimono-cut jacket she'd picked out for the wedding.

"Izzy," he murmured. "Run downstairs and get me a paper bag and a plastic Baggie."

I did as he said, clattering down the back stairwell as fast as my legs would carry me. I found a Baggie in a drawer by the stove, and I grabbed one of the white paper bags Rena used to package her pet treats.

When I got back upstairs and handed the items to Jack, he shook open the paper bag with a loud snap. He then put his hand in the plastic bag, creating a makeshift glove, and reached gingerly into Dolly's pocket. When his hand emerged, I was puzzled to see him holding a toothbrush. He dropped it into the paper bag, rolled over the bag's top, shook the Baggie off his hand, and tucked it in the pocket of his twill pants.

I shot him a questioning look. He lifted his shoulders in the universal sign for "I don't have a clue."

By then, Dolly was starting to regain her faculties. "Is he dead?" she asked.

"Yes," Jack replied simply, carefully studying her face for a reaction.

Poor Dolly's shoulders drooped in misery. "Oh dear. This is all my fault."

"What do you mean by that?" Jack asked.

"Not another word." I hadn't heard Sean coming up the stairs behind me, but I was glad he had. "Dolly? Do you want me to represent you?"

"Represent me?" she asked, clearly not grasping the gravity of her situation.

"Yes," I said firmly. "You do want Sean to represent you."

She still looked puzzled, but she shrugged. "Okay."

Jack glared at Sean, who kept his expression carefully neutral. "My client will not be speaking with the police at this time."

"Lawyers," Jack muttered.

"Cops," Sean muttered back.

Jack took a step toward him, and for an instant I thought they might come to blows. "You're not doing her any favors by telling her not to cooperate."

"Why don't you leave the legal advice to me, big guy? You stick with the crime-solving bit."

Jack growled low in his throat before turning away. He stepped around Dolly, and made his way gingerly up the stairs to my apartment, likely making sure the culprit hadn't escaped up instead of down.

Sean walked over to my aunt, grasped her hands gently, and looked her square in the eyes. "Don't you ever—*ever*—tell a cop that something is your fault."

"But it is," Dolly said, her voice soft but firm.

Jack reappeared on the second-floor landing, rocking on his heels to contain his nervous energy. He was ready to take Dolly in.

Sean glanced at Jack over Dolly's head and sighed in frustration. "Right this moment," he told my aunt, "I'm not concerned about the truth. I'm concerned about keeping you out of jail. Not another word, you hear me?"

Dolly's gaze slid to the side, staring into the middle distance, but she nodded.

I'd never in my life seen my feisty aunt look so small.

CHAPTER
Three

The rest of the evening passed in a blur. The police took extra time to ask Ama Olmstead about the pictures she'd taken, demanding copies of them all. Her husband, Steve, towered over her, protective of his petite wife. He had his finger in his mouth when I caught his eye, and he quickly removed it.

He must have snuck a taste of the cake icing. I didn't blame him. I could use a little cake right then . . . some sugar to bolster me through the rest of the evening. I sighed, realizing the cake would likely go to waste. What an awful evening.

The guests left after signing in with the police, and Ingrid and Harvey, still unwed, retired to my third-floor apartment. I think Harvey was more shaken than Ingrid, but she graciously claimed she needed to lie down.

That left Rena and my family: my sisters, Lucy and

Dru; my mom; and my dad. We quickly shooed Dad away, assuring him that we'd be waiting for Aunt Dolly and that there wasn't anything he could do to help. He'd spent his adult years in a house full of women and was used to being ordered about. With a gleam of relief in his eyes, he left, bussing my mother on the cheek, hugging his three daughters, and lifting tiny Rena right off the floor into his embrace. By the time my mom joined him at home, he'd probably be asleep in his big recliner, one of his beloved history books in his lap.

Rena brought out five pints of ice cream and spoons for everyone—even an extra for Dolly when she returned from booking—and our little coven gathered around the cherry red farm table. At first, we glumly dug our spoons into the cartons of comfort food and tried not to watch as the coroner removed Daniel's body from the floor of my store. Jinx and Packer were batting at the deflated helium balloons, knocking them all around the store. Eventually, Jinx managed to catch one with her claw, and we all jumped at the pop.

"Good heavens," my mother said. "I think this evening has taken years off my life."

Dru, the oldest and by far the most responsible of the stair-step McHale girls, reached out to take my mother's hand and give it a comforting squeeze.

Lucy pulled out her phone to check the time. "Are you sure Aunt Dolly will get out of jail tonight?"

My mother moaned. "I certainly hope so. I could barely stand to see that officer manhandle her into that squad car."

"Jack didn't manhandle her, Mom," Lucy said. "He didn't even put her in cuffs."

"Well, still, she won't last a night in prison."

My mom watched too much television.

"It's the Merryville jail, not Oz," I sighed. "And she should be here soon. Sean said they'd have to print her and take her picture, but that he'd call in a favor with Judge Lindsay and get her arraigned right away so she can bond out before bedtime."

"What on earth was she doing up there?" Dru asked.

"I don't know. Sean wouldn't let her say a peep while Jack was in the room."

"You know I love my sister, but she's always been a little wild, and I think she's getting a bit batty in her old age."

I smiled at the thought of Aunt Dolly as a wild child. I wondered if she'd ever burned her bra.

"Well, we'll have to wait until she gets home to ask her what happened," I said.

The last word had barely left my lips when the bell over the front door tinkled, heralding my aunt's return.

My mother dashed across the room to pull her sister into a tight hug. "Are you all right? Did they hurt you?"

Dolly tutted softly. "No one hurt me. It was actually kind of interesting." She held up her hand to show off the ink on her fingertips. "I've never been printed before."

"You crazy woman," my mother chided. "Only you would consider getting arrested for murder an adventure."

"You only get one ride in life. May as well make the most of it."

"Enough of this chitchat," Rena said, holding up a spoon for Dolly. "Sit down and tell us everything."

Dolly took a seat, and we all leaned in eagerly. "Well," she said around her first spoonful of cherry chip, "Sean said I shouldn't talk to anyone. He said that what I confided to him was privileged because he's my lawyer, but if I tell other people, it could be used against me in court. Something called a statement against my interests. That Sean boy is one smart cookie," she added, directing a pointed stare in my direction.

Lucy laughed. "Like any of us would ever testify against you. What you say here, stays here."

Rena nodded. "We've got your back, Dolly."

Dru frowned. "I don't know. People use lawyers for a reason. Maybe we should take Sean's advice."

My mother smiled fondly. "You're such a sensible girl, Dru." Dru rolled her eyes. She didn't appreciate people pointing out how sensible and straitlaced she was. It didn't help that Lucy and I—neither of whom would ever be dubbed "sensible"—teased her mercilessly for being such a stand-up citizen. "It may be more sensible for Dolly to keep her lips sealed," Mom went on, "but I for one want to know what happened up there. And I sure won't say anything. Scout's honor." She held up three fingers as a sign of her pledge.

Dolly waved her spoon through the air like a conductor. "I never had any intention of keeping this to myself. I trust you all completely."

"So?" Rena prodded.

"After I sent Ingrid down the front steps, I headed toward the back, planning to slip in through the kitchen and catch the whole wedding. But when I got to the landing, I saw that Daniel's back door was ajar. And you know how much I want to know what he's doing in Merryville, right?"

We all nodded. None of us had been spared Dolly's wild speculation about Daniel Colona. She'd pegged him for everything from a television host who was looking for a small town to make over to a terrorist.

"Well, of course I couldn't just walk past that open door."

Dru sighed. "You *could* have, and you *should* have."

"But I didn't," Dolly snapped. "I thought Daniel had left for the evening, to avoid all the hubbub down here, and when I slipped into his bedroom, I didn't hear anything except Daisy whining from her crate in the front room."

"Daisy," Lucy gasped. "Who's going to take care of poor Daisy?"

Every eye turned in my direction.

"Wait. I've already got a rambunctious dog, a huge cat, and two cantankerous houseguests. I can't handle Daisy, too." It wasn't just the extra work. Even though I ran a pet boutique, big dogs made me nervous. Ironic, I know, but there you have it.

Rena laughed. "Of course you can. This house is huge, stocked to the gills with animal food, and you know I'll help you with walks and stuff. Besides, it will only be temporary. We'll have to find Daisy a forever home eventually. But we can watch her until someone shows up to collect her or we find someone else to take her in. Just a week or two. Three, tops."

Three weeks. Great. But I sighed and nodded. I wasn't about to send the poor dog to an animal shelter, and I knew no one else was in a better position to take care of her.

"Sorry, Aunt Dolly," I said. "We didn't mean to interrupt your story."

"Well," she said. "As I was saying, I didn't hear anything other than Daisy whining. So I started poking around a little. Then, when I was in the bathroom—"

"The bathroom?" Mom squealed. "You were in a strange man's bathroom?"

"Oh, loosen up, Edie. I was looking for something with DNA on it, and I wasn't likely to find that in just any old place."

DNA. That explained the toothbrush in her pocket. I wasn't sure how Aunt Dolly thought DNA would help her in her quest to unmask Daniel Colona. I mean, it's not like she had access to DNA databases or anything. But gathering Daniel's DNA made about as much sense as her breaking into the apartment in the first place, so I decided not to raise any questions.

"Anyway," she continued, "I was in the bathroom when I finally heard the voices coming from the living room. They must have been whispering before, but now they were talking in normal voices . . . maybe even a bit heated. Then I heard the gun go off. I froze in the bathroom door, and I swear I saw someone dart past the bedroom door and slip down the back stairs."

"Well, who was it?" Lucy asked.

"I couldn't tell. It was really dark in there. I hadn't turned on any lights, and there was just a little ambient light seeping around those heavy curtains in there. There was a light on in the living room, but with the person in front of it, it didn't help. I just saw a shadow, and only for a second. Couldn't even tell if it was a man or a woman.

"As soon as the person went out the back door, I ran to the living room to see what had happened. Poor Daisy was whimpering in her crate, and Daniel was standing there holding his chest, this surprised look on his face. I tried to reach him to help, but before I could, he stumbled to the landing and fell down the stairs. That's when I saw the gun on the floor and picked it up."

"Dude," Rena said. "Why did you pick up the gun? Major mistake."

"Listen, young lady, you have no idea what you would do under those circumstances. I'd seen one person leave, but what if there were others? I was scared, and it was just a natural impulse to pick up something to protect myself with."

I had this crazy image of someone charging at my frail aunt Dolly and her whirling around to shoot. Dolly may have fancied herself a modern-day Cagney and Lacey, but she was really a Minnesota housewife. And not the hunting and ice fishing kind of Minnesota housewife. I doubted she even knew how to fire a gun. Lord knows, I sure didn't.

"So that's what happened," Dolly concluded with a shrug. "I didn't do anything wrong—"

"Except for the breaking and entering," Dru said.

"Uh, uh, uh," Dolly said, waggling her spoon like a schoolmarm's finger. "No breaking. Just entering. And some light theft. A toothbrush. Hardly counts at all. But I know I look guilty as heck. Who's going to believe that wack-a-do story?"

"I do," Lucy said. We all nodded in agreement.

"Did you find anything?" Rena asked. "When you were searching the apartment?"

I'd been so focused on the murder part of the story it had never occurred to me to wonder whether Dolly's ill-fated snooping had yielded any information.

"Not much. He is . . . He was definitely a reporter. I found a binder of newspaper clippings from the *Madison Standard* and a stack of photos he'd taken around Merryville. And I almost broke his camera. One of those big ones that newsmen use."

Lucy raised her hands above her head and crowed in victory. "I won! Investigative journalist. That's what Xander and I have been saying all along."

My mother shushed her with a quelling look. "Lucy, this is hardly the time."

Irrepressible Lucy smirked. "I know. But I *did* win."

"What were the pictures of?" I asked, curious about what would bring a reporter from Madison to our sleepy town.

Dolly raised one bony shoulder. "I just thumbed through them, but there were lots of things. Pictures of the downtown shops, some wildlife photos, a series of a dark-haired little boy playing at Dakota Park, and a few of our more colorful local characters. Basically, the type of pictures that any tourist might take."

"Forget the pictures. What did you tell the cops?" Rena asked.

Dolly sighed. "Sean wouldn't let me tell them much. In fact, he got mad when I said I would have used my own gun."

"Your own what?" my mother gasped.

"My gun," Dolly said with a shrug. "The derringer I carry in my pocketbook. I didn't have it with me tonight because I was carrying that tiny beaded purse Lucy gave me for Christmas." She leaned across the table to pat Lucy on the hand. "You have such good taste, dear.

"Anyway, I told them if I'd planned to kill Daniel, I would have brought my own gun instead of hoping I'd find one there. I was a Pioneer Girl back in the day, you know."

My mother sighed in frustration. "The Pioneer Girls are a church group, Dolly. They never once suggested we bear arms."

Dolly waved her off. "Whatever. I like to be prepared. I wouldn't have shown up for a gunfight without a gun."

Poor Sean must have nearly stroked out when Dolly blurted that out to the cops. I could picture him, slouched down in the chair next to Dolly, elbows on the table and his head resting in his hands, his dark wayward curls standing up in alarm at her pronouncement.

"Did they say whose gun it was?" I asked.

"It was his. Daniel's. They found the open gun safe in the living room where he was shot."

So whoever approached him didn't necessarily come armed. But something about their conversation made Daniel worried enough to get his own weapon . . . only to have it used against him.

"I don't know about the rest of you," Dru said, "but I'm exhausted. And Aunt Dolly's had quite a day."

My mom insisted that Dolly stay at my folks' house that night, and Dru and Lucy left with them while Rena and I cleaned up the remnants of our ice cream feast.

"What are we going to do with that cake?" Rena asked, pointing at Ingrid and Harvey's beautiful tiered wedding cake.

"I don't know," I sighed. "Tomorrow. Tomorrow we'll figure out what to do with the cake and how to prove that Aunt Dolly is no murderer."

Soon I was rattling around the big house at 801 Maple on my own. Even from the first floor, I could hear the call-and-response of Ingrid and Harvey snoring. Packer and Jinx had each looked up the stairs, ears twitching, before choosing to bed down on the first floor. Packer had done the three-circle-and-sniff dance around his fleece dog bed, and Jinx had picked her way up to the top of the oak armoire before settling into a cat-shaped loaf, her tail brushing lazily against the side of the wardrobe.

"Thanks, guys," I muttered. Ungrateful wretches, leaving me to face the ruckus Ingrid and Harvey were making on my own. Part of me wanted to bed down with them, and not just because of the noise. I was spooked about walking past Daniel's apartment, past the place he died.

But it was Daniel's plight that ultimately forced me up the stairs so I could retrieve poor Daisy May. Even if I'd been willing to step over Daniel's final resting place, the police had blocked off the front stairs with yellow tape. Jack had assured me it would be gone by the next day, so I wouldn't have to explain it to my customers. At that point, though, the tape forced me up the back stairs—the stairs the killer had probably taken to and from the apartment.

I'd walked the stairs a thousand times, but I'd never been more aware of them than I was that night. The fifth stair from the bottom squeaked. There was a rough spot on the railing halfway up to the landing. The pale cream paint had dripped onto the dark wood baseboard. The stairwell was very dark, perfect cover for nefarious deeds. I shivered.

I hesitated for a moment before opening the door to Daniel's apartment, but when I heard a whimper from Daisy, I steeled myself and went in. The apartment was spacious, but it had a shotgun layout. The back hallway opened onto two bedrooms and a three-quarter bath before spilling into the open living and dining area in the front of the house. The larger of the two bedrooms had a full bath en suite.

I flipped the light switch at the back end of the hall, and the trio of milk glass pendant lights that marched down the hallway flamed to life. I hustled through the apartment to the living room and over to the big dog crate in the corner. Daisy was lying on her belly; she cocked her ears and looked up at me with big soulful eyes. Poor girl.

I opened the crate, and she flew out in a jumble of large head and skinny legs, her momentum driving her right into my midsection. I huffed out a surprised breath and tried to quell the panic of so much dog coming at me so fast. But after her initial flailing, she settled on her haunches by my side, her head pressed against my thigh, her tail bouncing with barely controlled energy.

"Shhhh," I breathed. "Let's just simmer down."

Her response was to butt her head against my leg and whimper softly. It occurred to me that she hadn't been out to do her business in a very long time.

I found her leash and chew toy and pulled the bedding from her crate. I snapped the leash to her collar and left the toy and bedding in the back stairwell so I could carry it up after Daisy had a chance to relieve herself.

We clattered down the stairs, her toenails skittering on the hardwood, my own feet struggling for purchase as I tried to keep my balance with nearly seventy pounds of dog pulling me off my center. She danced at my side as we reached the back door, and I couldn't help but smile at that universal canine sign of desperation mixed with joy.

When we stumbled into the alley, she immediately began sniffing every available surface for a good place to go. Not surprisingly, her travels tripped the motion sensor on the back of the Greene Brigade, the military history boutique run by my neighbor Richard Greene.

As though he'd been waiting by the back door for precisely this moment, Richard's door swung wide and he stepped out onto his stoop with his massive German shepherd, MacArthur, at his side.

MacArthur and Richard were a perfect match, both grizzled and forbidding. But where MacArthur was all bite and no bark, Richard had bark to spare. He'd been suspicious of the ruckus my pet-based store would create on our quiet little block from the very start. He'd been trying to get Trendy Tails shut down since before it had even opened, and he never failed to remind me of his intent.

"What's going on out here, Isabel?"

"Our tenant's dog needed her evening constitutional." At that moment, Daisy found a spot outside the back door of the Spin Doctor, across the alley, to squat and tinkle.

"That's what the dog park is for," Richard reasoned, his voice suggesting I was too dense to grasp that simple fact.

"I know, but it's really late and it's been a long evening." I held up my roll of plastic poop bags. "We won't leave a mess."

Richard harrumphed, but the peeved sound morphed into a bone-rattling cough. "Well, I knew you'd be trouble, Miss McHale, and I see I'm right. First there was the debacle with that rodent nesting in my store."

Gandhi, an orphaned guinea pig, had indeed made his way into Richard's store and eluded capture for several days before dashing out the back door and into the wild. After the harsh winter we'd had, I feared

Gandhi had not survived, and I still felt a pang of sadness that I'd been unable to protect that little guy better.

"Now," Richard continued, "you've got the police swarming the place again and you're letting this animal use our *shared* alleyway as a latrine."

I didn't really have an answer for that. He was right. Today I was not the best neighbor. Instead of responding, I picked my way across the bricks to clean up the mess Daisy had left by the Dumpster, hopefully showing that I was at least trying to be more responsible.

Richard sneezed.

Daisy made her giddy way to MacArthur's side, and I gasped in fear of an altercation. Richard appeared unfazed, however, and sure enough, MacArthur sat perfectly still, the stoic soldier, while Daisy sniffed him all over. Still, unsure how long MacArthur's patience would last, I grabbed her leash and tugged her away as quickly as I could.

"So, Miss McHale," Richard said, his tone resonant and commanding. "What sort of shenanigans were going on in your store tonight?"

"It's a long story." I wasn't prepared to provide more ammunition to Richard, more reason for him to want my store gone.

"Nonsense, little girl. I may be old, but I know a gunshot when I hear one. I was loading my old Remington to come to your aid when I saw the first responders arrive. If they hadn't been so Johnny-on-the-spot, I mighta come in, barrels blazing. So spill it. What happened?"

I sighed. "Short story? Our tenant, Daniel Colona,

was shot in his apartment and tumbled down the stairs into the middle of Ingrid and Harvey's wedding."

"Sorry to have missed that," Richard said, punctuating his statement with another sneeze. "Terrible cold. Didn't want to spread contagion."

I couldn't stop my smile. "I know. Ingrid was sad you couldn't make it. But turns out you didn't miss the wedding at all. Daniel died before the 'I do's.'"

"Huh."

"Daniel dying was bad enough, but the worst is that the police actually arrested Aunt Dolly for the murder."

Richard's craggy features crumpled into a look of utter disbelief. "Dorothy? Hogwash! Why would Dorothy want to kill that man?"

Richard was the only one who called Aunt Dolly "Dorothy," and I found his use of her proper name charming.

"Right now, I think the cops are focused on the fact that she was literally holding a smoking gun, but you know how Dolly was obsessed with Daniel."

Richard laughed, the sound like gravel in a bucket. I'd never heard him laugh before, and it took me aback. "Dorothy has always had a vivid imagination."

Really? Richard had noticed Dolly's vivid imagination? He'd always seemed completely oblivious of her, even when she'd tried to exercise her feminine wiles on him a few months ago.

Daisy had stopped trying to get MacArthur to play with her and had turned her attention to Richard, himself, pushing her silky head up into the rough cup of his hand. He rubbed her ears absently while he continued. "She told me she'd seen that Colona guy taking pictures all around town and thought he might be a terrorist planning to plant a dirty bomb somewhere in Merryville. Said she might call those folks in Homeland Security."

He laughed again, this time the sound dissolving into a coughing fit.

"She didn't," I gasped, truly alarmed that Dolly's fantasies had taken such a dark turn.

"She did, indeed. I told her she had it all wrong. Terrorists aren't concerned with itty-bitty Merryville, Minnesota." He shrugged. "Twin Cities, maybe. Even Duluth. But not Merryville.

"He came by the store one time. Seemed like a nice enough fella. Interested in the history of the area. Looking for a local hunting and fishing guide. I told Dolly that whatever that man did outside Merryville, here he was just a tourist, taking it all in."

"And that's what you believed?"

"I didn't say that. Who knows what's going on in a man's head? And Dorothy was right that Colona was poking around into something. When did he move in?"

"It's been a little over four weeks. Thirty days, to be exact." I'd had to get that information for the police.

"Right. Four weeks during the month of March, looking for a hunting guide." He turned his head and coughed into his fist.

"So, he wants to hunt. Hunting and tourists are Merryville's lifeblood."

"Little girl, are you sure you're not from the Cities? Unless that fancy city man came up here to hunt for raccoons or beavers, there's nothing in season in March. Not a dang thing. Whatever that guy was looking for in Merryville, it was more than a little fresh game."

CHAPTER
Four

I snuck into my own bedroom and gently nudged Ingrid's shoulder. "Shhh," I soothed, when she woke with a start. Harvey was snoring next to her, and I didn't want her to wake him up.

"What's going on?"

"Shhh," I reminded. "Put on your robe and come downstairs."

I left her alone and scooted down the back stairs to the first-floor kitchen. I decanted the pot of piping hot coffee into a thermal carafe and took it and a pile of paper goods we'd planned to use the night before into the barkery portion of Trendy Tails. The cherry red farm table was already surrounded by my sisters, Dru and Lucy; Rena; and our friends Taffy and Jolly Nielson. My mom had called and said that she and Dolly were too wiped out from the night before to make it.

I joined the girls at the table, with the coffee, and

began passing it around. Everyone was a little hollow-eyed after the previous night's shenanigans, but there were still hints of smiles all around. The plate full of Rena's sinful pecan caramel rolls sitting in the middle of the table may have had something to do with it. I couldn't imagine how early she'd needed to get up to get those made; I suspected she hadn't slept at all. Jinx was draped across Rena's lap, and she was gently stroking the cat's big, silky head.

Ingrid thumped down the stairs wearing a cotton housedress over her flannel gown and a pair of untied hiking boots on her feet. Her silver hair fell over one shoulder in an unkempt braid. I promised myself right then and there that this was how I would always re-member Ingrid. The look was just so *her*.

"What the holy heck is going on?" she snapped. "Did someone else die?"

We all laughed. "Nope," I said. "We never got around to holding a true bridal shower for you before the wed-ding, so we're doing one right now."

"At the crack of dawn in the middle of a crime scene?"

Rena piped up. "Actually, you're the only one stand-ing in the crime scene. Come and join us at the table."

Ingrid stomped across the room and slid into a chair, her brow furrowed and lips smashed shut. She loos-ened a little when I passed her a cup of hot coffee with extra cream (just the way she liked it), and a smile came out when Rena handed her a caramel roll and a fork.

"When did you put this all together?"

"Last night," I volunteered. "After you and Harvey went upstairs and while we were waiting for Dolly to get back from jail. We all wanted something to get our minds off the ugliness, and this seemed like a good idea. We had to phone Taffy and Jolly, but they were both still awake."

Taffy shook her head. "I've never been so creeped out in my life."

"It *was* alarming," Jolly agreed. "I didn't ever think my heart would ever stop racing."

I caught an intimate glance between Jolly and Rena. Beneath the edge of the table, Rena took Jolly's hand, laced their fingers, and rested their small embrace on Jinx's black-and-white flank. Jolly and Rena's relationship was only a few months old, but they seemed to have fallen deeply in love. They made a good couple. Rena was exuberant, playful, and sometimes a little rash. Jolly, on the other hand, was a few years older and significantly more levelheaded. Rena was all edges, Jolly was all curves.

"Anyway," I said, trying to draw the conversation away from the murder, "we have presents!"

"Oh, heavens, no. I'm nearly eighty-five. I'm not some young blushing bride just getting her start in life."

"Nonsense," Dru said, pointing a caramel roll at Ingrid to emphasize her point. "Every new love should be celebrated."

"Besides," Taffy added as she brushed a stray honey gold curl from her face, "this is as much for us as for you. We'd been looking forward to throwing you a shower from the minute we knew you were getting married, but then the wedding preparations themselves pushed the shower to the back burner."

"But now, it's baaaack," Lucy said with a grin.

The tension in Ingrid's shoulders had been seeping away with every word we'd offered. I went in for the kill. "So what do you say, Ingrid? Will you let us shower you with joy so we can all breathe a little easier today?"

"All right, all right, all right," she ceded. "I'll put up with just about anything for one of Rena's caramel rolls."

We all heaved a collective sigh of relief.

"Me first," Lucy chirped. She passed Ingrid a tiny package wrapped in cherry red paper and topped with a frilly silver bow.

Ingrid carefully pulled off the bow and handed it to me to save before using her fingernail to carefully remove the paper in a single piece. Surreptitiously, I squished the bow onto the back of a paper plate.

Ingrid opened the tiny box and pulled out a slim metal item about the size of a cigarette lighter. "What's this?" she mused, turning the object this way and that.

"It's an MP3 player," Lucy said. "I'll show you how to use it later. But it has music on it. A lot of Johnny Mathis, of course, but Bobby Vinton, Sinatra, Tom Jones . . . all sorts of music Xander and I thought you and Harvey might like."

Xander ran the record store behind my shop, the Spin Doctor. He and Lucy had been dancing around each other like a couple of lovesick calves for months, each totally infatuated with the other, each way too cool to admit it. Even saying his name had raised a blush in my sister's cheeks.

"That's very thoughtful, Lucy." Ingrid still stared at the player with suspicion. I'm sure she was trying to figure out how something so small could hold more than a single song.

Taffy pulled a giant package from beneath the table. It was wrapped in cellophane and tied with a huge red bow (which was quickly added to the paper plate). The basket contained a delicate blue willow china teapot and two matching cups and saucers. The china was surrounded by small boxes and bags of various teas.

"Some are traditional black and green blends, but others have herbs for various illnesses. There are teas for indigestion, headache, and even one that's supposed to crank up your libido."

For the first time in forever I saw Ingrid Whitfield blush. "Well, uh, thank you, dear. I'm sure . . . Did you know my mother had a set of blue willow china. I loved it so much, but my sister got it when Mother died. I'm happy to own some of my own now."

Dru shyly pushed her package across the table. It was much larger but wrapped in the same red paper Lucy had used and topped by a trio of the silver bows. Ingrid went through her ritual of carefully preserving the wrappings as she opened the box, and once again, I added the bows to my collection.

Dru's gift was much more straightforward. Two purple-and-white-striped scarves. Dru shrugged. "I've been learning to crochet, but I haven't learned much beyond rectangles. I thought you and Harvey could keep your matching Vikings scarves here for when you come up to visit in the winter. Because I really hope you'll come visit during the winter."

Ingrid cleared her throat. "They're gorgeous, Dru. I'd like to place an order for your first tea cozy," she teased.

"We're up," Rena said, glancing at Jolly, who pulled another small package from her pocket.

The wrapping was all Rena: paper from the Sunday comics and brightly colored rubber bands holding it together. Even so, Ingrid's Depression-era instincts had her gently sliding the rubber bands so they wouldn't muss the paper and then pressing the paper flat so it could be used again.

With great care, Ingrid lifted a long chain and pendant from the box. It glinted as it twisted in her hand. She gasped. "It's beautiful."

"Thank you," Jolly said. Jolly was a jeweler who made exquisite pieces inspired by nature. Her usual materials were hammered silver and polished agate, but I could tell the pendant wasn't silver.

"I wanted it to remind you of home," Jolly said.

"Black Hills gold," Ingrid breathed.

Jolly chuckled. "Not exactly. Unless it's made in the Black Hills, it isn't Black Hills gold. But I have been playing around with the technique of combining different gold alloys to create colored gold."

Ingrid handed the necklace around the table. The pendant was a mellow gold, covered with sprigs of green leaves and pale pink roses. The pendant was large enough for a woman of Ingrid's stature to wear, but the delicate coloring gave it a fairylike lightness.

"It's a locket," Rena said when the pendant had made its way back to Ingrid.

She gasped again, as she found and opened the tiny lock on the side of the pendant. When it opened, she teared up. "It's us," she said. "However did you pull this off?"

Rena grinned and winked. "Like we said, we've been planning this for a while. The locket was Jolly's idea, but the pictures were mine. I went to the high school library and found the yearbook from the last year you and Harvey were both enrolled there. Digital cameras are amazing these days. It didn't take me long to duplicate the pictures, touch them up again, and—boom—cut them to fit the locket."

Ingrid passed me the locket and I gazed down on a very young Ingrid and Harvey. Ingrid's strong features were balanced by the rolls of blond hair that framed her face and the pert little netted hat perched on top. Harvey's short hair was slicked back by pomade that made it shine. Both of them were smiling like they hadn't a care in the world . . . like the end of World War II had cleared a pathway to a perfect future.

I fought back a lump in my throat. I was determined not to cry, even though my emotions were right at the surface.

"Here," I announced. "It's tradition." I displayed the paper plate with the red and silver bows decorating its back. I'd stapled a strand of ribbon on either side. With Ingrid's hesitant permission, I placed the plate on her head and tied the ribbons under her chin to make a hat.

"This is tradition?" Ingrid asked.

I laughed. "Yes. Maybe not an old tradition, but still."

"This is ridiculous, is what this is," she pouted.

"Oh, hush. At least I didn't keep track of the ribbons you broke."

"Why would you do that?" she asked.

"Because, according to *tradition*, you have a baby for every broken ribbon."

Ingrid threw back her head and howled. "I assure you, there's no danger of babies in our future."

I took my seat and an awkward silence fell over the group.

Rena kicked me under the table. "Your turn," she said. "Give her your gift."

"Right. Well, my present isn't so sentimental. And you may not even want it."

"Stop hedging," Dru said. "Just give the woman your gift."

I pulled the envelope from the back pocket of my jeans. It was a little rumpled, so I smoothed it on the table before handing it to Ingrid. There was no glitter, colored paper, or ribbons . . . just Ingrid's name written across the front.

She opened the envelope and pulled out a single folded sheet of paper. As it shook loose, a check fell to the table.

"A check? For twenty thousand dollars?"

"Just read the letter," I said, my voice tight with nerves.

I had expected she would read the letter silently, but instead she read it aloud.

Dear Ingrid,

In many respects, you nursed me back to life after
Casey left me. You kept a roof over my head and
food in my mouth by allowing me to work at the
Gift Haus, even though I know you never really
needed the help. More importantly, you gave me
a sense of purpose by encouraging me to develop
my pet couture skills. And you gave me a shot at
a life by allowing me to continue living and working at 801 Maple even after you left.

When we made this arrangement—that you
would move to Boca and let me use this space for
cheap—you made it sound like I was doing you a
favor. But I know better. You were supporting me
just like you always have. I know if it weren't for
me, you would have sold the building and used
the money to travel and live more comfortably
with Harvey.

So let me buy you out, let me free up this asset
for you. Consider this check a down payment on
a contract for deed. That way I can take over all
the bills here and still continue sending you pay-
ments to make your life better.

Never fear. You will always have a home here.
Just not so many bills.

All my love, Izzy

When she was finished reading, she let the letter fall to
the table. I couldn't read her expression to save my life.

"I mean, if you don't want to sell, then that's okay. I can just start paying you more rent or something. I just . . . You've helped me so much, and I think it's time I carried my own weight. You've given me the strength to do that, Ingrid."

She stood up and pulled me from my chair, throwing her arms around me in a crushing embrace. I felt the delicate drop of a tear on my shoulder, and that turned on my own waterworks. But I didn't know what we were crying about yet.

"I am so proud of you, Izzy McHale. I didn't give you anything but the gift of time. Even when you were reeling from that stupid boy's betrayal, I could sense the strength in you. You just needed to trust in yourself."

I squeezed her tight and let the tears fall.

I don't know how long we would have stood there if Rena hadn't broken us apart with a gagging noise.

"*Blech*. You two sound like a Celine Dion song."

I caught Jolly gently slapping the back of Rena's head and the two of them exchanged secret smiles.

"So?" Dru asked. "Are you going to sell the building to Izzy?"

"Oh, absolutely," Ingrid replied, wiping the moisture from her eyes and sinking back down to her chair. She tipped her head back to look me in the eyes. "You could have stayed on as a tenant for as long as you wanted, but you're right that I'm even happier without having to worry about taxes and utilities and maintenance." She paused and glanced away for a moment. "It will be strange to be a guest in my own home. Which won't be my own anymore."

"But there will always be a place for you here, both in this house and in my heart."

After the schmaltzy bit, our little hen party dissolved into gossip and laughter. I wanted to stay in that warm circle of joy all day, but at some point, I had to open up Trendy Tails. And before that, I had two dogs that needed some serious relief. I left Dru and Lucy tidying things up, let Ingrid go crawl back in bed with Harvey, and Rena accompanied me while I walked the dogs.

Packer was none too thrilled to share his morning walk with Daisy. Daisy lunged and tugged at her leash, sniffing the ground as she made her instinctive way down the sidewalk toward Dakota Park, where everyone—including Daniel Colona—took their dogs for morning exercise, but the usually irrepressible Packer hung back and sulked.

Rena skipped at my side, devouring a third caramel roll. I topped Rena by more than six inches, so she had to rely on her abundance of energy to keep up with my stride.

"Here," I said, "you take Daisy and I'll take Packer. At this rate, we'll never make it back to open up the store in time."

Rena took Daisy's leash and wrapped it twice around her hand. She was five foot nothing, and if Daisy caught sight of a squirrel, she could lead Rena on a merry chase.

"I can't believe the police are letting us open today."

"I'm a little surprised, too. I thought Jack would put

up a fuss. But I told him we couldn't afford to lose the business, and he rolled over just like that."

"Hmmm," Rena hummed. I glanced at my friend and watched her lips slide up in a sly smile. With her hair—currently bright pink—ruffled atop her head and the carnival of colors and bangles she wore, she looked like an imp.

"What?"

"Nothing," Rena said, but that smile said something else entirely.

I shrugged. "I suppose he might be getting some pressure from his mother. She's pretty gung ho about her Pearl marrying Romeo Tucker next weekend. I don't think she'll stand for a delay, murder or no murder."

"Yeah," Rena said. "I'm sure that's it."

Daisy tugged Rena away and into the park and made her way unerringly to a tree near an out-of-the-way park bench. Rena let her have her head and followed. We exchanged a sad glance as Daisy sniffed her way around the bench, where Daniel must have sat while Daisy played, then lay down on the ground with a tired whimper.

While Daisy had found her spot in the park, Packer had other things in mind. Now that he had me to himself, he danced around my legs and scampered his way toward a clutch of young mothers and their children.

Dakota Park covered a broad swath of green space, land that a timber baron had bequeathed to the town. One corner of the park was covered in vast slides, forts, swings, and other adventures for little kids, another corner was fenced off as a play area for larger dogs, and the band shell in the middle provided a focal point for picnickers coming in to enjoy fireworks and cookouts and even the annual Halloween Howl. There were also little nooks and crannies, quiet spaces occupied by one or two benches, where residents could sit with a book, hold a quiet conversation, or—occasionally—make out in peace.

Packer was great with kids, so I let his leash out and plopped down on a bench next to Ama Olmstead, who was watching her young son, Jordan, playing cars with another toddler.

Everyone in town loved Ama Olmstead. She was Merryville's darling. Tiny, pretty, blond, blue-eyed, and sweeter than a Christmas stollen, she looked like an old-fashioned china doll. She managed to greet everyone with a welcoming smile and a personal word. "How are your bunions, Martha?" "Did you get your green beans canned, Greta?" "How's your son down in the Cities, Roy?" It's why she was so good at her job.

Other than the editor, all of the *Merryville Gazette* employees were part-time. David Lusztig covered government business, the school board, and city council and such; Joyce Lambert covered the police beat; Amber Nash covered funerals and potlucks; and Ama Olmstead covered everything else. That meant writing stories on everything from town gatherings to tourist events to high school sports, and Ama handled it all with grace and good humor. I knew she was ambitious, eager to move up the journalistic food chain, but she was making the best of what she had.

"Morning, Izzy," she said, an unusual note of sorrow in her tone. Of course, she'd been on the scene when Daniel had died, and I imagined we'd all been affected. Heaven knows I wasn't feeling myself that morning. And Ama had seemed particularly shaken up by the sight of Daniel, making little choking sounds as she snapped pictures of the scene.

"Good morning, Ama. Hope you don't mind if Packer keeps Jordan company." My scrappy pooch had wormed his way into the boys' game and was vigorously licking a plastic yellow dump truck while Jordan giggled in glee.

A ghost of a smile drifted across her lips. "Don't worry. I'm not one of those sanitizer-crazy moms who won't let her kid get a little dog spit on him now and then."

I uttered a surprised laugh. Ama and I weren't close, and I'd forgotten how funny she could be. Unlike her husband, Steve, Ama wasn't a native of Merryville. She was a Wisconsinite, practically from Chicago, which in Merryville terms meant she was practically from New York City. She blended right in with the Merryville crowd, but every now and then the big-city edge made an appearance, either by way of a particularly edgy article of clothing—such as the chic Black Watch infinity scarf she wore with her black peacoat—or through her wry wit.

"You must be exhausted," Ama continued, her eyes never leaving her son.

"Yeah, it was quite a night."

"Quite a night."

"Did you know Daniel?" I asked.

She shot me a look of surprise. "Me?"

"Well, you were both reporters. I thought maybe he might have visited with you at some point during his stay here."

She turned her attention back to Jordan and Packer. "He was a reporter?"

"Yeah," I said. "I thought you knew."

"No."

"Too bad. I'd sorta hoped he'd given you some hint about what he was doing here."

A lopsided smile graced her face. "I'm just a small-town reporter," she said. "I've been to a few journalism conferences in Minneapolis, but the reporters from the big cities don't necessarily view me as their colleague. I never even met Daniel Colona."

I knew a little something about people looking down on you. I'd heard from some of my friends from college, men and women who'd gone on to work with some of the big design houses in New York or opened up their own boutiques, dressing wealthy women in Minneapolis and Chicago. They tried to act interested and enthusiastic about my pet boutique, but I could always tell they were faking it. Their undertones ranged from horror to hilarity. The fact that I was happy as a clam didn't seem to make much difference.

"Do you have any idea what he was doing here, though? I mean, what's going on in Merryville that could have been of interest to a reporter from another city?"

"Jordan, let Elliot have his Thomas back," she called. She shifted on the park bench. "I guess I'm not much of a journalist. I can't imagine what he was doing here."

Her tone was light, almost flip, but with a brittle edge to it.

"Huh. No idea at all?"

She shifted again. "Who knows?" This time, there was no mistaking the annoyance in her voice. "Maybe he just wanted to see how countryfolk live."

I watched Packer roll over on his back so Jordan and his friend Elliot could take turns rubbing his belly. While Elliot gave Packer his full attention, Jordan grabbed a handful of grass and toddled toward his mother.

"Ma!" He handed her the grass like a trophy.

"Thank you, sweets," Ama said. She set the grass on her knee and reached into the tote bag at her side for a baby wipe, which she used to wipe her son's ruddy face, cleaning it of mud and a drippy nose. He pulled back and squinted his chocolate-drop eyes. "Hush," Ama said softly, giving her son's face one final swipe before ruffling his hair and letting him go.

She glanced up at me with a smile, her son's presence completely dispelling her momentary annoyance. "I'm not one of 'those' moms, but I do have standards."

I laughed. "He's adorable. Growing fast. What is he, two?"

"Thanks," she said, but she looked uncomfortable.

"Yes, he'll be three in June. Party planning is already under way.

"You don't have kids, do you?" she asked.

Ah. It seemed a little personal, but everyone in Merryville knew about my spectacular breakup with my former fiancé, Casey Alter, and many felt it their right—heck, their duty—to pry right on into my business. It was like the story had become public property, an insult to the town as much as to me.

"No, Casey and I thought about starting a family a few years back, but decided to wait until he was done with his residency." Turned out that was a great decision, allowing us to break ties completely after he cheated on and then dumped me.

"Changes everything," she said. "It's definitely put a crimp in my career plans. I used to aspire to getting a job at a bigger paper, maybe in Brainerd or even the Twin Cities. I went to workshops and conferences, trying to network and hone my craft. Now, though, I stay home with Jordan. Almost no more work travel. I haven't given up on that dream of writing for a bigger paper, where it would be a full-time job, but the likelihood seems to shrink with every day. Still I wouldn't give motherhood up for anything, you know?"

"Yeah," I said, unsure what else to add to that. After all, I didn't have kids so I clearly *did not* know. "So you're sure you don't know what Daniel might have been doing here?"

Her lips thinned. "Like I said, I'd bet it was just some local color piece, promoting tourism or something."

"Seems like a puff piece wouldn't take so long. He was here for a month. Must have been something more serious than that."

She shrugged.

"You must have some idea."

She brushed at her face, as though an insect were bothering her. "I don't know what you want from me, Izzy. You're right. He was a reporter, and he wouldn't have been messing around in this town unless there was something going on. But I'll be darned if I know what it is."

If Ama knew something about the story Daniel planned to break, she was clearly going to keep it to herself. I guess I didn't blame her. Whatever brought Daniel all the way to Merryville, it must have been a juicy story, something the *Madison Standard* would be interested in. If Ama could pick up where Daniel let off . . . well, if she could scoop a story that landed in the big-city papers, she might actually secure full-time work at the *Gazette*, possibly even move to the front of the line to replace editor Ted Lang, who was about ready to hit the snowbird circuit, or even break into a bigger media market. She could have Jordan and the high-powered career she was looking for.

"Listen, Ama, if you know anything, you have to tell me. My aunt is in real trouble here, and if you know something that might help her get off the hook . . . you'd still get all the credit for the story."

Ama turned to face me, her brow knit in genuine confusion. She opened her mouth, but before she could say a word, a big hand descended on her shoulder and she about jumped out of her skin. I looked up to see Ama's husband, Steve Olmstead, smiling down at us.

"What are you two ladies up to?"

"Steve! What are you doing here?"

He leaned down to kiss his wife's cheek. She reached up to take his hand, and he winced.

"You okay?" I asked.

"What? Yeah, I'm fine. It's just a splinter. Got it cutting lumber for the wood paneling in Ken's new restaurant. Hazard of the job, you know. You should see my medical file."

His glacial eyes squinted as he turned his attention to his son and grinned. "Just got out of a meeting with Ken and Hal Olson. I was on my way back home to change for the site when I saw you here. Lucky me."

"The site?" I asked.

"Squeezing in a small roofing job while Hal and Ken get the finances for the restaurant straightened out. It seems like maybe Hal overextended himself a little when he decided to back Ken's restaurant and develop the old Soaring Eagles Campground at the same time."

I was familiar with the camp. Everyone in Merryville had either attended or worked at the camp back in its heyday. Now it was a crumbling mess, but Hal Olson had bought it for back taxes just a few months before.

"Have you seen what he's developing out there?"

Steve's fingers and smile tightened. "Just the plans. He's opting for semidetached condos instead of houses. They're going to look tacky as heck. But I haven't seen what's going on since they started building. I didn't get a piece of that project."

"Did you bid on it?" I asked, knowing full well I was being a nosey parker.

Steve's smile faded. "Yep, but this firm from Brainerd underbid me. No way can they build the condos at the cost they quoted Hal. No way."

"Well," I muttered. "It's Hal's loss."

Steve shook off his funk and planted a deliberate smile on his face.

"What have you two been chatting about? Planning something devious?"

Ama laughed, but it sounded forced. "No. We were talking about the dog wedding this Saturday. I decided I should cover it for the *Gazette*. It's the type of cutesy story that gets picked up on the wire, and it will make Hetty and Louise feel so special."

We had absolutely not been talking about the dog wedding, but it was still music to my ears that Ama wanted to do a front-page story about our event. I could post a copy of the column and the professional photos Ama took on the Web site Xander Stephens was helping me build. Xander and my sister Lucy had been dancing around, going out together for months, and I shamelessly took advantage of Xander's desire to ingratiate with my family. He'd helped me set up one of those little square dealies that allowed me to accept credit cards, he'd created an inventory spreadsheet that even I could operate, and now he was helping with the Web site. Part of me hoped Xander and Lucy would stay in this romantic limbo for a couple of years so I could milk Xander's body of tech and business knowledge for all it was worth.

"Hiya!" I turned away from Steve and Ama to find Rena was making her way across the park, the now-mopey Daisy in tow. "Hey kids," she shouted. "Izzy, we have to hit the bricks."

I pulled my phone from my pocket and glanced at the display. Sure enough, we'd just barely have time to make it back to Trendy Tails in time to tidy up and open the doors. With the spring tourist season just getting under way, every day was an important day for the store.

As Rena got a little closer, Daisy—who had barely made a sound since she and Daniel had moved in four weeks earlier—started to bark. Not an aggressive bark but somehow insistent. Like when a dog needs out of the house or when he thinks it's dinnertime. I don't know whether it was the kids, the other dogs, or her desire to go home, but she kicked up quite a little fuss.

"Whoa," Rena said, pulling on Daisy's leash to make sure she didn't charge.

Packer came dancing over, making twisty jumps in the air and barking just to be a part of the fun. Jordan followed him, running right into his daddy's arms. Daisy's attention immediately turned toward the toddler. She gave Jordan's pudgy ankles big sloppy kisses while the boy flopped over in a dangerous backbend in an effort to pet the doggy.

"Whoa, buddy," Steve said, righting his son in his arms. "Jordan seems to love dogs. We've been thinking about getting one, but, you know, there never seem to be enough hours in the day."

I tucked that little morsel of information away. If no one came to claim Daisy, she would soon need a forever home, and the Olmsteads might make the perfect family for Daniel's sweet girl.

I laughed. "Well, this suddenly turned into a party, but we really do have to scoot. Steve, Ama, it was good to see you both." I turned my attention on Ama and tried to capture her gaze with mine. "Think about what we were talking about, Ama. If you have any ideas, let me know."

Ama glanced up at her husband and then quickly away. "Sure," she said.

But something told me that Ama Olmstead wasn't about to tell me anything about anything. I was on my own.

"I'm telling you—she knows something." I carefully threaded a black bow tie onto a tiny collar. I'd made over two dozen of the little bows over the last couple of weeks. They were favors for Pearl Collins and Romeo Tucker's doggy wedding. Once they were secured to the matching black collars—all sized to the various canine guests—we'd pack them in boxes, wrap and tag them, and set them in an artful stack next to the canine cake Rena was baking.

Rena picked up a bow and began fussing with it. "These are cute." She gave the loops a gentle tug. "And sturdy."

I snatched the bow tie from her hand. "They're not that sturdy. Stop fussing." I tossed the bow back in the box with the others, and shooed Rena toward the barkery.

She slouched away, looking over her shoulder once to blow me a raspberry.

"Maybe Ama knows something, and maybe she doesn't want to say anything because she's hoping for a big story," Rena suggested.

"That's what I thought, but when Steve joined us, Ama lied about what we'd been talking about."

"Why would she do that?"

"I have no idea. It makes no sense. That said, I did get a little something out of talking to Steve Olmstead. Did you know that he put in a bid to help Hal Olson build condos at the old Soaring Eagles Camp on Badger Lake?"

Rena stopped in the middle of arranging a tray of fish-shaped kitty crackers and stared at me like I had two heads. "How on earth would I know that? I don't exactly travel in those circles. I didn't even know Hal had opted to build condos there."

It was true. Rena was my dearest friend in the whole world, but she definitely lived on the fringe of Merryville society. With her bubblegum spiky hair, her unconventional wardrobe, and her hostile, drunken father, Rena had never fit in well. When we were in high school, I'd even heard some girls whispering that she was a witch. Rena tended to stick with my family and Merryville's down-and-out crowd. She certainly wasn't privy to business dealings and development projects. She only knew that Hal owned the old camp because it came up during our troubles a few months earlier.

"Fair enough. Well, he is. He's going to call it The Woods at Badger Lake. Very hoity-toity. Anyway, Steve said that the firm in Brainerd that got the job put in a ridiculously low bid. You know Hal's always looking for an angle. I can't believe Steve would even want to work with Hal."

Hal Olson owned Olson's Odyssey RV, one of the largest RV lots in the Upper Midwest. He was also my rival Prissy Olson's husband. I'd gotten to know Hal a bit better—and actually accused him of murder—last fall. I knew he had one of the fattest bank accounts in the county, and he was in the process of running for mayor of Merryville. But I also knew that his good ol' boy, "dang glad to meet ya" persona masked a man of questionable ethics and a very flexible sense of right and wrong.

"Well," Rena said, "it's too bad Steve didn't get at least part of the construction deal. Xander"—who owned the Spin Doctor record store just across the alley from me—"said that Steve's having a tough time with money. I guess Steve stopped by to ask Xander if he needed a tear-off and offered him a fire sale kind of deal. Anyway, maybe Steve figures he's got to lay down with dogs if he wants to keep his wife and son from starving."

"First of all, comparing Hal Olson to a dog is an insult to dogs. But I see what you mean. Steve also mentioned that the construction at the old Grateful Grape has slowed to a crawl while Ken and Hal work out some of the kinks in Hal's financing of the restaurant. With work being so scarce, I guess Steve's got to do what he's got to do. Even if he has to do it with Hal Olson.

"Anyway, the whole conversation got me wondering if Daniel was up here to investigate shenanigans at Hal's development. It's certainly the biggest thing going on in town."

"Hmmm. Maybe. But what could Hal be doing that's worth an investigation from a big-city newspaper? A four-week investigation at that."

Before I could answer, the bell on the front door tinkled, signaling a guest. I turned on my brightest smile, anticipating a customer, but it melted when I saw Richard Greene wiping his feet on my welcome mat.

"Hi, Richard. What can I do for you?"

Richard glanced from me to Rena—who prompted the man to heave a big sigh—and back again. "Ladies. I've got some business to discuss."

It was my turn to sigh. Dour Richard had it in for Trendy Tails, and I doubted he came by to suggest cross-promotion of our stores.

He pulled a sheaf of printer paper from inside his jacket, unfolded the bunch, and handed them to me.

"Commercial Feed Program, blah blah, Minnesota Statutes 25.31–25.43," I read aloud. The entire sheet was covered with a single paragraph of text. I flipped through the other two sheets of paper and saw more of the same.

"Why don't we cut to the chase, Richard? What's this all about?"

"Miss McHale, I'm going to have your business shut down."

CHAPTER
Five

"Shut down?" Rena laughed. "And how are you going to do that? We've already gone one round with you at city hall, and we won that one."

"Yes, well, this time I'm going to the state. Turns out there are rules in Minnesota about selling animal feed. Including pet food. You have to have your products licensed and pay fees for each one. They have to be labeled, too."

"We have labels," Rena said, tilting her chin in defiance.

"Labels with ingredients, not just smiley faces and loopy letters."

I let the papers fall onto the glass display case at my side and rubbed my face with both hands. I didn't need this. Not now. The murder in my showroom wasn't enough? I had to deal with Richard Greene breathing down my neck about state regulations?

"Richard," I said, foreclosing any more back-and-forth between the cantankerous old man and my cantankerous young friend. "We didn't know. I promise we'll get this straightened out with the state. Just give us a week. Right now, I'm busy dealing with Aunt Dolly's murder charge."

Apparently I'd said the magic word: Dolly. Richard narrowed his eyes, but relented. "Fine. I'll give you a week. If you don't take care of this on your own, I'll have no choice but to report you to the appropriate state authorities. I don't want a lawbreaker for a neighbor."

"Thank you."

He harrumphed. "How is Dorothy holding up? Is there, ah, anything I can do to help?"

Wow. Richard must have been really taken with my aunt Dolly. I'd never heard him string so many kind words together before. Ever.

"Thanks, Richard. I'm not sure what anyone can do right now. We're trying to figure out who else might have had motive and opportunity to kill Daniel. If you have any thoughts . . ."

"I'll think on it some."

I had a sudden thought. "Hey, do you know Hal Olson is building condos on the old Soaring Eagles property?"

Richard frowned, the expression turning the lines around his mouth into gullies. "Vacation property," he spat.

"Well, isn't that a good thing?" Rena asked. "I mean, you rely on the tourist industry as much as we do."

He drew himself up. "Got nothing against tourists. But I got something against mucking up the natural beauty of Badger Lake. Won't be anyplace on the lake you can sit or float where you won't be able to see those condos or whatever."

I wouldn't have thought it was possible, but his frown deepened. "Come to think of it, I walk down to the lake near every day. Gotta stay fit. Saw that Daniel guy more than once."

"What was he doing?" I asked, my heartbeat starting to kick up a notch.

"Nothing. Just standing there by the build site. Watching."

I knew it. Something about the lakeside development had brought Daniel Colona to Merryville. And that something had gotten him killed.

That evening, Sean Tucker came over to join Rena and me for dinner and a movie.

The three of us had been inseparable from the day Sean moved to Merryville in the fourth grade until a week before we graduated from high school. Then, one night, Sean had stood beneath my bedroom window in the midst of a summer storm and declared his love for me. At the time, I was so lost in my infatuation with Casey Alter that I couldn't see the truth of Sean's words: that I was an accessory to Casey, not a real partner. By the time I caught on, fourteen years had passed and the rift between Sean and me had grown into a vast gulf of awkward silence.

A few months ago, Sean had reentered my life when

Rena's alleged involvement in a murder threw us together. The reunion had been rocky, to say the least. Sean's feelings for me had withered on the vine just as I started to think maybe Sean and I should have been more than friends. Still, we'd managed to mend fences enough to hold a conversation, and Rena was positively giddy to have the old gang together again.

The night after Daniel's death, we were all looking for a little lighthearted fun. I had DVRed *Clueless*, a movie we'd watched about forty-seven times when we were in high school, and Rena had promised to make her decadent cheese enchiladas. With Ingrid and Harvey's permission, we'd gotten rid of the wedding cake—a tier for the Merryville General staff, one for the police department, and one for the firefighters—so we didn't have dessert on hand. Sean brought the ice cream—he'd long since learned that we preferred a gift of ice cream to a gift of wine—and we had ourselves a party.

While Rena finished up in the kitchen, Sean and I leaned against the pass-through.

"So you think he was here to investigate the Soaring Eagles development?" Sean asked as he dunked a tortilla chip into a bowl of chunky salsa.

"It makes sense," Rena said. "Nothing ever happens in Merryville. That development is probably the biggest change to this town since the streets were paved."

"From what I hear, nothing much has happened yet," Sean argued.

"Still, what else would someone from Madison come all the way out here to investigate?"

Sean looked down, and my own gaze followed. Packer and Daisy were sitting at Sean's feet, wiggling excitedly on their haunches, their eyes following the path of another tortilla chip to Sean's mouth. Daisy whimpered and licked her chops while Packer tried to worm his way between her and Sean's loafers.

I looked up to find Sean staring at me, a quizzical twist to his brows.

"Unless you want those two trying to steal your enchiladas and fighting for your ice cream spoon, I would ignore them."

"Not even one little chip?"

"See, that's how they get you. First it's one little chip. Then, well, what's another? Pretty soon, they've eaten half the bag and consider you their dealer."

Sean laughed.

"You can laugh, but that chip is a gateway drug. Two hours from now, they're meth heads and you're their only supply."

"Okay. Fair enough." He looked down at the pitiful dogs. "Sorry, guys. Mom says no."

He shifted around so he could lean his side against the pass-through and face me head-on. "So, Daniel was working on a story. There's not necessarily anything sinister about it. Maybe it was just a human interest story?"

"Ugh. Enough with that already. Everyone keeps saying it might have been a puff piece about a cute tourist town. But that wouldn't take a month in the field to write, and Daniel wasn't that kind of reporter," I said.

"How do you know?" Sean asked suspiciously.

"Xander showed me how to go on the Internet and search the *Madison Standard*'s archives. I read a bunch of Daniel's columns and they were all about public corruption and corporate greed and sex scandals."

"Sex scandals?" Rena's face brightened at the possibility of some delicious tawdry sex story. "Tell me one."

I glanced at Sean. He shrugged like he didn't care about the detour in our conversation, but his lips were curled in just the faintest hint of a smile. I think he wanted to hear one, too.

"There was one about a personal chef—whom Daniel mercifully never named—who was sleeping with all his female clients. We're talking the wives of judges and city councilmen, and über-rich businessmen. Apparently all of the women thought they were the only one, that they were special. 'You're the center of my galaxy,' he'd tell them. But then two of them were chatting over a manicure, found out they were both sleeping with the chef, and pretty soon they'd told all their friends. Once all the women knew, some started telling their husbands about other women's affairs, and pretty soon the whole world knew that all of these powerful men had been cuckolded."

"Wow. And he didn't expose the chef's name?" Sean asked.

"That's just it. All these powerful people were exposed, but the women were still loyal to their lover and the men didn't want to give the chef any publicity. According to Daniel, they all refused to give the man's name. He's the 'Mystery Chef.'"

"What an awesome story," Rena said. "I mean, it's terrible that it happened and all, but still an awesome story."

I knew what she meant. Sometimes hearing about other people's bad choices made me feel a little better about my own situation. Specifically the whole Casey thing. I knew it was childish and maybe even a little catty. I wasn't proud of that fact, but since we're being honest here . . .

"So all of Daniel's stories are like that?" Sean asked.

"Yep. He wrote about the real underbelly of life in Madison. Not always hard-hitting journalism. I mean the sex scandal was a pretty tabloidesque bit of journalism. But he certainly didn't write anything about happy people and places and how great life was. In other words, I don't think he was here to write a story about how great Merryville is and how everyone should come for a visit."

"So let's assume he was here to check out the development," Sean said. "*What* about the development?"

"That, we don't know." Rena pulled the pan of enchiladas from the oven, and the apartment was immediately engulfed in the savory scent of chilies, corn, and just a hint of chocolate—Rena's secret ingredient.

The rattling of the wire rack in the oven acted like a dinner bell for the dogs. They came scampering in, Daisy's long legs serving her well but Packer trying his best to muscle his way in front of the canine competition. Rena lifted the pan high above their doggy heads and waded through their enthusiasm until she could set the pan on the pass-through. I couldn't see Packer, but I heard his snuffle of annoyance.

"Wow," Sean breathed, a dreamy smile on his face. His voice dropped an octave to a bedroom growl. "That smells delicious."

Rena laughed and I tried to muster a smile to hide the reaction that sultry voice had on me. I had to remind myself that Sean wasn't interested anymore. No point developing a crush fourteen years too late.

"Anyway," I said, "Rena and I were thinking about walking the dogs down to the lake tomorrow. It's Sunday, so the shop doesn't open until noon."

Sean groaned. "Are we really doing this again? Getting involved in another murder investigation."

"We're just going to walk by the lake. If we happen to see something interesting, well, then so be it."

"Right," he deadpanned. "Just an innocent stroll." He stood up straight and waggled his finger between Rena and me. "You two need to stay out of this. Jack Collins may not be my favorite person, but he's a perfectly reliable cop. Let him do his job."

I shrugged. "It's just a hunch at this point. If I told Jack about it, he would look at me just exactly like you're looking at me now. Like I'm a nut job. If we find something more concrete, I promise to take it straight to Jack."

He shook his head. "I still don't trust you two to stay out of trouble."

I took a plate of enchiladas from Rena and handed it off to Sean. "We're going. If you want to come along as a chaperone, you're welcome to join us. But with or without you, we're going. It's the very least I can do for Aunt Dolly."

With a deep sigh, Sean conceded. "Fine. I'll come with you. I'd never forgive myself if you two got yourselves killed."

As soon as we were seated, Daisy and Packer took up positions with clear views to all three of us. Smart dogs. You never knew which human would drop something or cave in and offer a little treat below the table.

"This is delicious," Sean said, lifting a forkful of melty cheese and sauce to his lips.

"I'll give you the recipe," Rena replied. "It's bachelor-proof."

Sean had been in a long-term relationship with a fellow attorney, but that had ended on a particularly sour note. I occasionally got a hint of a flirt from him, but I hadn't heard of him going on any other dates. He apparently needed some time to lick his wounds after the whole Carla Harper debacle.

"I'll have you know," Sean said, waggling his fork in Rena's direction, "I'm a pretty competent cook. It was a good way to unwind without feeling guilty during law school. After all, I had to eat, didn't I?"

"Prove it," Rena said.

"Fine. Next time we have a casual dinner party, we'll do it at my house. I'll make my famous eggplant parmigiana."

"Sounds like a deal."

We ate on in silence for a bit until Rena, whose chair faced the kitchen, heaved a sigh.

I followed her line of sight and watched as Jinx lifted her head out of the enchilada pan. A long string of melted cheese connected the cat to the pan, and the three of us watched her toss her head this way and that, trying to get that cheese into her mouth.

"Oh dear. I was so worried about the beggars here"—I indicated Packer and Daisy—"that I never even thought about Jinx's cheese obsession."

Sean snorted, trying to stave off a laugh.

Rena grinned. "I hope no one wanted seconds."

"You two can laugh. You don't live with her. That cat is lactose intolerant. She might drive Ingrid, Harvey, and me to a hotel for the night."

Rena and Sean broke up then, howling with laughter. After a few miserable seconds, I joined in. I watched in resignation and Jinx went in for another bit of cheese, this time sticking her paw into the pan and trying to shovel the cheese to her mouth.

I got up and took the pan away from the cat, earning me a pouty hiss, and then we went back to eating in relative silence.

After the dishes had been cleared and the tainted enchiladas dumped into a trash bag, I scooped up Jinx—who rumbled softly in her postbinge stupor—and we retired the few feet to my living area and piled on the couch, where I found myself wedged between Rena and Sean. My couch is not that big. In fact, I'd never realized just how small it was. From just a few inches away, I could feel the heat emanating from Sean's body, smell a faint whiff of juniper from his shaving soap.

"Okay," I said, my voice sounding unnaturally loud. "I need a good laugh."

I flipped on the television and started scrolling through menus looking for our movie. As soon as the opening credits began to roll, and the television started making noise, Daisy May came tearing out of my bedroom, big paws scrabbling on the hardwood floor. She slid to a stop in front of the couch and immediately leapt up between Sean and me. Or, more precisely, *on* Sean and me. One hindquarter rested on Sean's leg and one on mine, the dog wobbling until she managed to find her balance. In the process, she completely dislodged Jinx, drawing a full-throated hiss from my queenly cat.

"What the . . . ?" Sean leaned back to look around Daisy's back and meet my eyes.

I shrugged.

"She's watching TV," Rena said. "Look at her."

Sure enough, Daisy had settled and become very still. Her gaze was pinned to the television, her head cocked and ears perked up as though she were trying to follow the plot.

I managed to pull my leg out from under her weight, forcing her to waggle her butt to find her balance again, but her focus on the television never wavered.

"At least she's got good taste in movies," Sean quipped. We shared a smile over the back of the couch.

It might have been my imagination, but I thought I detected a spark in his eyes, a glint of heat that lingered just a smidge too long.

"I've never seen a dog watch TV," Rena whispered.

We were all staring at Daisy as if she'd suddenly started reciting passages on quantum mechanics.

"Seriously," I added. "Occasionally, Packer will pay attention to something moving fast on the screen, but he gets bored after about five seconds. What about Blackstone?" I asked Sean. Blackstone, Sean's elderly basset hound, didn't move much. I figured maybe he was enough of a couch potato to invest himself in some police procedurals or soap operas.

"Nah. If he hears an animal sound, his ears will perk up, but he never seems to put two and two together to realize that the sound is coming from the TV."

At that point, we were past the credits and Cher had been making vacuous chitchat with her vacuous friends for nearly fifteen minutes. Still, Daisy had not moved a muscle.

"You know," Rena said, "I've heard that some dog owners who are gone for long periods of time leave the television on for their pets, so they don't get lonely. Maybe that's why she's doing this."

I huffed a little sigh. "I guess that must be it. Still weird, though."

"Amen," Rena answered, raising her hand so we could high-five.

"Weird or not, I've got to get her off me," Sean said. "If she cuts off the supply of blood to my leg any longer, they're going to have to amputate."

Rena and I laughed, even as we hauled ourselves off the couch and physically shifted Daisy until she was resting with her narrow butt on the couch cushion.

"I guess Daisy has hijacked our movie night," Sean

said, as he stood and gingerly tested his weight on the leg Daisy had been sitting on.

"Yeah," Rena said. "I'll walk you out. But we're still on for tomorrow morning, right?"

"Absolutely. Let's meet on the porch at, say, nine thirty? You two can fight over who gets to handle Daisy's leash."

"I feel like Daisy and I shared a moment there. It would be the gentlemanly thing to do to walk her, right?"

"That's the spirit," Rena said, throwing her arms around Sean's middle.

He hugged her back. "Don't get your hopes up. I still think this is a terrible idea. But if it moves from terrible idea to terrible situation, I want to be there."

CHAPTER
Six

I gave Jinx some extra snuggle time that night, trying to make up for her rude eviction from my lap during the evening. As soon as I bedded down on the couch—having given my room to Ingrid and Harvey—she sprawled her massive, twenty-pound cat self across my torso and generously allowed me to scratch her chin and ears. Occasionally, she would scoot forward a bit until we were practically nose to nose. Eventually, she began to drift off to the sound of the quiet snores emanating from Packer's fleece bed.

Draped in that heavy cat blanket, I tried to unscramble some of the puzzle pieces we had at that point . . . which weren't much.

We knew that Ama knew more than she was willing to tell, but the substance of her knowledge could have been anything. And we knew that Ken West was being secretive about what he was doing in the alley the night of the murder. Either he was doing something he shouldn't have been doing, or he wasn't in the alley at all. . . . He could have been on the second floor killing Daniel Colona. But why?

At the moment our best lead was that Daniel was working on some sort of exposé; that's what he did. According to Richard Greene, he'd been looking for a hunting and fishing guide, someone who could help him find his way around the less populated parts of the Merryville area. And, currently, the most exciting event happening on undeveloped land was the development of the old camp by the always-slippery Hal Olson.

I drifted to sleep with visions of dark woods and dimly lit rooms, Daniel's broken and bloody body accompanying me through my dream-walk through Merryville.

Sunday morning greeted me with the scent of frying bacon and fresh brewed coffee. It had been years since I'd eaten meat, but that particular combination of smells sent endorphins running through my brain straight to my happy place. I crawled out of the nest of quilts on the couch and let my nose lead me to my kitchenette.

To my surprise, I found Harvey manning the skillet. Daisy, Packer, and Jinx lined up like little soldiers at his feet, each hoping some of that bacon might jump out of the pan and into their waiting mouths.

"Ingrid is busy getting gussied up. Wants to go to church this morning."

He speaks! I thought. *In full sentences, even!*

"Nice of you to make breakfast."

"Hope you don't mind me using your pans for the

bacon. I found some of that fake-on stuff in your freezer and I'm making some for you." He pointed toward a smaller skillet, where three uniformly rectangular pieces of mock bacon were sizzling softly in a little oil.

Every day, I understood a little more why Harvey was Ingrid's Prince Charming.

"Thank you, Harvey. You and Ingrid have a wild night last night?" The two had gone out before Sean and Rena had come over and hadn't returned home until long after I'd drifted off on the couch.

Harvey smiled, and I caught a glimpse of the boy Ingrid had fallen in love with. "Just a little supper and an evening at the Moose. Playing pull tabs and drinking beer."

"So romantic," I teased.

"That's what I love about Ingrid," he said, his voice rough with emotion. "For her, that is romantic. Every minute we're together, it's romantic."

I caught back a sigh. What must it be like to be so madly in love? I hoped I would get to find out someday.

"How are you two holding up after the wedding?"

He shrugged. "The attempted wedding, you mean. We're fine, I guess. We're both a little disappointed that we didn't officially get married yet, but that pales next to that poor young man's death."

"Oh dear! I hope we can figure out a time to reschedule. I want you two to have the wedding you deserve."

He looked past my shoulder, making sure Ingrid wasn't right behind me. "Ingrid says we should just go down to the courthouse. That it would be romantic, like eloping. But I know she wants to get married with her friends and family around her."

"Harvey." Ingrid had come out of nowhere to stand at my shoulder. "I told you I want to be married to you more than I want anything else."

Good heavens, these two were killing me. All this lovey-dovey stuff was so out of character for Ingrid, and a little too saccharine for so early in the day. Still, it was hard to be immune to so much romance.

"We could try again," I suggested. "Downstairs."

"When?" Ingrid asked. "Trendy Tails is getting busy these days."

She was right. As the first wave of tourists hit the streets of our tiny burg, Rena and I had seen traffic in the store pick up tremendously. We got lots of compliments on both the merchandise and the treats, so we were hoping that word of mouth would boost business even further.

I had a sudden thought. "Would you . . . ? No." I hummed to myself, trying to figure out whether my question would be insulting. In the end, I took the plunge. "We already have next Saturday afternoon blocked off for Pearl and Romeo's wedding. Would you mind sharing your festivities with a couple of pooches?"

Harvey looked horrified, but Ingrid laughed. "Harvey, can you even imagine? We'll live on in Merryville lore forever: our first wedding cut short by a dead body, our second shared with a couple of dressed-up dogs?" She hooted. "I love it!"

Harvey raised his eyebrows and bobbled his head

like he was weighing the pros and cons. "Darling, if it makes you happy, I say let's do it."

The three of us feasted on Harvey's amazing scrambled eggs—apparently the secret ingredients were mountains of butter and rivers of heavy cream, bacon (both fake and real), sourdough toast, and a fruit salad of strawberries and cantaloupe in some sort of light, minty syrup. As I chewed, I idly tried to come up with an excuse for Harvey to stay on in Merryville and cook for me every day. And then I idly tried to imagine just how many pounds I could gain eating Harvey's fare.

"Harvey said you're going to church."

Ingrid nodded. "I'd say that I want to go to say an extra prayer for Daniel Colona, but it would be a lie. I want to go to hang out with all those Methodist biddies and find out what I've missed over the past few months."

At least she was honest.

"Do you have a few minutes to help me out downstairs before you have to go?"

She glanced at the clock on my stove. "Absolutely. I don't have to leave for another half hour or so."

Ingrid practically skipped down the stairs when she followed me to the shop after breakfast. Sean and Rena and I had our trek to Badger Lake all planned out, but I had about half an hour before we left, just like Ingrid, so I figured we'd work on making the big display cabinet in the middle of the store more springlike.

"What do you think, Ingrid? Should we go with gauzy pastels or brighter spring colors like crocus purple and daffodil yellow?"

Ingrid rolled her eyes. "Why would you even ask? You know what I'm going to say."

"Right. Bright colors."

Ingrid popped into the barkery and came back with a huge vase of lilacs, the bouquets and smaller vases from her wedding consolidated into a single vessel. She set the overflowing vase on the display case and took a step or two back. "Definitely bright colors."

Looking at her beautiful wedding flowers, already starting to wilt, I felt myself tear up. "Ingrid, I am so, so sorry that you couldn't get married. It's completely unfair."

Ingrid looked me square in the eyes. "Hey. Do you see me crying or moping around?"

"No. But you're Ingrid. You never cry or mope around."

She laughed. "That's not entirely true. I've had my down days before. But this isn't one of them. I'm sorry that poor man died, and I wish Harvey and I were an old married couple already. But the bottom line is that I'm surrounded by good friends, I have Harvey at my side, and we already have a new plan for a wedding in just a week."

Most people thought of Ingrid as a tough old broad. They weren't wrong. But she could whip up a silver lining for any cloud that came her way. She grouched a lot, but she was also surprisingly optimistic.

Ingrid pulled me into a brusque hug and then set about pulling together the brightest of the wares I had on display, putting together little outfits for our specially made dog and cat mannequins (each carved and painted picket-fence white by Chimpy Lassiter, a local woodworker whose intricately carved bedsteads and dining tables were a hot commodity among the hipster crowd in Minneapolis).

I swiped the dampness from my eyes and joined in. We had already put together a hot pink tutu with a ridiculously cute Daisy Duke halter top and picked out a dozen of the most flamboyant collars in my inventory when there was a knock on the door.

I spun around, expecting to find Sean waiting on the doorstep—after all, Rena had her own key—but I was stunned to see Jane Porter.

I glanced at Ingrid. She had pulled herself up to her full height and had wiped all expression clean off her face. My friend had suddenly become a totem pole.

Jane knocked again, and I bustled over to answer. I only cracked the door enough to wedge my own body in the opening.

Jane wore a cloak the color of ripe strawberries over a pale blue dress. Her feet were encased in a pair of low heels that matched the dress to perfection, and the feathered hat perched on her snowy head mirrored the cloak's vibrant red.

At first glance, her pale skin and wide blue eyes made her look like a china doll. But even in the kind light of morning, Jane was showing her age. The powder that coated her cheeks rode unevenly across her wrinkles and made her skin look more papery than flawless. She'd built a Hadrian's Wall of lip liner to prevent the savage red of her lipstick from overrunning her white, white skin.

The march of time had taken its toll, but she was still a pretty woman. I guessed that in her day she would have been a great model for a sailor's pinup tattoo, all exaggerated curves and lush femininity.

"Good morning, Jane. I'm afraid you've caught us a little off guard. We don't open until noon on Sundays."

"Oh no, dear. I didn't come to shop. I was hoping to chat with Ingrid."

I didn't know Jane Porter well. She was Lutheran; I was Methodist. She lived in Quail Run, an upscale housing complex; I lived in a downtown apartment. I'd heard she had an enormous cage full of lovebirds, but I didn't really sell to the bird crowd. Short story, our lives rarely overlapped.

Still, I'd heard Dolly mention Jane's cutting wit at the canasta tables, and I knew the history between Ingrid and Jane. Maybe Jane's intentions were pure, but for all I knew, she had come to rub Ingrid's nose in her failed wedding. And I couldn't let that happen.

I shot a quick glance back at Ingrid, who gave her head a tiny shake.

"Gee, Jane. I still can't help you. Ingrid isn't available at the moment."

Jane closed her eyes, revealing wobbly black eyeliner.

"Dear, your door is made of glass. I can see her standing behind you."

I felt heat licking up my cheeks. "Well, yes. But she isn't actually available."

Jane's ruby lips thinned in a tight smile. "What you mean is that she isn't available for me."

"Oh, no, of course . . . I mean . . ."

She held up a calming hand. "Don't worry, dear. I don't blame Ingrid, and I certainly don't blame you. I meant to give this to Ingrid before her wedding, but never seemed to find the right time." She flicked the kiss lock on her black patent handbag and pulled out a flat rectangular package wrapped in pink polka-dot paper. "Would you mind giving it to her now? Tell her to call me if she wants to."

I took the package from hands that trembled ever so slightly. She snapped closed the lock on her purse and made her way down my steps before climbing into a burgundy Lincoln and driving away.

I closed the door slowly and turned to face Ingrid. Her expression was grim. She nodded toward the package in my hands. "That for me?"

I nodded, and held it out to her.

She shook her head. "I don't want anything from that woman."

I looked from the package to Ingrid and back again. "Are you sure?"

"Yes," she said firmly, but I saw a twinge of uncertainty in her eyes. She had to be burning with curiosity just like I was.

"Well, then, what should I do with it?" I asked, starting to make my way to the trash can we kept behind the front display counter.

"Oh, here," Ingrid blustered, shoving her hand out to take the package. I handed it to her, and she ripped open the paper . . .

And gasped.

"What is it?" I asked, growing worried by the wavering emotions on Ingrid's face. All I could tell was that she was holding a picture frame in a white-knuckled grip. I couldn't imagine what the picture could be that would upset her so.

She handed the picture to me, as much to get it out of her hands as to show me what it was. I turned the frame around so it was upright and saw a picture of a man. The tones of the picture were washed-out, suggesting it was old, maybe from the sixties or seventies. The man himself looked to be middle-aged, hair thinning on top even as it brushed his collar below. He was handsome, with strong features and a firm, square jaw, broad shoulders and a trim physique. In the photo, he was staring off into the distance, his mouth turned up in a smile of quiet joy.

I tried to place him. He was vaguely familiar, but since the picture seemed to outdate me, if I knew this man, he was much, much older.

"It's Arnold," Ingrid offered. "I've never seen that picture before. Jane must have taken it."

I felt a little sick. I wished I could dial back time about five minutes and throw the package in the trash without even showing it to Ingrid.

"Why would she give you such a thing?" I asked.

"I don't know. To hurt me, I guess. Maybe to remind me that she wooed my husband. Maybe to suggest she could do it again. I have no idea what goes on in that woman's head, and I certainly don't want to."

"I'm sorry, Ingrid."

She waved her hand dismissively. "Don't be. I've

spent the better part of thirty-five years putting that period of my life in the past, and I'll be gosh darned if Jane Porter is going to send me back there with a single picture. What I have now is what matters, and what I have is the love of a very good man."

"That doesn't mean that you have to be immune to Jane Porter's meanness."

Ingrid nodded and drew in a deep breath. "You're right. I think it's time I headed to church. Maybe the good Lord can squash my impulse to drive out to Quail Run and punch Jane Porter in the kisser."

I watched her leave, her pocketbook tucked under her arm. She held her head high and she talked tough, but I could still see the sadness of that old wound hanging over her head.

CHAPTER
Seven

Rena, Sean, and I must have made quite a sight as we traipsed down Maple Avenue. Rena walked Daisy, who was doing the sniffing dance with Hetty Tucker's greyhound (soon-to-be groom-hound), Romeo. Sean struggled to keep hold of the antsy greyhound while still tugging along his own lethargic basset hound, Blackstone. And, of course, my Packer was leaping in crazy twirls trying to get everyone's attention at once. The dogs were all so interested in one another that we moved at a snail's pace down Maple, past Dakota Park, through the historic Birch Mound neighborhood, and eventually up Walking Bird Lane to Badger Lake and the old Soaring Eagles Adventure Camp.

By the time we approached the site where Hal Olson was building his vacation community, I think the humans were all ready to drop the leashes and let the dogs fend for themselves. Sean had taken to cursing under his breath, tiny Rena—whose stride was so much shorter than the rest of ours—was panting softly, and I was clenching my teeth in annoyance.

"Dogs! Enough!" I said, trying to inject my tone with as much steel as I possibly could.

Surprisingly, all four mutts turned their faces up to mine with comical expressions of wide-eyed wonder, as though they'd forgotten there were people involved in this walk at all.

We all stood there, a frozen tableau, getting our respective minds back on track.

"Well," Sean said, "what now?"

"I don't know," Rena responded. "I guess we look around."

"For what?"

Rena and I shrugged in tandem.

"Ahh," Sean said with a little laugh. "Like Justice Stewart on obscenity: we'll know it when we see it."

Rena and I looked at each other. She frowned and raised her hands in the universal expression for "What the heck?" I frowned and shrugged in the universal expression for "I have no idea."

Sean started to laugh, and his laughter grew until he'd plopped down to sit on the ground, Blackstone crawling into his lap as if on cue. "Lord love a duck," he said. "We have absolutely no reason to be here, do we? I mean, what could we possibly find that is at all relevant to Daniel's murder just by meandering around the work site?"

"Maybe nothing," I conceded, "but you never know.

We're talking about Hal Olson here. Not exactly a master criminal. He's a manipulative womanizer who plays fast and loose with ethical norms, but he's not very discreet about his exploits."

"But that's exactly it. Hal is not a master criminal. How could he be responsible for Daniel's murder? Heck, Hal wasn't even at the party."

"One step at a time," I said. "I just know that if we figure out what Daniel was writing his story on, we'll figure out why he was killed . . . and then it's just a hop, skip, and a jump to who killed him."

Sean heaved a sigh. "All right, then, let's see what there is to see."

Leading the dogs, who were now much more subdued, we skirted the fence surrounding the construction site and picked our way through the debris to see what Hal was building.

I knew they were building condos, but the terrible sameness of all the units hit me only when I saw them in person. I suddenly understood Richard Greene's frustration that these cookie-cutter buildings would obscure the view of the lake from every other point along the shoreline.

"Hmmm," Sean muttered.

"What?"

"Most of the people who can afford waterfront property like this expect high quality. This house wrap they're using is the most cut-rate stuff on the market."

Rena stopped in her tracks, her Doc Martens kicking up a little cloud of dust. "How on earth do you know that?"

Sean smiled like the cat who ate the canary. "I'm a man of many talents."

"Right."

"Oh, fine. My cousin Bubba runs a construction company just outside of Oxford. When I was doing my undergrad at Ole Miss, I worked summers and weekends for him. I remember him talking about this particular brand of house wrap and how one of his competitors was using it. It allowed the other guy to come in with lower bids, but Bubba wouldn't touch the stuff. Said it was a rip-off."

"Doesn't really surprise me," I chimed in. "Hal can squeeze a dollar until it squeals. Maybe that's how the Brainerd contractor was able to underbid Steve, because he plans to use substandard materials."

"True," Sean said, turning his head to survey the delicate curve of Badger Lake's shoreline, "but what a waste to erect shoddy condos on this beautiful property."

We wandered through the huddle of buildings, each the same as the last.

"Given how much work they have to do to finish these out, they don't seem to have many building materials lying around. I would expect huge stacks of shingles and bags of plaster, not to mention an earthmover or two to clear out that last section of property." He pointed to the far end of the old camp, where stakes were set in the ground indicating new builds, but the land was still covered in low brambles and mounds of dirt.

"So what does that mean?" I asked.

"Well, it makes me even more curious about what Daniel was doing out here. It doesn't look like there's that much work going on. Nothing to watch."

We completed our tour of the property, finding nothing else of interest, and were just about to give up and start the long walk home when a voice called out from the trailer parked right by the water's edge.

"No trespassing." The voice was little more than a growl, so gravelly it was difficult to understand. "I gotta gun." That statement was punctuated by the unmistakable sound of a round sliding into the chamber of a pump-action shotgun.

The three of us turned around slowly. There, in the trailer's open doorway, stood a woman in a purple flowered muumuu, a cigarette dangling from her coral-painted lips, and her weapon leveled right at the three of us.

"Son of a—" Sean muttered beneath his breath. "I knew you two would find a way to get killed."

I shushed him softly, trying not to agitate the woman who could blow us all away with a twitch of her finger.

Rena raised her hands in a sign of surrender. "Dee Dee? Dee Dee Lahti?"

"Yeah. Who're you?"

"It's Rena Hamilton."

Dee Dee cracked a laugh, the sound like the rasp of sandpaper over raw wood. "Dang, girl, I didn't recognize you with your hair that color. Last time I saw you, it was kind of a teal."

Rena had a pretty distinctive look. Apart from barely

clearing five feet, she had a ladder of earrings marching up her lobes, a studded collar around her neck, an old Ramones T-shirt hanging off one shoulder, and enough black eyeliner to write out a novel. No matter what color her hair happened to be, it was hard to mistake her for anyone other than who she was.

"Right," Rena replied. "I think that was last Veterans Day. I brought Dad to the party at the VFW and you were there with Kevin."

I had never had the pleasure of meeting either Dee Dee or Kevin Lahti, but the couple had quite a reputation. Dee Dee was Merryville's resident crazy dog lady. She and Kevin lived in a little house on the edge of town, where Dee Dee kept at least a dozen dogs. She was known for her ratted bleached-blond hair, the circles of brilliant lipstick she used to outline her mouth, and the endless stream of Parliaments hanging from her mouth, often with a precarious inch-long column of ash shivering at the end.

In short, Dee Dee was crazy, but—the shotgun aside—basically harmless.

Her husband, Kevin, on the other hand, was as dangerous as an angry badger. He'd done a couple of stints in Stillwater for aggravated robbery and made his money off the books, leading hunting, fishing, and canoeing expeditions. He was too rough around the edges to appeal to Merryville's tourist crowd, and his knowledge of the wilderness was a little too "real" for the tourists' neatly tailored bird-watching trips. Still, somehow he was keeping body and soul together.

"Who you with, Rena?" Dee Dee squinted her eyes as she tried to make us out, a note of suspicion lingering in her voice.

"These are my friends Izzy McHale and Sean Tucker."

"McHale? You related to Edie and Clem McHale who taught there at Eisenhower High?"

"Yes, ma'am. I'm their second daughter."

"Oh, well then. I had your folks in high school. Never really took to your dad's history class, but he was a nice man. And your mom let us write poetry in English. Didn't even care if it rhymed. Good people."

Apparently the goodness of my parents gave me, too, a patina of goodness. At least in Dee Dee Lahti's eyes.

"Well, come on over here so I can meet all those dogs you got." Dee Dee didn't put the shotgun down, but she did tuck it under her arm. I led the way as the three of us walked our menagerie over to meet Dee Dee.

As soon as the dogs got close, Dee Dee dropped to her knees in the dirt and began loving on all four animals, laughing like a rusty hinge on a windy day as the pooches licked her face and bonked their heads into her hands.

"Why don't you all come inside while I get some treats for your fur babies?"

I still hadn't figured out what Dee Dee was doing at the construction site, so I had no idea what to expect when I climbed the steps into the giant trailer. Still, I was surprised at what I found: an office space, neat as a pin, complete with architectural drawings and whiteboards lining the walls. The only flaw in the otherwise perfect little office space was an ashtray overflowing with Dee Dee's cigarette butts. The air was heavy with the dueling scents of the smoke and a lemon air freshener.

We piled into the trailer, four people and four dogs, and Dee Dee waved toward the tan twill sofa to indicate that we should have a seat.

She made her way around one of the desks, plopped into the chair, and dug through a drawer for a handful of dog treats for our critters. It was only then that I saw Dee Dee's dog, a Shih Tzu with flowing auburn and white hair. The dog was perched on a purple velvet pillow resting on top of the desk. Next to the pillow, there was a china plate with what appeared to be scrambled eggs and sautéed chicken livers. This was one pampered pooch.

Dee Dee must have tracked my attention. "This is Pumpkin. She's mama's special baby, isn't that right, Punky-kins?"

"She's beautiful."

"So what are you three doing out here again?"

Rena, sitting on the arm of the sofa, jumped in. "Just taking a walk. Trendy Tails opens late on Sundays, so we thought we'd take advantage of the beautiful weather and give the dogs some exercise."

"You're really not supposed to trespass on the work site."

"Sorry about that. Curiosity just got the better of us. We've heard so much about the development that we wanted to see how it was coming along."

Rena sounded so casual. Technically, she wasn't lying, but she certainly wasn't telling the whole truth. Personally, I'm completely transparent. I can't lie to save my life. But Rena was born with a streak of grifter in her soul, and she could sweet-talk the devil.

"What about you?" she asked. "You working on the site?"

Dee Dee drew herself up proudly. "Yes. I'm working the office here. I answer the phones, take lunch orders, that sort of thing. It's not a glamorous job," she said, her sly smile suggesting otherwise, "but I've got my foot in the door now. Figure if I do a good job, maybe I can get Mr. Olson to hire me out at the RV lot. That's why I'm in today. Get some files tidied up so Mr. Olson can see what a hard worker I am."

For Dee Dee, who lacked some basic social skills and bordered on mental illness, this position at the work site probably represented a huge leap in her career opportunities. Still, I couldn't imagine Hal Olson letting Dee Dee Lahti get in front of customers at his lot. Frankly, I was hard-pressed to figure out how she'd gotten the job at the construction site.

As though she'd heard my thoughts, Dee Dee answered my question.

"Steve and I were never all that close. I'm twelve years older than he is, and I married Kevin when Steve was still in grade school. But I've managed the desk for him on some of his projects and he remembered his sister. He knew I needed a job pretty bad, so he wrote a really nice letter of recommendation for me, even though he was pretty mad at Hal at the time. He's so successful. Got that pretty wife and that beautiful baby boy. I'm so proud of him."

Sean and I shared a glance. Really? Steve Olmstead and Dee Dee Lahti were siblings? I'd known Steve for years, but if Dee Dee Olmstead had become Dee Dee Lahti when I was in grade school, I suppose it wasn't shocking that I'd never made the connection. And I had to give Steve props for putting his reputation on the line for his loony sister.

Hal Olson's motivation for hiring her, on the other hand . . . that I could not begin to puzzle out.

"So you're here just about every day, then?" Rena asked.

Dee Dee nodded. "Yep. This place couldn't run without me."

Sean leaned forward. "You ever see other people lurking around here?"

For an instant, Dee Dee looked surprised. Then her eyes shifted to rest on Pumpkin.

"What do you mean, 'lurking'?"

"You know. Just someone who didn't belong here spending a little too much time hanging out."

Dee Dee turned her face back to us, her brow lowered and the suspicion on her face now unmistakable. "You mean the way you three are lurking?"

Apparently Dee Dee was a little sharper than I gave her credit for.

Sean just took it in stride, smiling back at her. "You could say that."

Dee Dee twisted her mouth to one side like she was contemplating something. Finally, she said, "Well, that fella that just died. He was here a lot. Never came on the work site, mind you. Not like you all. But he'd stand right at the edge of the water so he could see around the fence and watch what was happening."

"Didn't you find that a little odd?"

A hint of pink crept across Dee Dee's cheeks, and her gaze drifted back to Pumpkin. "Maybe. But it wasn't really my place to say anything."

"What did he do out there?" I asked.

"Nothing," she said. "He just stared."

Just stared. That's what Richard Greene had said, too: that Daniel Colona had just stared at the work site.

I was more convinced than ever that Daniel's death had something to do with the development, but we were no closer to knowing why he died or who killed him. We would probably never find the answer unless we could figure out what, exactly, Daniel had been staring at.

CHAPTER
Eight

As Sean, Rena, and I made our weary way home, we'd just turned onto Maple for that final block when my friend Taffy Nielson, owner of the Happy Leaf Tea Shoppe, bustled out of her store to grab me.

"Izzy," she said, her sugar-sweet voice tight with tension. "I need your help. I think I have a . . . a vermin."

"A vermin. Singular?" Rena asked.

"Yes." Taffy shot a glance just up the street to where Richard Greene was sweeping the steps of the Greene Brigade.

"I'm not really sure I'm going to be of much help, Taffy," I said.

"Yes. You will be of tremendous help. Just come with me." She looked like she was trying to control my mind with her fierce gaze. I'd never seen Taffy, a tender biscuit of a woman, show such fierce determination.

For whatever reason, she wanted me to follow her, so I handed Packer's leash to Rena. "Thanks for indulging us," I said to Sean. "It may seem like a dead end, but who knows? Maybe we saw something today that will unlock the whole mystery."

"Anytime, Izzy." Sean smiled one of his lopsided smiles, and I felt my heart twist in my chest. When he smiled like that, all I could see was my dear friend from high school who had harbored an unrequited crush on me. It made me want to travel back to that more innocent time, before I'd broken Sean's heart and Casey had broken mine.

Rena and Sean went their separate ways while I allowed Taffy to pull me into the tea shop. The inside of the store was as sunny and soft as Taffy herself. The walls were painted a pale buttery yellow, and blue chintz tablecloths draped the tiny round tables, each set for tea service with china pots covered in quilted cozies and a scattering of votive candles arranged artfully. The cash register sat on a pastry counter that, come Monday morning, would be overflowing with finger sandwiches, macaroons, and petits fours. Behind the counter, the walls were lined with apothecary jars filled with teas in all manner of flavors, from simple English breakfast to complex herbal concoctions.

"Okay," I said, "what's really going on?"

"I really have a vermin. Ish. Vermin is kind of judgey, but he's been getting into the bags of herbs I keep in back, and I'm terrified he's going to dash across the floor when I have customers in here."

"What on earth are you talking about?"

"It's that guinea pig," she stage-whispered.

"That guinea pig?" It took a second for the penny to drop. "Gandhi? Gandhi is alive?" I couldn't believe it. Last I'd seen poor Sherry Harper's orphaned guinea pig, he was fleeing from the wrath of Richard Greene. He'd dashed out the back door, right past my aunt Dolly, and disappeared into the cold winter night. I figured there was no way he could have survived a Minnesota winter, but I guess the pig had more sense than I had given him credit for. I suppose if he had survived Sherry's benign neglect, he'd learned a thing or two about fending for himself.

"Where is he?"

"I don't know where he is right now. I've only caught a couple of glimpses of him. I can't bear to bring in an exterminator, but I can't have him in the shop. Besides, if Richard Greene finds out he's still around, he's going to be even more determined to close down Trendy Tails."

She was right, of course. One of Richard's primary objections to our store was the possibility that nuisance animals would affect the buildings around 801 Maple. Gandhi had proved him right once before, and another pig sighting would send Richard into the stratosphere with righteous indignation. He was already giving us a hassle over the barkery. . . . Giving him more ammunition could prove fatal to our business.

"Thank you so much, Taffy. I'm sorry if Gandhi is causing you problems, but I swear I'll help you catch him."

Taffy sighed. "I know you will. And it's hardly your

fault. I just need to protect my herbs from the little guy and make sure no one sees him."

"Maybe we can get him to wear a tiny mask and cape."

"Phantom of the tea shop," Taffy giggled.

"I can make that happen."

We both cracked up.

"Would you like a cup of tea?" Taffy asked when we came up for air.

"I would love one. Too bad there aren't any goodies."

Taffy slid around the counter to begin boiling water and getting the leaves ready to steep. Her head was down as she worked, but I could see her blush.

"What?" I asked, my eyes narrowed as I searched my friend's face for some sign of what was causing the flushing that crept across her cheeks.

"What, what?" she parried back.

"Oh, come on. I mention treats and you look like you've just accidentally flashed Reverend Wilson."

That teased a smile from her.

"It's nothing," she demurred.

"Uh-uh. Spill it."

She poured boiling water from the electric kettle into the pot and covered it to steep.

"Okay, fine. I've started having a caterer provide my sweets and savories."

"Mmm. I've noticed that you've had a bigger selection lately. But that's hardly a reason to blush," I prodded.

"Well, my caterer is Ken West. And, uh"—she squinched one eye closed as though she was already wincing from my reaction—"we may be dating."

I confess, Ken West would not have been my choice for my sweet friend. He'd engaged in some sketchy shenanigans to secure the capital for his new restaurant—shenanigans that involved Hal Olson, a strip club, and a certain someone who went by the name Cherry. I could hardly criticize the man for fighting tooth and nail for his business, but there had to be a line, and blackmail was surely over it. Besides, he rubbed me the wrong way. He always seemed disdainful, like Merryville and everyone in it were somehow beneath him.

Still, if my friend saw something good in Ken and he was smart enough to see what a catch she was, I'd darned well keep my mouth shut.

"What do you mean you 'may' be dating?"

"We've been hanging out a lot. Talking and, uh, stuff. But we haven't really had an opportunity to go on a real date. Like dinner or a movie."

"Oh."

"And you can't tell anyone. Ken's busy running his catering business and putting together all the renovations and menu for his new restaurant. He doesn't want his backer, Hal Olson, to think that there's any competition for his time and energy."

"Oh."

Alarm bells were ringing like crazy. Ken's reasons for keeping his relationship with Taffy secret seemed pretty lame. I'd had so many girlfriends in college who'd had that kind of relationship with guys. *Baby, I'd rather hang out here with you than go to some stupid party. I'm really into you, but why don't we keep this to ourselves? Our little secret. Just so none of our friends try to break us apart*. And then, after the novelty wore off, the guys disappeared, and the girls realized they'd been played.

Still, Taffy was a grown woman, and I was hardly one to give romantic advice. After all, I'd been duped for fourteen years, not just a few weeks.

"Well, I can't say that I saw that coming," I said.

Taffy laughed. "Me neither. We're so different. I'm such a homebody, and Ken is an aggressive businessman. He's incredibly fit, and I'm a little soft around the middle. We're really just night and day. But somehow it works. He actually treats me like I have a brain, and he's an interesting man when you get past all the brash talk."

I must not have looked completely convinced.

"Sorry, Izzy. The heart wants what the heart wants."

This I knew. I'd only learned that my childhood BFF Rena was gay, but since she came out to me, we'd talked a lot about our respective love lives (or the lack thereof). I knew that Rena's attraction to curvy ladies was as much a part of who she was as my attraction to tall men. We don't get to make decisions about whom we desire, only about what we do about that desire. Finally, Rena was starting to act on her emotions and had gone on a couple of dates with Jolly Nielson, Taffy's older sister and a truly talented jeweler. And I was starting to let the light creep into my soul to uncover any feelings I might be harboring for Sean Tucker, who'd been relegated to the role of friend ever since I'd gotten dizzy and puked all over him in the fourth grade.

With Rena on my mind, I decided to pick Taffy's brain for gossip on my good friend.

"You know that Rena and Jolly have been seeing each other, right?"

Taffy nodded, but she didn't look thrilled.

"What?" I prodded.

"Well, I love my sister so much, and I really cherish my friendship with you and Rena. I'm just afraid that if something goes south, it will make it hard for me to remain neutral."

"Do you have any reason to suspect that things will go south?"

Taffy took a dainty sip of her tea. She shook her head, sending her halo of golden curls bouncing around her cherubic face. "No, not really. It's just that my sister has been burned a few times in the past couple of years, and I know Rena hasn't dated anyone for a very long time. I just hope that Rena's not using Jolly as a trial run. That it isn't a training relationship. Because it definitely isn't to Jolly."

I grinned. "So Jolly's pretty into Rena, huh?"

Taffy moaned. "My sister falls hard and fast. And then when it ends, she's a total disaster."

"Don't be so sure it will end. Rena and I have actually been talking about our love life, and she's told me that she'd like to spend more time with Jolly. They're both so busy that it's tough, but I think Rena is smitten."

Taffy tipped her chin down and smiled up at me through her lashes. "Wouldn't that be wonderful? Oh gosh, if they got married, we'd practically be sisters."

"We shouldn't get too far ahead of ourselves. After all, they've only been on a few dates. But they do make an adorable couple, and love does seem to be in the air in Merryville these days."

Now, if I could just catch a little of that romantic juju for myself . . .

When I got home, I called Jack Collins at the station to thank him for expediting the clearing of the crime scene so Trendy Tails could open normally the day before. When he answered the phone, he was wearing his full-on cop persona.

"Happy to do it," he said in his no-nonsense, you-have-the-right-to-remain-silent voice.

"Just thought I should let you know, we talked to Dee Dee Lahti at the construction site on Badger Lake. Did you know she's Steve Olmstead's sister? Well, any-way, she is, and so he helped get her a job there. She confirmed that Daniel was snooping around down by the work site, but she didn't know what he was looking for."

"Wait. Who's 'we'? And why on earth were you out at Badger Lake talking to Dee Dee Lahti?" Jack's tone had gone from all business to mild alarm in the space of a few sentences.

"Relax. It was just me and Sean and Rena, and we went out there to see if we could find something hinky."

"Why?" Now he was starting to sound a little angry.

"Because Richard Greene said that he'd seen Daniel down there several times, and we figure whatever story he was working on must involve the construction site. And the story he was working on is what got him killed."

"Okay." Yep, definitely angry. "First, you and Sean and Rena are not cops. You should not be doing coplike things. Second, there's no hard evidence to suggest that Daniel was working on a story at all, much less one that got him killed. And third, if you are *right*, if something at that construction site got him killed, you should be running like crazy in the other direction."

"Nonsense. Of course he was working on a story. And of course it got him killed."

I could practically hear Jack's teeth grinding. "Izzy McHale, you're missing the point. You need to back off so you don't get *yourself* killed."

"Would you miss me?" I teased.

"Yes. As a matter of fact I would."

I was taken aback. I'd known Jack Collins all my life. He was one of those boys who pulled pigtails and planted whoopee cushions. Every year, when we taped our brown paper bags to the back of our chairs, he got caught stealing my valentines. But we'd never been all that close. Sean, Rena, and I were the three musketeers, and once I started dating Casey, I hardly had time for anyone else. Besides, Jack hung out with the jocks. He was in a couple of my AP classes, but he was real quiet there, kept to himself; it was only when he was with his fellow football and hockey players that he came out of his shell.

"Thank you." It sounded lame, but I couldn't figure how else to respond. "I appreciate your concern and all, but I really need to make sure my aunt Dolly doesn't go to prison. You can see that, right?"

I heard him shift his posture on the other end of the line. "Yes," he said, voice softer now. "I know how much Dolly means to you. And for what it's worth, I won't let them close the case until we've examined every possible angle on this murder. I can't save your aunt if she's guilty, but I'm going to make sure we look under every rock before we prosecute her."

"Thanks, Jack," I said, genuinely touched.

He laughed gently. "Don't give it a second thought. My mother would have my hide if I didn't look out for Dolly. Your aunt has quite a fan club. I've had half the Methodist Ladies' Auxiliary call me, and Richard Greene has 'just stopped by' the department twice already."

"That's my Dolly. Always the life of the party."

"Emphasis on 'life,' Izzy. Like I said, protect your own. Stay out of this investigation."

I hung up the phone with nothing more than a simple good-bye. I wasn't about to make a promise I couldn't keep.

CHAPTER
Nine

As we were wont to do, the whole family gathered at my parents' house for Sunday dinner. The immediate family—Mom, Dad, my sisters, and I—were always in attendance. We rounded out the ten-person dining table with a variety of people. I had asked Rena to join us, which she usually did. In fact, I think my mother would throw me out to make room for Rena.

This particular week, though, she'd asked if she could bring Jolly with her. Jolly was luscious, a cloud of raven black ringlets surrounding soft features and balancing out a tiny, curvy body. She and Rena had been hanging around more with each other over the past couple of months. I think it started as Jolly helping Rena find entrée into the Merryville gay community, but all signs now pointed to a budding romance. The two of them showed up together with a bottle of merlot and a hand-tied bunch of tulips.

The big surprise, however, was that my sister Lucy brought Xander Stephens. Xander was tall but scrawny, six foot three but no more than one hundred and seventy-five pounds. I saw the glint in my mother's eye when she showed him to a place at the table. Xander was a challenge my mother appeared determined to conquer. She would make sure the boy left at least five pounds heavier than when he arrived.

She immediately handed him a basket of cheese straws. He ducked his nearly hairless head and, without looking my mom in the face, took one and passed the basket. My mother's sigh was dramatic. Like William Shatner dramatic. I shot her a quelling look, but got nothing but a shrug in return.

Dolly was the last guest to arrive. She hustled in wearing a silk tank top, a pair of skintight jeans, and brilliant white track shoes on her feet.

"Sorry, sorry, sorry," she said breathlessly as she plopped into her usual seat at the table. "Didn't mean to keep everyone waiting. I was on the phone with Nora Miller, telling her all about my ordeal."

"Nora Miller?" Mom asked. "Why, she hasn't lived in Merryville for at least fifteen years. You've never once mentioned that you keep in touch."

"Don't really," Dolly conceded. "But extraordinary times call for extraordinary measures."

"What's that supposed to mean?"

"Just that I've been going through my old address book making sure I call everyone. Had to track Nora down through her niece Miranda Stone. Thought I'd never find her."

Mom sank slowly into her chair. "You mean you're actually telling everyone you know about being arrested?"

Dolly flipped her hands palm up and shook her head. "Well, of course. I want them to hear it from me and not on the nightly news."

Dad chimed in, "Dolly, I don't really think—"

"Oh hush, Clem," my mom said. "Dolly, the national news isn't going to cover this story."

"You never know, right, Clem?"

We all looked at my dad.

There was no right answer to this question. If he agreed with Dolly, my mother would give him the silent treatment for the rest of the night. If he disagreed with Dolly, she'd yammer at him all night. Either way, he was hosed.

Taking the only prudent course open to him, he grabbed a cheese straw and shoved it in his mouth.

"I still can't believe you're worried about what people you knew eons ago are thinking about your arrest. You were *arrested*. . . . Shouldn't you be worrying about that? I mean, Dolly, you could really go to jail. Aren't you a little bit afraid?"

Dolly closed her eyes and cocked her head. "As a matter of fact, I am not. I've decided I like that big, sweet cop, and I know he's still investigating. He's not giving up on me yet. Plus, I have Izzy and Rena and everybody helping me out, too. They'll find the real killer, and I'll never even go to trial."

Rena and I shared a panicked look. Sure, we were trying to find the real killer, and we'd even done it once before, but we couldn't offer Dolly any guarantees. It worried me that she was putting so much faith in us. It was a mighty weight to bear.

I helped my mother bring in a carved ham, fresh green beans, mashed potatoes, creamed corn, and two seitan sausages for me and Rena. We began the ritual of passing the plates around, everyone serious in their efforts to load up on my mom's incredible cooking.

As we settled down to dig in, my dad cleared his throat. "So, Jolly. I've seen your work. You do a fine job."

"Thank you, Mr. McHale."

"Mmm. Well, I was just wondering if you and our Rena are a thing?"

Jolly had her mouth open to answer, but my mother beat her to the punch with a shocked gasp. "Hush, Clem! That is none of our business."

"I just . . ." He let his sentence trail off into silence in the face of my mother's withering stare.

"I'm so sorry, Jolly. We don't mean to intrude. But . . . we do care very much for Rena and we won't take kindly to someone breaking her heart."

Both Jolly and Rena turned bright red.

"Now, Xander, tell us a little about yourself."

Xander looked up, but it was Lucy who spoke.

"Xander is from Milwaukee. He's got a degree in math from Lawrence, and he's supersmart."

Mom cut in. "Lucy, why don't you let the boy speak for himself?"

Lucy thinned her lips and looked pointedly at my father, then back to my mother.

"Well, I . . . " Mom sputtered before clamping her lips closed. "That is different. Clem has had his whole life to talk at this table. This is Xander's first time."

Mom's logic made no sense at all, but that didn't really matter. From the outside, my parents seemed to lead a very average life. They were both retired high school teachers (Mom in English, Dad in history). Edie and Clem McHale had three stair-step daughters, Irish triplets, some might say. They lived in a comfortable suburban house. Clem did woodworking and Edie played canasta with all the other ladies in town.

But once you got a good look inside, you could see how cockeyed it all was. Dad didn't carve spoons or walking sticks. . . . He carved little trolls and demons and mushrooms, and he was building himself his own orc-filled kingdom. And my mom had started reading all these books about self-actualization. According to Dolly, Mom was trying her hand at writing erotica, and she'd let her inner bossiness come out in full force.

My sisters took after our mom. They were strong-willed, set in their ways, and tended to run roughshod over people whenever it suited them.

I, on the other hand, was like Aunt Dolly: flighty, trusting, easily distracted, and sometimes downright foolish.

We were the perfect Midwestern family with a heart of pure neurosis.

"Go ahead and tell us your story, Xander."

"There's not much to tell, ma'am. Like Lucy said, I'm from Milwaukee."

"And . . ."

"And I own a record store?"

My mother sighed. This was not going as she had hoped. She turned to Lucy, who smiled smugly.

"Xander doesn't just own a record store. He has a whole Internet empire where he sells to collectors all around the world. He scours estate sales and flea markets finding the most gems in the dirt. Oh, and did I mention that he moved to Merryville to start this record business *after* he sold this app he created in college for like a bazillion dollars?"

We all turned to look at Xander, who ducked his head and forked up a big bite of mashed potatoes.

He was wearing a button-down shirt of indeterminate color, its collar all wonky, and a pair of jeans that were cut for a scarecrow and still were falling off his scrawny hips. His left leg bobbed up and down like he was ready to bounce right out of the house.

I couldn't blame him.

"I, uh," he mumbled. "I did okay. It wasn't a bazillion dollars, though."

Everyone just kept staring at him, like the poor boy was an alien who had beamed into my parents' dining room.

"So," I said, taking pity on him, "how've you been doing, Dru?"

"What's that supposed to mean?"

"What do *you* mean, 'what's that supposed to mean'?"

"You know there's nothing new going on. I go to work, I go home, I cook dinner, I knit, I snuggle with Poppy, and I go to bed. You don't need to rub it in."

"I wasn't trying to rub it in," I insisted. "I was just making conversation."

"Girls," Mom cut in, "that's enough. At the end of the day, all I want to know is when I'm going to get some grandbabies."

"Mom!"

"Mother!"

"Holy crap."

On that one point, the McHale sisters agreed. Baby pressure was entirely off-limits.

Mom stuck her tongue out. Then she turned to Rena and Jolly. "That goes for you ladies, too. Rena's babies will be my grandbabies, too. And I don't care how you get them, whether you adopt or do that in vitro thing."

"Mom," I hissed. "Rena and Jolly are just good friends." I wasn't sure that was true, but I wasn't about to give my mom ammunition. "You can't be pushing them to have babies yet."

"She's right, Edith," Aunt Dolly said. "You've got three beautiful girls who are making their own way in the world, all with good jobs, none of them in jail or high or anything. Count your lucky stars and stop with the baby nonsense."

"Well, fine," Mom said. "You know I love you all to pieces. I just sometimes get carried away."

I reached over and patted her hand. "We know that, Mom. But can we just eat now?"

She laughed. "You'd better. I don't want this food going to waste."

Xander looked up at my mom with a crooked smile. "I won't let that happen, Mrs. McHale," he said as he reached for the plate of ham and served himself another slice.

My mom smiled like he'd hung the moon just for her.

She leaned toward Lucy. "I like this one," she whispered. Before Lucy could respond, Mom held up a hand. "I know. I know. I'll be quiet now."

The rest of the meal was filled with casual chitchat and gentle teasing. Mom even let Dad tell a few jokes. They weren't funny, but we all laughed anyway.

When Mom and Dru disappeared into the kitchen to dish up peach pie and vanilla ice cream, I leaned over to speak quietly with Dolly.

"What you said earlier? I'm really touched, Dolly. But you shouldn't put too much faith in us."

"What exactly is too much faith, dear?"

"I mean you should be relying on Jack Collins, not a bunch of rank amateurs, to get you off the hook for murder."

Dolly gently patted my hand. "I have a great deal of faith in Jack Collins, but he's just doing his job. You and Rena and Sean love me."

I felt a well of panic building in my chest. "Yes, we love you so much, Dolly. But we're not professionals. There's no guarantee we can pull this off."

"Oh dear," Dolly soothed. "I didn't mean to upset you. I know you have other obligations, and you're an amateur. You may not be able to help me, but I have faith in your efforts. That you won't give up on me. That's all I could possibly ask."

Despite the crowd in the room, I couldn't resist pulling Dolly into a fierce hug.

No matter what, I wouldn't give up on her.

CHAPTER
Ten

Monday morning dawned as bright and clear as the sound of church bells. I crawled out from the pile of quilts I'd been nesting in on my couch and made my way to the shower, where I indulged in a long soak.

Once downstairs and ready to face the day, I got to work swapping out some of my winter fashions for more summery outfits. I tucked the fleece-lined hoodies and striped sweaters (all repurposed from human sweaters I'd found at thrift shops) into sturdy plastic totes and used the clear space for spring slickers, fluttery chiffon ruffs, and a few ridiculously tiny swim trunks.

Packer did his best to help, dogging my every step and generally getting underfoot, drooling around the rawhide toy he had in his mouth. Daisy mostly stayed put at the foot of the stairs, but occasionally tiptoed toward Packer, her eyes on that rawhide. Whenever she got close, Packer would hunker down and growl. Finally, I found a rawhide for Daisy. She was delighted and dug into the chew toy with abandon. Packer, however, looked like I'd given another kid his ice cream. Sharing wasn't Packer's strong suit. He renewed his efforts to get under my feet, to gain my attention.

Meanwhile Jinx sat on top of the counter and watched us all with narrow-eyed ennui.

"For the love of Mike, Packer, can you settle down?" I snatched the nasty rawhide out of his mouth before I pulled one of the new rope toys I'd just gotten in from its shelf—making a mental note to pay the store for the lost inventory—and tossed it in the direction of the barkery. I was hoping the novelty would keep my little guy distracted from Daisy and me for a while. Sure enough, Packer went scampering off, toenails clicking on the hardwood floor. When he got the rope toy, he gave it what for, shaking it fiercely and growling to let it know who was in charge.

He was a dork, but he sure was cute.

By the time Rena rolled in to set out her organic pet treats beneath their sparkling cake domes, I was hip deep in receipts, trying to make sure that my sales matched up with my bank deposits.

"Better you than me," Rena said, idly scratching her ferret Val's head as the animal lay draped around her neck.

Val, short for Valrhona, was a chocolate roan ferret. Her rich brown coat was sleek like an otter's, and she adored being close to Rena. In fact, Val had been known to ride around inside Rena's shirt. Val was adorable, frolicking around the store, pestering Jinx and frustrating Packer (who never could catch her in their chasing games). Val's one flaw, and it was a biggie, was her kleptomania. Like many ferrets, Val had a way of slithering here and there, picking up shiny or interesting objects, and stashing them in hidey-holes she maintained throughout the shop. Rena was used to returning watches with a loaf of banana bread, or earrings with a plate of fudge.

"Yeah, well, I'd be completely underwater if Xander the Wunderkind hadn't installed that bookkeeping software."

Rena laughed. "What exactly were we thinking when we decided to open our own business?"

"That starving didn't sound like fun."

The bell over our front door jingled and Pris Olson made her elegant way into the store. She carried a flowered hatbox in one hand and a plate of pastries in the other.

"Sorry to drop by unannounced, but I've just been so swamped lately. The master gardeners want to do a tour of gardens in late May, so I've been up to my eyeballs in new shrubs and eighteen potential lilac varieties. I figured I should stop by while I could."

With her hair in a perfect French twist, her nails immaculate with a fresh French manicure, and the enticing aroma of some fabulously expensive French perfume wafting with her every move, it didn't seem like Pris had been gardening. But I imagined that Pris's gardening involved a lot of pointing and yelling and not very much actual digging.

"I brought a peace offering. I stopped by the Happy Leaf and picked up a handful of pastries for us to munch on while we chat about Romeo and Pearl's upcoming wedding."

"Pastries?" Rena craned her head around the corner from the barkery, trying to scope out what exactly was on offer.

Pris's eyes fluttered gently, as though she was trying to keep her composure in the face of a crude display. "I brought cherry Danish, pecan twists, and bear claws . . . two of each."

"Mmmm," Rena hummed, making her way toward the plate of goodies, her eyes never wavering from her prey.

Her lips twisted in an indulgent smile, Pris set the hatbox on the counter as well. She popped off the lid and began lifting out its contents.

"We have more crepe paper, because I don't imagine we can reuse the paper from Ingrid's would-be wedding. I have the tiny bottles of bubbles for the humans to use after the ceremony is over."

That had been my idea. I couldn't wait to watch the dogs all lose their minds chasing the bubbles around the store. I would have to hide all the breakables—and Jinx.

"Finally, I have a CD of the music Louise and Hetty picked out. 'Puppy Love' leads the list and Elvis's 'Hound Dog' ends the show. Very clever, those two little ladies."

I ran my fingers over the ridges of one of the bubble wands. "For the first time, I feel like this is going to work."

Pris laughed softly. "You're so trusting, Izzy. Any number of things can go horribly wrong. The bride or groom may pee at the altar. One of the four-legged guests may devour the cake before the service starts. Or try to devour a guest. Cats are quite refined, but dogs are rambunctious and unpredictable."

I managed to keep my eyes from rolling. Pris was the definition of cynical. "If we do our parts, I'm sure the dogs will do theirs. Let's not borrow trouble."

Pris shrugged as she took one dainty bit of a pecan twist. She'd barely taken off a corner of the pastry, but she set it back in its box and picked up a paper napkin to remove the crumbs from her fingers. No wonder she was still as skinny as her high school beauty queen self.

"I've got to get back to work," Rena said around a mouthful of her second bear claw.

As she skipped back toward the barkery, I saw an opening, and on impulse, I took it. "Speaking of trouble, how are things going with the real estate development that Hal is working on?"

If it had been any other wife in the world, I wouldn't have bothered asking. But Pris made no bones about the fact that her husband was uncouth and a little dense. She stayed in the marriage because he also happened to be filthy rich, and she had signed a prenup before they got hitched.

She narrowed her eyes. "Fine, I guess. I haven't been out to the site. I don't do wilderness and marshes and such. But Hal hasn't mentioned any problems. Why do you ask?"

"Oh, nothing really. I just thought that Hal might be a little overextended between managing the building site, helping Ken with his new restaurant, and keeping up with sales at the RV lot."

Pris's lips curled in a feline smile. "*Tsk, tsk, tsk,* Izzy. Surely there's no need for pretense between us. I've already told you that I would like nothing more than for my husband to get caught with a mistress. After an admission like that, secrets seem inappropriate."

I studied Pris's face for a moment, looking for some hint that she was being disingenuous, but she looked as honest and forthright as Pris ever looked. Maybe I could just come right out and ask my questions.

"Look, I was out walking the dogs by the lake, and I couldn't help but notice that there didn't seem to be much activity, so I wondered if maybe Hal was having a little cash flow issue."

Pris tipped her head back and laughed.

"Oh dear," she said as she dabbed at the corners of her eyes. "Oh my."

Her response wasn't quite what I was hoping for. In annoyance, I started playing with the fringe of a red crocheted poncho that I hadn't set out for display yet.

"Gracious, Izzy. That's too funny. No, we are not having money problems. You should know better than anyone that if the cash was drying up chez Olson, I would be skating out of there faster than Apolo Ohno."

She had a point.

"No, when Hal told me he wanted in on this project,

I set a very precise spending limit. He was not to spend a penny past his limit, and he knows better than to try to sneak something past me. Besides, Hal is a dolt most of the time, but he has good business sense. He's way too savvy to sink a chunk of his working capital into a real estate deal. Not as volatile as that market has been over the past few years."

Pris was usually so surface—perfect face, perfect clothes, perfect hair—that I tended to forget how smart and savvy she really was. She clearly had a strong grasp of her husband's business and finances.

"Anyway, he had a budget, and he's just about hit the limit."

"So are they going to just stop building? Leave those half-finished condos there?"

As bad as the condos would be for the view of the lake, a scattering of half-finished buildings slowly being reclaimed by the forest would be an even bigger eyesore. Richard would have a cow.

"Oh heavens, no. He's just regrouping by bringing in some additional investors."

I tried to think of who in Merryville had the kind of cash to keep the development moving. If there were any more solvent Harpers in town, that family could probably help. As it was, though, they were all dead, in jail, or living in warmer climes.

"Who?" I asked. I hadn't meant to ask the question out loud, and could feel myself blush as soon as the word left my mouth.

Pris laughed again. "I promise you—you wouldn't

know them. And they prefer to remain silent partners. Very silent, if you catch my meaning."

I wasn't a hundred percent sure I caught her meaning. Maybe just about ninety-five percent sure.

"Well, listen," Pris said, placing the lid back on her now-empty hatbox. "This has been delightful. I'm always intrigued by your little theories, Izzy. But I'm afraid I have to boogie. I have peonies to pick out and a business to run."

She left without looking back, nothing but a pageant wave over her shoulder to say good-bye.

I hadn't heard Rena creeping back into the room, but she suddenly yelled "Booyah!"

"What?" I snapped, startled.

"I was right. 'Very silent partners.' That means the mob. I knew Daniel had something to do with the mob," she crowed.

"You thought he was a crime boss. I didn't hear anything in there that suggested Daniel was a made man."

"Oh, come on. Don't be a stickler. This all makes perfect sense. Daniel was up here investigating the mob connection to the Olson development. Maybe he wasn't a member of the mob, but his reason for being here had to do with organized crime." She bounced up and down in excitement. "Xander and Lucy may have been right about him being a journalist, but I was right about the mob connection, too."

I began stashing the supplies Pris had delivered in the cupboards behind the counter.

"You're making some pretty big leaps here, Rena.

First, you don't know whether Hal is really getting into bed with the mob. And, even if he is, we don't know that Daniel was aware of that connection. Why would Daniel feel compelled to watch the construction site if he was really interested in who financed it?"

Rena plopped down to sit tailor-style on the floor. On cue, Jinx jumped off the top of the wardrobe—her second-favorite napping spot—did a downward dog stretch, and crept onto Rena's lap—her favorite napping spot.

"It makes perfect sense. If Daniel was investigating organized crime in Madison and he caught wind that the mob was investing in the Badger Lake development, it would explain why he moved up here. As for spending time at the development site, maybe he suspected something other than building was going on down there. Or maybe he was staking out the place in the hopes of catching one of the mob guys visiting the site."

My punk pixie friend was a smart cookie. It was all pure conjecture, but this was a better explanation for why Daniel would be in Merryville and haunting the shores of Badger Lake than anything I'd come up with.

I called Sean and asked him to perform his legal mumbo jumbo to figure out who was investing in The Woods at Badger Lake other than Hal Olson. Sean had a client to meet, so he told us it would probably be a couple of hours. Sean ran a general practice, willing to handle all kinds of cases. Divorces, DUIs, and minor assaults (read: bar fights) were his bread and butter. Given the raised voices I heard in the background, I was guessing he was working on a divorce case.

While Rena and I waited for Sean to call back, our lives slipped out of investigator mode and into entre-preneurial mode. Rena got to work trying a new flavor of pupcake—an apple-carrot creation with a maple glaze. I spent about half an hour on the phone with a woman from Duluth who made jewelry out of Lake Superior agates. We were discussing the possibility of her making collar dangles with the stones, so they would serve as pet adornments and as souvenirs of a family trip to Minnesota.

After reaching an agreement about a trial run of ten dangles, I quickly said my good-byes so I could wait on the genuine customer who had walked through the door.

She was a stately woman with straight black hair framing a face as bloodless as marble. She wore a camel-colored turtleneck and a pair of deep brown trousers, her outfit set off by a massive topaz pendant that rested right on the crest of her bosom. She carried with her a black patent bag. A sleek feline head poked out of the bag, a Burmese by the looks of her slender skull and chocolate fur.

"Welcome to Trendy Tails. Can I help you?"

"Perhaps," the woman said. "My name is Pamela Rawlins, and I'm on the board for the Midwestern Cat Fancier Organization. Tonga, here, and I are visiting Merryville to determine whether it might be a good fit for next year's Cat Fancier Retreat. I'm visiting the pet-related businesses in the area.

"It seems you have two." She concluded her introduction by pursing her lips and tilting her head at the exact angle as her feline friend Tonga.

My heart began to race. She was right. Merryville had two pet-related businesses, but having the retreat here would be incredible exposure for our businesses and the whole town.

"True. We're a small town. But Pris, from Prissy's Pretty Pets, and I have coordinated on several large events, and we make a pretty dynamic duo. Plus, Merryville has so much to offer your human guests: pet-friendly hotels and cabin rentals, great restaurants, and beautiful scenery."

Pamela narrowed her eyes. "You sound like you work for the town's convention bureau."

That was good, because I was ninety-eight percent certain that Merryville didn't actually have a convention bureau.

"For now," she continued, "we're just looking around. I thought I might pick up a little something for Tonga."

"Let me show you a few of my newest items."

I led Pamela around the store, pointing out an exquisite silver acorn dangle that Jolly had made, a hand-studded collar in an aqua blue that would really set off Tonga's fur, and a few sundresses. I caught sight of Jinx on the top of her armoire, lazy eyes following every move Tonga made around the store. Tonga, too, kept her eyes on Jinx. I felt like Pamela and I were standing in a Cold War demilitarized zone, just waiting for someone on either side to fire the first bullet.

The visit ended without any cat melee, and Pamela ended up buying both the acorn dangle and the collar, a nice sale for me and hopefully a good sign that the organization would give us fair consideration.

Rena popped out of the kitchen in all her dive bar glory, causing Pamela to shrink back and hold on to her cat carrier a little tighter. But when Rena smiled her contagious smile and offered Tonga a bag of freshly baked salmon crackers, Pamela softened a bit.

"It's been a pleasure meeting you," I called as she left. She didn't respond, but I tried not to let that dampen my enthusiasm.

"Can you even imagine having a cat fancier retreat right here in Merryville?"

Rena let out a low whistle. "That would be the bomb."

Just then the phone rang, and I snatched it up, eager to tell someone else about our visit from Pamela Rawlins, but it was Sean and he had even more important news.

"It looks like the incorporation papers for The Woods, Inc., have recently been updated to show a new partner. Something called Ma Pa, Unlimited. I've searched the Web high and low, and I can't find a trace of this corporation anywhere."

"So it really could be a mob front."

Sean hedged. "Well, it could be. But there are a lot of other reasons that people set up shell corporations for the purposes of conducting business."

"But you'd think you'd find *something* about them out there on the Internet."

"Yes, it's a little strange, but I still don't think you should go jumping to conclusions."

I didn't want to jump to conclusions. I wanted to wade right into the thick of things and find the truth.

CHAPTER
Eleven

I formulated my plan for the rest of the day while I sucked down another cup of joe and nibbled on a grocery store toaster pastry . . . my go-to meal for every occasion. Rena had popped out to take her dad to his podiatrist appointment, so she wouldn't be back for at least an hour, which gave me plenty of time to savor the slightly dry pastry, the overly sweet filling, and the shellac of icing that covered the whole thing. With the exception of cheese puffs and ice cream, my kitchen-savvy friend had little patience for prepackaged food. But, for me, ripping open the shiny silver wrapper of overly processed sugar brought fond memories of eating "brunch" with Sean and Rena during our third-period study hall.

I'd just popped the last piece of pastry in my mouth when the bell above the front door tinkled. I quickly swept the crumbs and wrapper from my lunch into a trash can and managed to form a tight-lipped smile around the last bite of strawberry preserves.

When I saw it was just Lucy and Xander, I promptly chewed and swallowed. No need to hide my sweet tooth from my sister.

Lucy stretched her face forward and sniffed three times. "What is that? Strawberry. Strawberry Toasties! I want one."

Reluctantly, I pulled the box from behind the counter and let her grab a silver package. I offered the box to Xander, and he was raising his hand to accept my offer, but Lucy butted in. "We'll share."

Xander sighed and his expression of boyish disappointment brought a laugh that I worked hard to suppress. There was no doubt about it. Lucy was bossy. Actually, so was Dru, but in a very different way. Lucy took for granted that her vision of the way the world was and how it ought to be was the correct vision. She had no qualms about telling people they should or shouldn't eat something, that they had pitiful personalities, or even that their butts looked fat in their jeans.

Poor, passive Xander didn't stand a chance. It was the one fear I had for their relationship: that Xander would get swallowed up in Lucy's massive ego and we'd never see the boy again.

Lucy broke off a piece of her pastry and handed it to Xander.

"I've decided that Xander needs a dog," she announced.

I glanced at Xander for confirmation that he wanted a dog, but he just shrugged and took a bite of the Toasty.

"Why does Xander need a dog? He's already got George." George was Xander's iguana. She—yes, she . . . she was named after George Eliot—was still the brilliant green of youth, and would likely live another seventeen to eighteen years. She was a whole lot of pet, her cage taking up much of a spare bedroom in the apartment above Spin Doctor.

"George shmeorge. You can't cuddle with an iguana."

"Not true," Xander piped up. "I've told you before, she likes to sleep around my neck, and she practically purrs when I stroke her head."

"I don't believe you. The only sign of sentience that I've seen is that she tries to avoid the carpet."

"And I keep telling you that iguanas are very territorial. You're a threat. She won't let her guard down when you're in the apartment."

Hmmm. Lucy had been in Xander's apartment. He was a shy and private young man. Getting into his apartment was the near equivalent to getting him to utter the "L" word.

"Still, I think you need a dog and Izzy has one that needs a home." Lucy faced me and batted her eyelashes. "Could Xander meet Daisy?"

While I was certain that Xander and Daisy had crossed paths in the past, they'd never really gotten a chance to interact. I saw the color drain from Xander's face, but I really did need to get rid of Daniel's dog, and I knew I could trust Xander to take good care of her.

I pulled a bag of treats off one of the shelves behind the counter and gave it a good shake. Packer, Daisy, and even Jinx came running. I gave everyone a couple of treats, and they all hunkered down to gobble them up. Jinx was the slowest, but when Daisy tried to sidle up and horn in on Jinx's snack, the cat managed to keep chewing while letting out a high-pitched keening sound that sent Daisy stumbling back. Packer glanced up, but he knew better than to try to steal food from my massive Norwegian forest cat.

"Go ahead, Xander. Play with the dog."

"Lucy," I snapped, suddenly channeling my mother.

She rolled her eyes. "Please play with the dog."

Xander dropped to his haunches and Daisy promptly came to sit before him. He scratched her ears, and she leaned in for the pet. He stroked her head, and she licked his hand. They went through the rituals of nice man meets nice dog, but I could tell there was no love connection there.

"See," Lucy said. "They're a perfect match."

Xander looked up at me with an imploring gaze.

I sighed. I wanted to find Daisy a home, but this wasn't it. "I don't think it's a good idea, Lucy. I appreciate your interest, Xander"—ensuring he would not catch the fallout later—"but like Xander said, iguanas are very territorial. They also have long sharp claws and tails that can be used to bludgeon other animals. I don't think it would be safe for either Daisy or George to share the same space."

Lucy snorted. "You just don't want to give up the dog."

"Not true," I said. "For the love of Mike, don't go telling people I'm keeping Daisy. I need to find her a forever home ASAP. But Xander and George just aren't the right family for her."

She heaved a sigh. "Fine. Xander, let's go. You can drive me to work." Clearly Lucy was in full-on princess mode. The courthouse where she worked was only three blocks away, yet she was summoning Xander to be her chauffeur. It would take them longer to get to his car than it would take for her to just walk it.

She handed me the empty wrapper from the strawberry Toasty, turned on her heel, grabbed Xander by the hand, and headed toward the door. Before they left, Xander looked back over his shoulder and mouthed a big "Thank you."

I'd saved both Daisy and Xander from a horrible fate, and I'd managed to resist my sister's manipulation, but Lucy was right: I needed to find Daisy her own home, where she would be loved as much as she deserved to be loved. Maybe even with someone who had more time for her than Daniel had. And I needed to do so stat.

When it came time to go confront Hal, I had to leave Rena in charge of Trendy Tails. I would have loved to have her at my side, but we truly did need to mind the store. Since Dru, Lucy, Taffy, and Sean were all working, I settled on bringing Aunt Dolly with me. Not only was she a foxy old pistol-packin' mama, but people tended to be truthful in her presence. Especially when she gave them her patented look: a stare so pointed and intense that it actually hurt your eyeballs to meet it.

As we made our way into the showroom of Olson's Odyssey RV, Hal was right there to greet us. He held out his bear-paw hand to shake ours with a little more vigor than was strictly comfortable. "Good to see you, good to see you. Got a button yet?"

Without waiting for an answer, he reached into his pants pocket and withdrew two three-inch-round buttons. They said MAYOR in a stripe across the middle with VOTE FOR HAL, HE'S YOUR PAL curving around the edges.

Hal and I were a long way from pals, but I dutifully pinned it to the front of my bright pink Trendy Tails button-down.

"Looks good on you," he said, his smile blinding against the perpetual golf tan that had leathered his face.

"You looking for some camping equipment? I can hook you up with Joel—Joel!—and he can help you find everything you need. Knows all the ins and outs."

"Actually, Hal, I was hoping we could talk to you."

Hal's eyes narrowed. Last time I'd had a chat with Hal, I'd ended up accusing him of murder. Given the information I had at the moment, today might not end much differently.

"As much as I'd like to, Izzy, my schedule is pretty full. You know I'd love to give all my customers the Big Hal treatment, but when you're the manager, you don't always get a chance to do the fun stuff."

He started to pivot and walk away when Aunt Dolly chimed in.

"Not so fast, son." Her voice wasn't especially loud or forceful, but it stopped him in his tracks. As underhanded as Hal could be, he'd been raised, like most of us, in the tradition of "Minnesota nice." People from far and wide talked about the knee-jerk politeness of most Minnesotans, how we'll smile at you even while you're serving us with divorce papers. Minnesota nice dictated that you did what your elders told you to do.

"We're not here for camping equipment. This old gal does not camp." Dolly spread her arms to draw attention to her low-cut silk blouse, her jeggings, and her short, pointy-heeled black boots. "We just have a couple of questions, and I'm sure you won't mind answering them."

Hal blew out a lungful of air, but then ducked his head like a chagrined child and waved at us to follow him back into his office. His office was surprisingly Spartan for a man whose outward persona was so much larger than life. Despite what he'd said about not being able to give personal attention to his customers, Hal actually did spend more of his days walking the lot, shaking hands and kissing babies, than he did in the bare white-walled room.

Dolly and I sat in the wooden chairs set in front of Hal's desk, while he took the seat behind it. "So. What kind of questions do you ladies have for me?"

"We're interested in The Woods at Badger Lake," I said.

"Sorry to tell you, we're not ready to start selling units yet," Hal said.

"Honestly, we're not really in the market," I said. "We're more interested in how the development is being built."

Hal cussed beneath his breath. "Look, if you want to harass me about the house wrap and the siding panels we're using, you can save your breath. Steve Olmstead has already given me an earful about how RJ's Construction only outbid him because they're using substandard materials. I've talked to a few other friends I have in the real estate world, and they assure me those products are perfectly adequate."

"Adequate" sounded like a far cry from good, but I really didn't care whether the siding would last more than six months or whether the condos would be drafty in the winter.

"That's not what we were interested in," I said, trying to slide into our rather inappropriate questions. Dolly had another plan altogether.

"Look, Hal, we know you're in bed with the mob, and Daniel Colona was on to you, and you killed him to keep his mouth shut."

I groaned softly. So much for subtlety.

"Mob? Are you kidding me?"

"Not at all," Dolly responded. "You need capital to complete the Badger Lake development. You need it bad. And Pris said your investors are pretty insistent about remaining behind the scenes. That sounds like the mob to me."

Hal waved his hands like he was calling a strike. "Good golly, no. I'm not getting wrapped up in any mob business. I saw *The Godfather*. I'm not waking up to a horse head in my bed. Pris would kill me."

I made a mental note that Hal was more concerned

about Pris's ire than he was about the actual damage the mob could do him.

"Well, if it's not the mob, who else would want to keep so quiet?"

"I don't see that it's any of your business," he said.

I made a move like I was about to get up. "I guess I can just call Ama Olmstead and tell her about this secret outside investor. I'll bet she could get to the bottom of it, and then the whole town would know."

"Oh, for crying out . . ." Hal craned his head to look behind me, then hunkered down low to his desk. He spoke in a whisper. "It's the Japanese."

"The Japanese? Why would they care about keeping their participation secret?"

"Izzy McHale, you should know as well as anyone. Why do people shop in your fancy little boutique— your *expensive* little boutique—when they can go to Wally World and get all the pet clothes they want?"

"Because my stuff is cuter and better quality?" I proffered.

Hal waved off that answer, making a face like he'd smelled something rotten. "Oh, that's part of it. But part of it is because it's homegrown goods. Made in small-town USA, emphasis on the USA. We live in one of the most pro-union, pro-buy-American states in the country. People find out The Woods at Badger Lake is part owned by the Japanese, and there goes the business. I'm a savvy enough businessman to know that."

"Then why take them on at all?" I asked.

He laughed. "Because I'm also a savvy enough businessman that I don't turn away money when it walks through my door. This bigwig from a Japanese electronics company, his wife read the Little House on the Prairie books and decided she just had to live in Minnesota. On a lake. In the woods. Frankly, I think she may be getting some of the details wrong. Anyway, that's what she wants, and he wants to indulge her but wants to make a few bucks in the process, and voilà, our deal was born."

Ma Pa, Unlimited. It made perfect sense now. Ma and Pa Ingalls. This electronics tycoon sure was one doting husband.

"Still," I said, "Daniel was clearly doing a story on The Woods at Badger Lake. Unless he had something else to interest him out there . . . ?"

Hal shook his head, his face turning the red of raw steak. "No. Absolutely not. Everything with the development is strictly aboveboard."

"So the investor angle must have been what Daniel was investigating. Either he thought it was the mob, too, or he knew it was the Japanese and that was his angle. . . . He was threatening to expose a secret you very much want to keep. One that, if spilled, could cost you the thousands of dollars you've already sunk into the development and leave you with a half-developed eyesore hanging around your neck like an albatross."

"What are you implying?" Hal blustered.

Dolly perked up in her seat, sending her blouse swaying precariously close to a wardrobe malfunction. "We're not implying anything, son. We're accusing you of killing Daniel Colona."

I groaned again. I was never ever taking Dolly on one of my little investigative excursions ever again. Ever.

"Well, I never . . . ," Hal growled, his Minnesota nice melting from the heat of his anger. "I can't believe you'd accuse me of murder."

I wasn't sure why he was that surprised. After all, it hadn't been even six months since I'd accused him of murder, right here in this very office.

"Look, I don't know what Daniel Colona was messing around in up here, but I sure as heck didn't kill him. I had an alibi."

"An alibi?"

"Yeah." He paused for a moment. He looked like he wasn't sure whether he should share his alibi with us. This made me think that Handsy Hal had taken up with another woman. Pris would literally be thrilled.

"Yeah," he repeated. "I was with Kevin Lahti."

"Why on earth would you be hanging out with Kevin Lahti?"

"Let's just say we were doin' stuff. If you ask him, I'm sure Kevin will confirm that I was with him that night."

Dolly and I exchanged a look. I, for one, planned to check out Hal's alibi, but it was starting to look like our grand theory had just crumbled before our very eyes.

CHAPTER
Twelve

When Dolly and I arrived back at Trendy Tails, Packer, Jinx, and Daisy May were lined up staring at the front door just like they knew we would be walking through any minute. Rena stood next to them, holding her ferret, Val, up like a trophy.

"You'll never guess what happened," she said.

"Is it something bigger than Dolly here accusing Hal Olson of murder?"

Rena grinned. "You didn't!"

Aunt Dolly drew herself up and looked down her nose. "I absolutely did. As it happens, he is not connected to the mob"—Rena's smile slipped—"and he purports to have an alibi for the night of the murder."

"So he didn't do it?" Rena asked.

"At the moment, the signs point to no, but we have a few details to follow up on."

"What's your big news?" I asked Rena as I fetched treats for Packer, Jinx, and Daisy May.

"Well, it's a long story."

"Does it have to be?"

Rena stuck her tongue out at me. "Yes. It started just after you two left. Taffy Nielson stopped by and said she'd lost a gold necklace that had belonged to her mother and that it might have ended up here."

"Here?" Dolly asked as she made her way to a chair. As perky as she was, Dolly wasn't a spring chicken anymore.

Rena shrugged and draped Val around her neck. "Who knows? Taffy's always been a bit daffy. Oh! Daffy Taffy. We should totally start calling her that."

I rolled my eyes. "We should totally not call her that. She's our friend, and I would like to keep it that way."

"Well, whatever, she was looking for her necklace, and so I went to our 'lost and found.'" She used air quotes as she said it. Our unofficial lost and found is a cranny between Jinx's armoire and the wall where Val the ferret hides all her ill-gotten loot.

"And?" I started boxing up a few items that I needed to get to Prissy's Pretty Pets so Pris could work her magic on our four-legged bride, Pearl.

"Turns out she was right. The necklace was there . . . though how that happened and why she thought to ask us is completely beyond me. Anyway, the big news is what else Val appears to have stolen."

She paused dramatically. "I'll bite," Dolly said. "What else did you find?"

"One of Daniel's pocket journals." She squeed and did a little jig of pure excitement, sending Val hurtling down her shirt and into her sleeve, where it was safe.

Dolly and I gasped in unison. "Really?" I breathed.

"I kid you not."

"Well, let's have a look," Dolly said.

We gathered around the folk art table, and Rena produced the journal: a trendy little leather-bound book, not much bigger than an index card, held closed by an orange elastic. As though it were a holy book—or a vial of the plague—Rena slid the elastic off and opened the journal.

"I can't believe you waited for us," I said.

"I thought it would be more fun if we read it together."

It was so small, we had to take turns thumbing through the journal. Most of what he'd written appeared to be in some personal shorthand that would require a cryptographer to decipher. And we were all out of cryptographers at the moment.

There were, however, a few things we could make out. The first was near the front of the booklet. He'd written "DNR" and drawn what appeared to be a narrow-necked vase with two big olives in it. Later, about midway through the journal, he'd scratched the date "June 10" with three question marks following it. Finally, on the back cover, he'd written two names and phone numbers: Dee Dee Lahti and Ama Olmstead.

Prissy's Pretty Pets Spa and Salon was Pris Olson's pet project. Hal made a fortune selling RVs and other camping equipment, so Pris certainly didn't have to work, but I think she was bored just sitting around the house and directing other people to plant flowers in her yard. She owned and doted on a show-quality silver chinchilla Persian named Kiki, and I guess it just seemed natural to pamper other pets the way she pampered her own.

The pet spa boasted the whole array of bathing and grooming services along with animal massage, aromatherapy, and a posh kennel in which all the animals slept on velvet pillows and were fed fresh organic meats and produce. While our businesses didn't precisely overlap, we were definitely competing for the pet lover's dollars. What's more, Pris's inner mean girl wasn't quite so "inner." In her natural habitat, Pris had a nemesis, and since I'd opened Trendy Tails, that nemesis was me.

When I entered her store, a subtle chime sounded somewhere in the back of the building. I was juggling an expandable folder with all of my notes on the Tucker-Collins wedding, a plastic box with a sample of the doggy cake Rena was making, and the rhinestone tiara and veil that Pearl would wear on her special day.

Prissy's Pretty Pets was not your average dog groomer's. The waiting room looked like that of a high-end human salon. Gilt-legged purple wing chairs were scattered about the plush chocolate carpeting in intimate conversation groups, and down-filled dog beds were tucked beneath and beside about half the chairs. There was a whole wall of glass shelves filled with the finest pet grooming supplies—shampoos, serums, and clippers—and another wall adorned with arty black-and-white posters of animals in motion. I was fairly sure the trotting Persian in one of the posters was Pris's Kiki. Finished with soft lighting, new age music, and carefully chosen essential oils wafting through the air, the front part of the store was an oasis of comfort. When the curtain to the back of the spa parted, I could see that the soft lighting continued into the work space, though I knew there had to be more brightly lit rooms for precision hair and nail clippings.

Pris emerged from the back of the store like a phantom rising from the mist. I swear the woman's feet never touched the ground. She glided above the floor like a Macy's parade balloon, serene and effortless.

"Izzy," Pris cooed, her lips sliding into the perfect cocktail party smile.

She did not dress like a woman who spent her days with animals—and their fur. That morning, she wore a turquoise shirtdress that made her blue eyes sparkle like the Caribbean, her blond hair pulled into a smooth, low pony, and a matching set of seashell-shaped gold earrings and pendant. All she was missing was the sun hat and the mai tai.

"Hey Pris. I brought Pearl's headpiece for the wedding so you can attach it after she's been groomed and clipped. And Rena thought you might want to try the cake."

"The dog cake?" Pris asked as she took the tiny tiara and lace-trimmed veil from my hands. "I think I'll pass."

"Honest, it's really quite tasty. Not very sweet, but

made with bananas and carob with a yogurt-based frosting. Better than those health bars they sell in the supermarket."

"Hmm. I think I'll just take your word for it."

"Are we all set, then? You have everything you need for the big day?"

Pris turned the tiara this way and that, studying the struts that would attach to Pearl's collar and the elastic that would slide under her chin. She nodded in approval before handing the veil back.

"I think so. I'll groom both dogs in the morning, and then bring them to Trendy Tails along with my assistant Tammy. With your help, we'll get both of them dressed in that kitchen of yours. The dress and veil should be a piece of cake, but the tux looks like it's going to require a bit more wrangling."

"Mercifully, I think Romeo is okay with clothes. Hetty Tucker has been haunting Trendy Tails for months now, and she always brings him in different outfits. He must be reasonably patient."

Pris cocked her head. "This is a little bonkers, isn't it?"

I laughed. "Maybe a little, but Hetty and Louise are over the moon about this event. And now that we're combining the pupptials with Ingrid and Harvey's nuptials, I think it's going to be crazy fun."

Pris opened her mouth to respond, but before she could say a word, the door chime rang softly. I looked up to find Dee Dee Lahti standing on the threshold, looking around with wide eyes as though she weren't quite sure how she'd come to be standing at the entrance of Prissy's Pretty Pets. She wore another muu-muu, this one a dark teal with brilliant fuchsia hibiscus flowers all over it. Her lipstick matched the flowers and her hair was caught up in a dark teal scarf.

"Dee Dee," Pris crooned. "Tammy is just finishing up Pumpkin's blowout, and then she'll pull her hair up into the topknot you like so much. She shouldn't be more than another five minutes or so. I'll go check on her now."

Rena, Dolly, and I had had quite a conversation about which phone number we should pursue first, but since Dee Dee was standing right in front of me, it was like fate had made the determination for us.

"Hi, Dee Dee," I said.

She grunted back.

"I've been meaning to stop by your place."

"Really?"

"Yes. I wanted to ask you a little more about Daniel Colona."

Dee Dee looked down at her feet, cloaked in white athletic socks and strappy silver sandals. "More? I told you, he just came out to the lake and stared."

"Hmmm. That's odd. We actually found one of Daniel's notebooks, and he had your name and phone number written in the back."

"Huh."

"Did he call you?"

"No."

"Any reason why he might want to call you?"

She shrugged.

I took a few steps in her direction, and she took one

back. I froze. She was acting like a skittish colt, and I was afraid she'd bolt.

"Dee Dee," I soothed, "it's okay. No one thinks you did anything wrong."

That was the truth. I couldn't imagine Dee Dee finding her way into Daniel's apartment. Even if she did and she shot him, she seemed like the type who would just stand there until she was caught.

"It's just that whatever Daniel was researching up here got him killed, and he seemed to spend a lot of time at the construction site. I know how important you are there. If you have any idea what Daniel was looking for out there, it would help us so much."

Dee Dee shuffled her feet.

I decided to play the Dolly card.

"Do you know my aunt Dolly? Scrawny lady with platinum hair?"

That drew a smile from her. "Sure. She's real nice. She brought me a tuna and Tater Tot hotdish when Kevin had that surgery for his sciatica."

Where the rest of the country has casseroles, Minnesota has hotdishes. They come in a huge array of flavors, themes, and variations, from venison and potato to chicken and cheese puffs to tuna and noodles. Whenever there's a birth, death, wedding, or illness, Minnesota women circle the wagons and bake comforting hotdishes. I happened to know that my aunt Dolly's tuna hotdish was particularly tasty. I think it's because she used buttery crackers instead of chips or saltines on the top, and she threw in a teaspoon of paprika.

"Right. That sounds like Dolly. Dee Dee, Dolly's in a

lot of trouble right now. The police have already arrested her for Daniel's murder, and if we don't figure out who really did it, she might go to prison. No one gets hotdish in prison."

She tucked her lips between her teeth, clearly weighing her options.

Having apparently reached a decision, she glanced around the store to make sure we were alone. "Okay, Mr. Colona called me a couple of times. But it didn't have anything to do with the development on Badger Lake. He was trying to reach Kevin."

"Kevin."

"Yes, my husband. Kevin doesn't have a phone like I do. He doesn't like to be disturbed. So Daniel would call me and then I would hand the phone off to Kevin."

"Could you get a sense of what they were talking about?"

Dee Dee looked aghast. "I would never eavesdrop."

More's the pity. In her shoes, I would be trying to catch every last word.

"Not even a little?" I nudged.

"Never on purpose," she said.

"But maybe by accident?"

She paused a few moments before nodding. "Once I had to run into the living room to catch Mr. Jingles, my Chihuahua, and I heard Kevin say something about goggles."

Goggles? "Are you sure that's what you heard?"

Dee Dee sniffed. "I know what people think. That I have a screw or two loose. That maybe I'm a little slow. I'll admit I might be a bit eccentric, but I'm neither stupid nor deaf. He said 'goggles.'" She paused and held up a quelling finger. "And before you ask, I have absolutely no idea what it means. I only heard the one word, and I freely recognize that it sounds nuts."

Before I could push Dee Dee any further, Pris emerged from the back of the shop carrying a dinged-up dog carrier holding a lovely-looking Pumpkin.

"We gave her a spritz of that glitter spray, just to give her some extra sparkle," Pris said. She waved her hand. "Completely on the house."

When Dee Dee saw her companion, her eyes lit up. "Oh, thank you for taking such good care of my Punkykins. She looks like an angel."

"Well, she's always a joy to work with," Pris said.

I didn't think Pris did much of the actual "work" with any of the dogs, let alone Pumpkin, but that hardly mattered.

Dee Dee left the shop with an irrepressible smile on her face.

"I heard you two chatting away out here. Was she talking your ear off? She does that sometimes. I think she may be a tiny bit bipolar."

"Actually, I was the one asking her the questions."

Pris lifted one perfectly plucked eyebrow. "Really. And what did you learn from Dee Dee Lahti?"

"That Merryville is way more mysterious than I thought."

CHAPTER
Thirteen

"Goggles?"

"Goggles."

With the store closed for the evening, Rena, Sean, Dolly, and I were sitting around the cherry red folk art table in the middle of Trendy Tails tying new bundles of Jordan almonds for Ingrid and Harvey's Wedding: The Sequel. I had to shoo Jinx away because she wouldn't stop gnawing on the ribbon ends. She swished her tail in annoyance and walked over to the corner, stuck one leg straight up in the air, and began grooming. Clearly, I was dead to her.

"That's weird," Rena said.

"Maybe not," Dolly said. She rocked forward in her seat from excitement, and that got Packer wound up. He immediately jumped from his dog bed and came prancing over to Dolly's side, hopping back and forth beneath the table. "Construction workers wear goggles to protect their eyes from splinters and bits of metal and such. Maybe Daniel wasn't investigating the financing of the condo project. Maybe he was investigating workplace safety."

Sean was struggling to tie the thin satin ribbon in a bow around the gathered tulle holding the almonds. I reached my hand out to take the packet from him, letting him and his man fingers off the hook.

"Thanks," he muttered. "So that's a possibility. Again, we have no idea what was drawing Daniel to the construction site. Safety violations may well have been the allure . . . though I can't imagine why a reporter in Madison would come all the way to Merryville to report on occupational safety issues. Surely Madison has plenty of examples of much more egregious violations."

"Besides," I added, "if Daniel was interested in the workers wearing safety goggles, why would he call Kevin Lahti? Other than the fact that Dee Dee works on the site, Kevin has nothing to do with anything."

Rena giggled. "Kevin Lahti wouldn't know a safety measure if it bit him on the—"

"Rena!"

"Oh, come on, Dolly. You've said worse. Heck, I've heard you say worse in church."

Dolly harrumphed. "That may well be, but I've earned my right to cuss. You're a young lady. You can keep it clean. Besides, you're a professional now."

Rena laughed again, this time with her head tipped back in abandon. "I bake snacks for pets. I'm not sure that qualifies me as a professional. And this"—she waved her hand down her body to point out the Green Day T-shirt she wore over a man's thermal shirt, her military-issue pants, and her Docs—"this does not exactly scream 'professional.'"

Sean chimed in. "Speaking of baking pet snacks, have you two heard anything more from Richard Greene about the pet food regulations?"

"What's this?" Dolly asked.

"Oh, Richard's trying to shut us down again, this time because we didn't register our pet food products with the Minnesota Department of Agriculture."

"That man," Dolly huffed. "I should go give him a piece of my mind."

"You going to dress like a hooker again?"

A few months back, Dolly had tried to intervene between me and Richard, and her efforts to employ her feminine wiles were a little over the top.

"Smart aleck. I looked good in that vest."

That sequined vest. That she wore over nothing but her birthday suit.

"But no," she continued. "I think Richard responds best to plain speaking, so I'm just going to reason with him."

Secretly, I guessed that Dolly was leaping at an excuse to spend time with Richard. They were an unlikely couple, but I caught sight of sparks when they were together.

"That would be great, Aunt Dolly," I said. "I've been on the phone with the Department of Agriculture, and no one there seems to know whether we really need to register our products and, if so, how we're supposed to do that when our inventory changes so often. It's going to take a team of bureaucrats to figure out their own rules, and I can't do much of anything until they do."

Rena yawned loudly.

"Hint taken," I said. "It's getting late. We can finish these tomorrow in between customers."

Rena had walked to the store that morning, so Dolly offered her a ride home. After the two of them left, Sean lingered to help me put away the scraps of our crafting project.

"Izzy," he said, "Dolly's in trouble. I appreciate all your efforts to connect Daniel's murder to the development at Soaring Eagles, but . . ."

I plopped into a chair and covered my eyes with my hands. "I know," I moaned. "It feels like we're swimming in circles. What was he doing out there?"

"We may never know."

I spread my hands flat on the table. "Maybe not, but I'm not giving up yet. If Daniel was calling Kevin Lahti, then Kevin Lahti must know something. And whatever that is, I'm going to find out."

Sean sat next to me and covered one of my hands with one of his. His fingertips curled around my palm ever so slightly. It felt heartbreakingly close to holding hands.

"No," he insisted. "Absolutely not. Dee Dee is harmless, but Kevin's a genuine bad guy. You are not confronting that man."

"Not alone," I countered. "Rena will come with me."

He sucked in a big breath and rubbed his face with his free hand. "Jeez, Izzy. I'd bet Rena could take you in a fight, but that's not saying much."

"Hey!"

"Come on, it's true. You've got heart, but it's all soft and gooey. You'd be terrible in a fight. Rena's got that edge, but she's a terrier: fierce, but too small to do much damage. The two of you are no match for Kevin Lahti."

"You know what? I'm getting a little tired of men telling me what I can and cannot do. Between you and Jack, you'd think I didn't have the sense God gave little bunny rabbits. But I'm a grown woman, and I can do as I wish."

"Jack? Well, I may not be his biggest fan, but if he's telling you to drop this investigation, then I'm with him one hundred percent."

"Men," I huffed.

"Izzy," he countered.

He was staring at me from under his dark brows, a hint of a smile playing on his lips.

"Oh, don't look at me like that."

"Like what?"

"Like you're flirting."

He tilted his head and considered me for a moment. "What if I am?"

I'd broken his heart in high school and had done nothing to mend fences until a few months earlier. At first, he was wary of me, as though I still had some power to hurt him, but it eventually became clear that he'd gotten over me well and good. My tentative gestures of affection had been soundly rejected.

We were more comfortable with each other now. At least when Rena was around. And it seemed like Rena was always around. It was like we'd made an implicit agreement to avoid private time together.

"You're not," I said. I couldn't hide the hint of pain in my voice as I spoke the truth we both knew.

He slowly withdrew his hand from mine. "I suppose I'm not."

Did I detect a note of sorrow? Or was it only a reflection of my own hurt?

I cleared my throat, breaking the tension between us, and returned to the more urgent issue: Dolly's predicament.

"Look, one way or another I'm going to talk to Kevin Lahti. If you're so worried about my safety, you could do the chivalrous thing and come with me."

"Heck, I'm not sure I would be much protection against a river rat like Kevin, but I guess I don't have any choice."

"You have a choice. You could let Rena and me go on our own."

"That's not really a choice at all."

I felt very country come to town when I met Ama Olmstead at her office door, the entry to a mother-in-law apartment on the side of the Olmstead residence. I looked fine in my good jeans and a kelly green twinset, but Ama looked incredible. The lean spare lines of her body were cloaked in a snow-white suit and dashing red silk scarf at her neck. The early-morning light picked out the myriad shades of blond in her perfectly coiffed hair.

Ama Olmstead's office suited her perfectly. Clean

lines of Danish modern furniture, soft white walls, and occasional pops of vibrant color in the artwork and pillows and desk accessories. A handful of plaques and certificates hung on the wall: Ama's diploma from Loyola of Chicago, a certificate for completing a workshop called "Shot Heard Round the World," an award for a story she'd written on Merryville's football team the year they went to the state finals in their division, and a commendation from the mayor for service to the community. Artistic black-and-white photos of Jordan, likely taken by his own mother, filled in the blank spaces, making the wall a monument to Ama's many accomplishments.

I'd promised Sean that I would meet with Ama to get her take on Kevin Lahti before we went knocking on his door. After all, the two were related, and Ama had her ear to the ground as a writer for the *Merryville Gazette*. What's more, Ama's number had been in the back of that journal, too. It wouldn't hurt to ask her about Daniel's calls.

She directed me to sit down on one of the curved, blond wood chairs in front of her glass-topped desk.

"I take it this is a Jordan-free zone," I teased.

She laughed. "You'd be surprised how good I am at hiding crayon drawings and spit-up. But you're right—this is my grown-up space, decorated long before Jordan came along. And I only wear this suit on days that Steve is getting Jordan ready for day care."

"Like you said, having a kid changes everything."

"What can I do for you today, Izzy?" she asked, her voice as crisp as an August apple.

"I was wondering if you'd be willing do a longer feature on the double wedding we're having at Trendy Tails this weekend."

"*Double* wedding?"

"Yeah. As you know, we had already planned a doggy wedding between Louise Collins's and Hetty Tucker's dogs. And since their wedding was cut short, Ingrid and Harvey have agreed to get in on the fun and tie the knot along with our four-legged couple."

Ama looked puzzled at first, but then she laughed.

"I wouldn't miss that for the world. And I'll give you this, Izzy McHale, you are all in on this pet boutique."

I pulled a face. "I don't have much choice at this point. Every dollar I have is wrapped up in the boutique and I owe Dolly and Ingrid a pretty penny. I mean, business has been pretty good, and we're running in the black, but that doesn't happen by magic. I have to hustle if I want to keep on bringing in cash and keep up with my bills."

Ama waved her hand. "Oh, I didn't mean to make fun. Steve's the same way. The money he earns from last week's roofing job is spent buying edging rock for next week's landscape business. It all comes out in the wash eventually, but it feels like he's always one step behind. That's why this opportunity to build The Woods at Badger Lake was such a big deal to him, and why he's still a little bitter about not getting the contract."

Ama began tapping her finger on the desk, her manicured nails making little clicking sounds.

"Are you okay?" I asked.

"Fine," she replied. "Just having a nicotine fit. Would you mind if we stepped outside so I can have a smoke?"

"No problem."

We both headed out her office door and then around the side of the house. Ama peeked at the driveway, which was empty, before pulling a pack of cigarettes and a lighter from an inside pocket of her purse.

She lit the cigarette and gave it a long pull, then slowly let the smoke seep from her nostrils. A look of profound relief washed over her face.

"Sorry. Steve was home almost all day yesterday, so I haven't had a chance to get a smoke since yesterday morning. If I light up in the office, he smells it in the house, and he'd kill me if he knew I was still smoking."

"Really?"

"Yeah, we both quit when I was pregnant with Jordan, and Steve was all gung ho to stick with it after the baby was born. Keep his environment clean and all that, make sure we both live long healthy lives. But I don't have many vices, and this is one I just cannot give up."

"Steve's quite the convert, huh?"

"Yep," she said after taking another heavy drag. "Won't even let his crew smoke on outside jobs. A couple of times, he's even asked people in public places to put out their cigarettes because of Jordan. It's a little extreme."

She took one last drag, then snuffed out the cigarette on the bottom of her shoe, dropped the butt in a plastic Baggie she'd pulled from her purse, and sealed it up tight so the odor was contained. Finally, she pulled out a little canister of breath spray and gave herself a couple of healthy squirts.

"Anyway," she said after she finished her postcigarette ritual, "I'd love to do a full-length feature on the double wedding, hopefully for the Sunday paper. I'll run it by my editor Ted, but I can't imagine he'd be opposed."

"Thanks so much, Ama."

Frankly the request for extra coverage of the weekend's nuptials had been a thin cover story for my real reasons for bothering Ama.

"I don't mean to beat a dead horse, but did Daniel Colona contact you after he got to town?"

Ama's mouth dropped open. "Seriously, Izzy? How many ways can I tell you that I didn't know Daniel Colona and he didn't know me?"

"It's just that he had your phone number in the back of his journal."

"Maybe he got my number from someone, called the paper or something. But he didn't use it. I. Never. Met. Him."

I offered a timid smile of apology. "I get it. I'm sorry. I'm just so anxious about my aunt Dolly."

Ama sighed. "It's okay. Family is important. I'd do anything to protect my family. I understand that you must feel the same way."

"Listen, I had another question, if you don't mind."

She stiffened, but she didn't say no.

"I was wondering what you know about Kevin Lahti. If maybe you've learned anything about him in your time as a reporter."

Her shoulders relaxed.

"Joyce Lambert is the one you should ask. She covers the police beat, and from what I know of Kevin, his whole life is just a series of criminal acts."

I decided to dip my hook in the water to see what I might catch. "I'd heard"—from Rena's rambling speculations—"that Kevin might be involved somehow with the development out by the lake."

"Kevin? I can't imagine that. Hal Olson may be a shady character, but no one in their right mind would trust Kevin Lahti with any kind of job at all. He's horrible to Dee Dee. I mean, don't get me wrong, Dee Dee and I are not exactly sisterly, but no one should be treated the way Kevin treats Dee Dee. And he lies every time he opens his mouth. He used to borrow money from Steve all the time, coming up with emergency after emergency, until I finally put my foot down and said 'no more.'"

She'd gotten pretty worked up during her tirade, so she took a moment to calm herself before continuing. "Why on earth do you ask?"

"Just something I heard," I hedged. "That he was hanging out down there."

"It was that Richard Greene, wasn't it? For a man who insists he wants to be left alone, he sure does spend a lot of time prying into everyone's business."

Amen.

"After he found out that Steve got beat out of the bid by a firm in Brainerd, he decided to take it personally. Like Hal's decision had been an affront to Merryville."

I wondered how Richard would feel if he knew that Hal had brought in overseas investors for the project.

"In this case, he's probably right. Steve has driven . . ." Her voice faded away when she realized what she was about to spill. She cleared her throat and continued on bravely. "Steve has driven out to the site now and then to see what they're doing, how it's coming along, and he's mentioned that he's seen Kevin a couple of times, getting out of that rust-bucket truck of his with a guy in full Cabela's camo gear, both of them carrying guns."

"That sounds ominous."

Ama waved off my concern. "Just hunters."

"But I'd heard that Kevin wasn't getting much business from the hunters and fishermen anymore. Too sketchy for the wealthy tourists who are visiting now."

I couldn't help but wonder if Kevin was leading some sort of survivalist group, or maybe even a white supremacy group that had set up a command center in the woods. You hear about these things happening in Wyoming and the UP of Michigan. Why not Minnesota?

Ama laughed grimly. "You're so naive, Izzy. You're right that the high-toned hunters and fishers and birders wouldn't be caught dead with Kevin Lahti during the daytime. But at night? Guides who'll take you on night hunts are few and far between."

"Night hunts? Isn't that illegal?"

"Precisely."

Night hunting would explain the discussion of goggles. Hunters used night-vision goggles to see their prey in the dark.

"Why hasn't Steve called the police?" I asked.

Ama shrugged, her mouth set in a thin line. "I've told him to do it a hundred times. But he just says he's only guessing about what they're doing. Even the time he actually heard a shot in the woods, he claimed that he didn't know if Kevin and his companion were actually shooting at a living thing or just doing target practice."

"What?"

"Exactly. I think he doesn't want to call the cops because he's afraid of what will happen to Dee Dee if she loses Kevin. He treats her worse than a dog, but without him, she couldn't afford to keep the house, and there really aren't that many job opportunities for someone who's so far off the rails. Somehow Steve convinced Hal to hire her to work on the site, but that won't last forever, and she'll be back to relying on Kevin for every penny."

"I'm sorry you're caught up in all this," I said, genuinely sad that Dee Dee, Ama, and Steve were dealing with the fallout of Kevin's illegal activities.

"So let this be a warning to you, Izzy. If I were you, I'd stay as far away from Kevin Lahti as I could."

CHAPTER
Fourteen

Needless to say, I chose not to take Ama's advice.

Kevin and Dee Dee Lahti lived in a ramshackle house on the edge of the city. It appeared to have been a tidy 1950s bungalow at one point, but additions, sheds, and slant-roofed porches had grown out of the original building like tumors. The property had been fenced in so that dogs and chickens could roam freely. Most of the dogs were not getting blowouts at Prissy's Pretty Pets. Most of them looked semiferal and defeated.

Rena had been called away to spend the afternoon with her father, who suffered from severe alcoholism and the myriad physical complaints that came with that. So Sean and I were left to deal with the ravening pack at the Lahti house on our own.

Okay, that wasn't fair. While the dogs didn't appear domesticated, as we stood there at the gate, they looked like they didn't give a rip what was happening around them.

Gingerly, Sean opened the gate and we stepped through. One of the dogs stirred so he could watch us more closely, but there was no aggression in his stance. Still, Sean held his hands out to his side, keeping me safely behind him. The chivalrous gesture made me smile.

When we mounted the porch and made it to the front door, Sean's knock was met almost immediately by a cry of "Dee Dee, get the damn door."

Charming.

The door swung wide, and Dee Dee stood there in another extravagant, brilliantly colored caftan—tonight in a chevron-stripe pattern of apple green and purple that made me slightly queasy when I looked at it. She took a drag on the ever present Parliament and squinted at us suspiciously.

"What do you want?"

"We were actually hoping to have a word with your husband," Sean said gently.

Dee Dee's eyes grew round with alarm and she stepped out onto the porch, pulling the door behind her. "Are you trying to get me killed? Kevin don't like folks knowing about his business. If he knows I told you that that reporter called him, he'll have my hide."

"We'll keep you out of it," I soothed. "Promise."

She glanced over her shoulder, apparently weighing the probability that she'd be caught out no matter what we said with the damage Kevin could do.

Before she reached a decision, Kevin yelled from in-

side, "Who the heck is it, woman? Who you dillydallying with?"

Dee Dee winced at the sound of footsteps approach-
ing the door.

"What's all this about?" Kevin asked as he pulled
the door open wide.

Kevin Lahti was as tough and spare as his wife was
colorful and exuberant. His grungy jeans hung off his
bony behind and it looked like he hadn't shaved in a
good five days: not long enough to have a genuine
beard, but too long for that sexy five-o'clock shadow
look. Though, frankly, no amount of shadow could have
made Kevin Lahti sexy. One look in the man's black
eyes, flat as flounders, and I shivered clear to my toes.

He, too, squinted at us in the dim light. "I know
you," he said, nodding his head toward Sean. "You that
lawyer from in town. Helped get Nick Haas out of that
loitering beef last month."

My Sean. He moved in such lofty circles.

"Yes, sir," Sean replied, holding out his hand to
shake. "Sean Tucker."

Kevin looked at the proffered hand and snorted.

Sean pulled his hand back to his side. "This is my
friend Izzy McHale."

"McHale, McHale . . . Were your folks those teachers? Both flunked me."

"I'm sorry."

Kevin laughed with a chain-smoker's harsh cackle.
"Don't be. Hated school. Just marking time until I
could drop out. Anyways, what do you two want with
my Dee Dee, here?"

"Actually, we were hoping to speak with you."

Kevin cocked his head. "Now, what would two fine, upstanding folks like yourselves want with me?"

Dee Dee was doing her best to squeeze her body around Kevin's to get back in the house.

"Quit your wiggling, woman," Kevin demanded. "Why don't we invite our friends here inside?"

Dee Dee looked mortified, but she mustered a smile.

The four of us made our way into the Lahti living room. Dee Dee's fingerprint was stamped squarely on this room. Macramé hanging baskets filled with spider plants, avocado green furniture, and a plethora of owls in paintings and sculptures and even one crafted of macramé all served to date the room horrifically. But while it was a trip back to Brady days, it was also neat as a pin. Smelled like an ashtray, but every item had a place and every surface was dust-free. Pumpkin, her hair still flowing and shining from her trip to Pris's, sat on a plush gold ottoman next to the wood-burning stove. Dee Dee didn't have the best taste or the funds to update her home, but she clearly cared for it.

"So what can I do for you?" Kevin asked as he plopped down into a black pleather recliner.

At Kevin's urging, Sean and I took a seat on the green velveteen couch. Sean leaned forward, taking the lead.

"We're trying to figure out what happened to Daniel Colona. Do you know him?"

"Who?"

"Daniel Colona."

"Don't know him."

A hint of frustration crept into Sean's voice. "Mr. Lahti, we have it on good authority that he called you a couple of times while he was in town."

"You making some sort of accusation?" Kevin's voice cut through the air like a razor blade.

Sean held up his hands. "Not at all. We're just trying to retrace Daniel's steps during his stay in Merryville, figure out how he spent his days."

Kevin looked back and forth between us, trying to judge our motives. We must have looked pretty darned innocent, because he didn't throw us out immediately.

Eventually, he sighed and leaned back in his chair. "I don't know what that fella was doing up here. He did call me a couple of times, trying to get me to lead him on a night excursion of some sort."

"Night hunting?" Sean prodded.

Kevin grew very still, and I think Dee Dee stopped breathing. I slid my hand into my jacket pocket and got a death grip on Aunt Dolly's derringer.

"That's illegal," Kevin said, stating the obvious.

"It sure is," Sean said. "Don't worry. We're not interested in your poaching."

Kevin relaxed against the back of his recliner. "What poaching?" he asked with an oil slick of a smile.

"We're interested in what Daniel was interested in," Sean explained. "And if *Daniel* was interested in your nighttime activities, then that raises the question of whether Daniel got himself killed over your poaching."

That ominous stillness hung over the room again, until Kevin laughed. Tipped back his head and howled at the ceiling.

"You think I'd kill some guy because he thought—*thought*—I was engaged in a little dirty hunting? Even if I did, on occasion, take a select few clients on night hunts—and I'm not saying I do—I didn't take that reporter fella out on any excursion at all, let alone one that skirted the law. I may not be educated, but I'm not stupid. Don't trust reporters, that's what I say."

"But your sister-in-law is a reporter," I chimed in softly.

"Damn straight. Don't trust her, either. Too perfect. All that perfect has to be hiding something. Anyway, Daniel didn't have a story. At least, he didn't have anything on me. Why would I kill him?"

Sean shrugged.

"Can I get anyone an iced tea? Or maybe a beer?" Dee Dee asked. Her whole body was vibrating with anxiety. This conversation might kill her.

Kevin growled. "No one wants a drink, Dee Dee. These folks won't be here much longer."

Sean threw Dee Dee a smile. "Thanks for the offer, Mrs. Lahti, but I think Izzy and I are just fine."

"You all finished accusing me of shit?" Kevin said.

Sean's smile never wavered. "Not quite," he admitted.

Kevin laughed again, the sound less amused this time. "You really have some nerve, mister. Most people know to keep their distance from me. Stay out of my business."

"Yes, well, I've never been one to cower in the face of bullies. And I don't think you're going to hurt me, Mr. Lahti. A half dozen people know that Izzy and I are here. If something happened to us, the cops would be on your doorstep in a heartbeat. And while you're not stupid, you're not smart enough to commit the perfect crime."

Kevin grunted in response, eyes narrowed in simmering anger.

"So what do you want now?"

I scooched closer to Sean. This was the tough part, our Hail Mary pass, fourth down with only seconds left on the clock.

"We talked to Hal Olson," Sean said. "He might have had a bone to pick with Daniel, too. But Hal said he was with you at the time of the murder. 'Doin' something.'"

"Mmmm," Kevin hummed, clearly unsure where we were going with this.

"The way we look at it, one of three things is the truth. First, you and Hal really were together that night, doing God knows what. Second, Hal is lying to cover his own ass. Or third, Hal is lying to cover your ass. Hal isn't in the mood to be forthright, but we're hoping you will be."

"And why would I help you with this? Hal sends me a lot of business. I don't see why I should throw him to the wolves."

I held my breath. It sure sounded like Kevin was about to blow Hal's alibi out of the water.

"You might want to help us because, while we're not interested in your poaching, the police would be."

Kevin realized he was trapped.

"For crying out loud, okay. Hal and I were together that night."

"Hunting?" Sean pushed.

"No, as a matter of fact we weren't hunting," Kevin said smugly.

What? Mind. Blown. What on earth could Hal and Kevin have in common beyond a little shady hunting action?

"So if you weren't hunting, then what were you doing?" Sean asked.

Kevin looked pointedly at Dee Dee, who wordlessly got up, scooped up Pumpkin, and disappeared into another room.

"We were socializing. Hal was after a little action. He's got varied tastes, if you know what I mean, and that wife of his is watching his every move. If he wants a little nooky on the side, he has to go out of town to find it. I know about a little place down near Brainerd where the ladies are pretty and the price is right. Place is very discreet, very careful not to open their doors to cops. So, for a small fee, I agreed to drive down with him and get him in the front door."

How interesting, I thought. *Kevin has no problem treating his wife like dirt in front of other people, but he doesn't want her to hear about his infidelities. I guess different people have different priorities in their relationships.*

"When did you leave?" Sean asked.

"About nine. Hal was supposed to meet me at the RV lot at eight—it's a long drive to Brainerd, and I wanted to get there before the really cute girls were otherwise employed—but Hal was late. He's lucky I didn't just drive off without him."

I did the math in my head. Just because Hal was

with Kevin that night, he didn't have an alibi. Ingrid and Harvey's wedding had started at seven. Daniel was killed around seven twenty. That left Hal with over an hour and a half to make his way home, clean himself up, and get to the RV park to meet Kevin at nine.

"You know, Hal's been a good partner over the last few years, sent a lot of specialized clientele my way, but dragging me into this? Not cool," Kevin said. He might have been cagey when we brought up Hal's name, but by then he'd clearly crossed some threshold and was more than happy to dish all the dirt on Hal.

"I'm gonna give you a little free intel. That reporter fella, Daniel Colona, he did call me a couple of times, but he wasn't interested in hunting. He was interested in the owls."

"Owls?"

"Dryden burrowing owls, to be precise. A whole bunch of them, hunkered down living in the woodlands right by the marsh. Just a stone's throw from Olson's construction site."

"Dryden's burrowing owls? I've never heard of them," I said.

Kevin cackled. "Probably haven't heard of them because there aren't very many of them to hear about. They're endangered. And that's a big problem for ol' Hal. Because his building activities are disturbing the ecosystem of a highly endangered animal."

I thought about Daniel's journal. The initials DNR— Department of Natural Resources—next to the vase with the olives. Which wasn't a vase with olives. It was a burrow in the ground occupied by a wide-eyed owl.

Daniel wasn't investigating Hal's investors; he was investigating the environmental impact of the development.

Sean didn't seem impressed. "You keep up with the endangered species list? I thought you didn't care about all those hunting regulations."

Kevin eyed Sean from head to toe and back again. "Mr. Fancy Pants Lawyer," he mocked. "I absolutely keep up with all the hunting regulations. Look, as far as I'm concerned a critter is a critter and men were meant to hunt. Deer doesn't care if it's killed in October or June, whether it's day or night, so why should I care? Still, I keep up with everything the DNR does. I offer a very specialized service, and those regulations and lists help me keep up with just how much that specialized service is worth."

Ah. So the more endangered the species, the more Kevin could charge the men who wanted his help in hunting it.

I felt the hair rising on the back of my neck. This could be it. If The Woods at Badger Lake was threatening an endangered species, that would be a heck of a story for Daniel Colona. And if Hal was in danger of being shut down by that story, that gave him a powerful motive to get rid of Daniel before he filed his report with the *Madison Standard*.

"Did Hal know about the owls?" I asked.

"Sure did."

"How do you know?" Sean asked.

"Because I was the one who told him. Went white as the road to Fargo when I mentioned it."

"Did he know that Daniel Colona was interested in the owls?"

Kevin chuckled, the sound as dark and unctuous as crude oil. "Yep. I told him that, too. Like I said, I felt like I owed Hal for all the years of mutually beneficial business dealings. But when he tries to use me as an alibi, gets me wrapped up in a murder investigation, well, I'm done with him."

That night I'd promised to bring home pizza from Del Monico's for Ingrid, Harvey, and Rena. After our stint with the Lahtis, I was a little on the late side, but Del Monico's was still open. Stewart Paglio owned the place—a classic Italian restaurant three buildings down from Xander's Spin Doctor record store. He was a short, pale, balding man in his midfifties, a widower with two grown children who lived in Chicago. His whole life was wrapped up in his restaurant, and the menu—and the food—showed his commitment to quality.

Because we were practically neighbors, we had a deal that I could phone in an order and pick it up at his back door, so I only had to walk a few yards down the alley instead of walking clear around the block. I'd called from Sean's car, and the food was ready as soon as I got to the restaurant.

I carried my bounty up the back stairs to my apartment: a pizza box holding a pie that was half sausage-and-onion (for Ingrid and Harvey) and half mushroom-and-olive (for Rena and me), a bag of Stewart's world-famous garlic rolls, a plastic clamshell containing a beautifully dressed salad, and yet another smaller clamshell holding four cannoli.

I'd managed to get through the back door with the towering stack of food, but halfway up the first set of stairs, I started to lose my balance. I quickly reached out to grab the railing, and I felt my finger slide across a rough spot on the back of the railing and then the quick slice of a splinter working its way beneath my skin.

I gasped in surprise, pulling my hand back immediately, and yet somehow I managed to catch my now flailing body against the wall on the other side. In all the juggling, the cannoli box slid precariously close to the edge of the salad box, but all of the food managed to remain upright, intact, and in my arms.

I felt a wave of gratitude that no one had seen that astonishing display of grace, but then realized I'd have to fess up when I asked someone to help me remove the splinter in my finger . . . a splinter so massive I could see its dark shadow beneath the skin of my fingertip even in the relatively dim light of the back stairwell. I stuck my finger in my mouth, sucking gently, trying to ease the pain.

I climbed the rest of the steps to my apartment, and bumped my rear against the door in lieu of knocking.

Rena opened the door and ushered me into the warm glow of my apartment. Harvey and Ingrid were sitting at the table playing a game of gin rummy, Packer somehow draped across Harvey's lap. Honestly, I didn't know how those two would survive if separated. Jinx had stretched her long self across the back of the couch, balancing precariously on the top edges of the cushions. Her tail swished in a "come hither" motion, but her narrowed eyes clearly read "keep away." I could see where Rena had been curled on the couch by Jinx's head, a tangle of yarn and knitting needles from her newest hobby lying in a chaotic heap on the sofa seat.

Both of my animals, whom I fed and sheltered every day, and who had enjoyed the luxuries of frequent grooming and vet care at my expense, continued to relax . . . Packer only bothering to raise a single curious eyebrow before stretching and relaxing further on Harvey's legs. Daisy May, however, the interloper whom I desperately wanted to find another home for, came galloping over, all legs and excitement.

"Food!" Rena announced, as Daisy tried to shove her nose between Rena's arm and body.

"Chill, dog," Rena said, pulling Daisy away from me and my precious pizza. She put one hand on the dog's head and the other on her rump, pressing down until the dog sat. Daisy whimpered once, but then she did, indeed, chill out. Rena's way with animals was a constant source of wonder.

"We're starving," she said, waving at Ingrid and Harvey. "You?"

"Yeah," I said around my throbbing finger, "but first I need a little help digging out a splinter."

"Oooh, me," Rena said, raising her hand. I didn't like the eager glint in her eye, but when my other two options were octogenarians with fading eyesight and trembling hands, Rena seemed like the best pick.

I set the food on the kitchen pass-through and encouraged Ingrid and Harvey to dig in, while Rena and I retired to the tiny bathroom to try to extricate my splinter. She washed her hands with antibacterial soap—mmmm, plumeria!—doused the finger with a little rubbing alcohol, and poured a little more on a pair of tweezers. With surprisingly deft fingers, she manipulated the splinter until it popped out from the skin. Then, with the tweezers, she gently tugged the whole splinter. What had felt like a tree branch in my finger actually looked more like the tip of a toothpick.

As Rena worked, I kept up a steady monologue about Sean's and my visit to Kevin Lahti . . . more to distract myself than to actually convey information. But Rena managed to nod at all the right times.

When she was done pulling out the splinter, Rena opened the medicine cabinet and grabbed a tube of antibacterial ointment and an adhesive bandage.

"It sounds like you and Sean had a productive day," she said, slathering goo over my small wound.

"I suppose," I said, holding my finger rigid as Rena wrapped it in a bandage. "I just feel exhausted. Spending time in the Lahti home was absolutely toxic. How can two people survive together with so much contempt and fear between them?"

Rena finished her nursing work by planting a brief kiss on my boo-boo. "There, you're all set."

She leaned back against the bathroom wall. "It's all about the conditions we place on our love. You and I would never tolerate what Dee Dee tolerates, but she doesn't place any conditions on her relationship with

Kevin. And that makes her vulnerable. On the other hand you have other people, like Pris Olson, who place tight constraints on their emotions, and so her love died early and she's just waiting for a lucrative time to bury it. That doesn't work well, either."

"Speaking of conditional love, how are things with your dad?"

"He won't stop drinking. Which means he won't stop dying. And he won't stop being a total ass. Today he drank half a fifth of rotgut Canadian whiskey while I cleaned his house and did his laundry. He yelled obscenities, and I kept my mouth shut."

She paused to rub her eyes, but I didn't see any tears.

"I guess my love is unconditional, but my patience is not."

"I'm so sorry, Rena."

"Why? It's life. We all have our special crosses to bear."

"You're bringing me down here, Rena."

She laughed, folding her arms across her chest. "I don't mean to. I think there's a perfect balance where we hold our loved ones accountable but don't demand more than they're able to give. That's when love flourishes."

"My, aren't you the philosopher tonight?"

"Mmm. I'm meeting up with Jolly for a drink in a little bit."

"Ahh. So that's why you have love on the brain."

"Let's not get ahead of ourselves. We're still testing the waters."

"But you dig her?"

"Oh, yeah."

We made our way back to the living room, where I caught Harvey feeding pieces of sausage to Packer. Ingrid held up her hand. "I know. I know. It's my fault. I know Packer's not supposed to have people food, but he was killing us with those big eyes and plaintive whines."

"You two are suckers, and that dog played you," I said. I couldn't help laughing at their expressions of shock and remorse. "I'm only kidding. He's a manipulative mutt, and he always gets what he wants. Do you have any idea how much ice cream I've fed the little guy over the last few years?"

Ingrid and Harvey both visibly relaxed.

At the sound of Packer's gleeful and greedy chewing, Daisy May slunk her way over to the couch. Her head was down, but she peered up at Harvey like a penitent seeking absolution. Or, in this case, sausage.

Harvey turned to me with the exact expression.

"Oh, go on. It's only fair."

Harvey picked a couple of choice morsels of meat off his slice and held them low for Daisy to gobble up.

Rena and I fixed ourselves plates and joined our elders at the dining table. We spent the next hour eating, making small talk, and engaging in a little friendly bickering.

Harvey and Ingrid got into a betting war over when Johnny Mathis's first album was released, but when Rena suggested we go to the Internet to get the answer, both of them said no. It was the back-and-forth they enjoyed; they didn't really care about the answer.

Then Rena turned on me. "So. What are you going to do about Sean?"

"What's that supposed to mean?"

"It means, are you two cool again? You thinking about striking up a romance? What?"

I glanced over at Harvey, who barely knew me and didn't know Sean from Adam. He bobbled his eyebrows at me in encouragement.

"There's nothing to do, really. We're working together, and neither of us has started a fight with the other, so that's good. We've even shared some meaningful conversation, which suggests we're friends . . . though you'd want to check with Sean about that. As for romance, I don't know if that will ever be in the cards, but it sure isn't now."

Rena sighed. "Bummer."

"Why is it a bummer? We have perfectly wonderful separate lives, and they get a little better when our paths happen to cross. That's not so bad."

Rena reached across the table to pinch my cheek. "I just want my Izzy-bear to be happy," she baby-talked.

I shoved her arm away playfully. The question was awkward, but it was nice to know she cared.

While Ingrid and Rena were debating the quality of different flours, a subject I couldn't have contributed to if my life depended on it, I thought about what a lovely evening we'd had. It was bittersweet. I couldn't help but think that Dee Dee—with her abusive husband and distant brother—probably never enjoyed such relaxed and spirit-lifting evenings. And I also couldn't help but think of Dolly, and how she was going to miss out on these evenings, too, if we didn't find the real killer.

But Rena was right. Sean and I had made a lot of progress that day.

I felt a renewed sense of purpose. Dolly and I had taken a run at Hal, but we didn't have all the information. Now we knew for certain that Daniel had been investigating the development site and we knew exactly what he'd been after. We also knew that Hal's alibi was hogwash. I couldn't wait to confront Hal again.

CHAPTER
Fifteen

Turns out I didn't have to go looking for Hal Olson. He came looking for me the morning after Sean and I met with Kevin.

The jingle of the Trendy Tails door preceded him.

"Hello, Izzy." His voice practically dripped with suspicion.

"Hal. I'm surprised to see you here." Surprised didn't actually cover it. Astounded, stunned, gobsmacked, aghast . . .

He pulled a face and patted his ample stomach like a child trying to self-soothe. "I admit, I'm a little surprised I'm here, too."

I caught sight of Rena standing off in the corner. Her eyes were huge and she mouthed "Oh my God." I subtly tried to settle her down with a wave of my hand.

"What brings you by?"

"Well, you've got that dog wedding thing coming

up, and Pris is going to be busy with the, uh, bride and groom."

"Pearl and Romeo?"

Hal sighed. "I gotta say—this just doesn't seem right. Holding a wedding for two dogs . . . well, it seems to belittle the institution of marriage."

That was rich, coming from a man who slept with every woman he could get his hands on, even those he had to pay. But I kept my lips sealed for the moment.

"Well, anyway, Pris wants me to bring Kiki. She said I should come by your store to get something fancy for Kiki." He sighed. "But here's the thing. Whatever I get, I have to put it on her, and that cat hates me. I don't want to be torn to shreds, so this needs to be easy on, easy off."

Okay, so I thought Hal might be a murderer, but I still felt a stab of sympathy for him. Kiki generally showed all the enthusiasm and character of a piece of dried toast. But she hated me every bit as much as she hated Hal. I'd been on the receiving end of that wrath more than once, and that little fur ball was vicious.

"I think I've got just the thing." I stepped back behind the counter and pulled out a tray of chiffon ruffs. The ruffs were just circles of fabric with a hole cut out and elasticized so the whole thing would slip over the cat's head and stay put. Some were playful, made out of cotton and meant to be everyday adornments. But the tray I brought out for Hal was my special inventory. These were made of chiffon and lightweight silk, hand dyed so they had a ombré pastel coloring. Some of them even had multiple layers.

I knew Pris well enough to know that she'd want a

feminine color—like pink or peach—and that she'd want the fluffiest three-layer ruff I had to offer.

I held out three options for Hal to consider.

"Can't you just pick for me? I don't really know anything about this cat-costuming business."

The lavender was my favorite and would go beautifully with Kiki's brilliant blue eyes and snowy fur. I put the rest of the tray back in the case and pulled out a box and some tissue paper for the ruff Kiki would wear.

"It's really simple. Just hold it wide and slip it over her head. Once the elastic contracts, she won't be able to get it off. It won't hurt her, though, so don't worry about that."

"I'm not terribly worried about the cat's well-being," he muttered under his breath.

"But speaking of hurt," Hal began more loudly. He paused to clear his throat. "I gotta say, Izzy, I don't take kindly to you coming by my place of business to accuse me of murder. You should at least get your facts straight before you do."

My eyes narrowed and I tipped my chin back so I could meet Hal's eyes. I didn't appreciate being chastised by this man who himself had all the tact and morals of a cockroach. "I'm sorry you feel that way, Hal. You're right. We didn't have our facts straight when Dolly and I came to visit you, and I didn't expect Dolly to be quite so blunt."

"Hell, I don't mind the bluntness. Don't have a lot of patience for games."

"Okay, then. No games. We didn't have our facts straight then, but we sure do now. We know about the

Dryden burrowing owls, we know you knew about the owls, and we know that you knew that Daniel knew about the owls. We also know, thanks to your good buddy Kevin Lahti, that your alibi is pretty flimsy. You were with him that night, but not until nine . . . giving you plenty of time to kill Daniel, get cleaned up, and then meet up with Kevin.

"Is that blunt enough for you?"

Beyond Hal's shoulder, I watched Rena mouth "Oh my God" again. She crossed her hands over her heart dramatically and pretended to swoon.

Hal's face had reddened again, turned the color of boiled beets, and I swear there was steam coming from his ears.

He handed me his credit card. It was surreal, but with that accusation of murder hanging in the air between us, I rang up his purchase, slid the box into a baby blue Trendy Tails bag, and handed it over to him.

"I've had it up to here," he said, holding his hand several inches above his head. "So far you're just harassing me, which is bad enough, but if someone else hears your accusations, it's going to be slander. I'm a reputable businessman and I'm running for office. Your wild accusations could cost me a lot. So just back off."

He turned sharply on his heel and strode out of the store.

"Holy cow," Rena said. "I can't believe that just happened. Twice in two days. That must be some kind of murder accusation record."

"I'm not setting out to break records. I'm just trying to save Dolly."

"Well, that should certainly save Dolly, once you tell the police what you know."

And that's exactly what I did. I called Jack Collins's number. He didn't pick up, but I left a long and detailed voice message. If I could just get the police to take me seriously, Dolly might finally be cleared.

"I hope you don't mind that I brought Daisy with me," I said as I stepped through the door of Louise Collins's house.

Jack, who'd held it open for me, shook his head. "Not a problem." His voice was tight and hard. He must have gotten my message from earlier in the day.

I hated to impose by showing up with an animal in tow, but I had finally managed to get Daisy in to see the vet late that morning. I should have done it before I let her mingle with Packer and Jinx, but better late than never. Thankfully, Daisy got a clean bill of health.

However, the wait at the vet had been long, as Dr. Sheridan had been called away to attend a cocker spaniel who was having problems birthing a litter of pups. As a result, I had to choose between being late for my appointment with Louise—our last consultation before the doggy wedding on Saturday—or bringing Daisy along.

As Jack ushered me into his mother's living room, Daisy politely stayed at my side.

Louise had been a widow for some time, and her house had reverted to a state of unadulterated femininity. The plaster walls had been painted a deep rose, the room dripped with lace, and delicate porcelain figurines—

mostly of children and animals—littered every available surface. Two TV trays had been moved to the side of the sofa, the remains of sandwiches and baby carrots on the plates they held. Jack must have come over to have lunch with his mother.

Jack pointed me toward a cream wingback chair, and he sat next to his mother on the damask striped Queen Anne sofa. There was something endearing about seeing such a big man perched on such a dainty piece of furniture. I couldn't help but smile.

The television was on when I came in, and Louise simply turned down the sound instead of turning it off. Daisy was, of course, thrilled. She made her way to Jack's side, managed to worm her head up into the palm of his hand, and watched TV in absolute silence.

"Would you like a hard candy?" Louise asked.

"Yes, ma'am. That would be lovely." I chose a butterscotch candy wrapped in golden cellophane.

"So, we're getting mighty close to the big day," Louise said, her eyes sparkling behind the lenses of her cat-eye glasses. Her eyes were the same violet blue color as her son's.

"We sure are. And I think we have all the details worked out. We've got white wedding decorations, tissue bells and such, and I'm almost finished making the bow tie favors. Rena's tested the cake recipe and both she and Packer have given it their seal of approval."

Louise cut me off to click her tongue against her teeth, summoning Pearl the bride.

"Here's my girl," Louise said as Pearl wobbled into

the room. Pearl was an old girl, with some serious curves, and not entirely steady on her feet.

Louise leaned down to rub the dog's velvety ears. "She's looking so fine these days. You know, I adopted her from Dr. Sheridan's office. Someone had found her living behind the Bread Basket. She'd grown quite rotund on cinnamon rolls and bear claws, and her small beagle frame was carrying a good forty pounds. Dr. Sheridan worried that I wouldn't be able to provide Pearl with enough exercise to get her down to a healthy weight, but I just asked Jack if he could be her personal trainer and he said yes."

She reached across to pat her son's hand, and I saw a hint of red creeping up his neck.

"He started just walking her to the mailbox and back, and now they jog almost a mile every day."

"That's wonderful," I said. I meant it sincerely, but Jack flushed harder.

"She's going to make a beautiful bride," Louise said.

"She sure will. Listen, we do have a little wrinkle that I hope you won't mind. As you know, Ingrid and Harvey never officially tied the knot last Friday, so they're hoping they can join Pearl and Romeo in a joint ceremony. I've asked Reverend Wilson, and he's free Saturday afternoon. He even promised to do a blessing of the animals during the ceremony for Pearl and Romeo. You should feel free to say no, but would you mind having Ingrid and Harvey horn in on Pearl's special day?"

Louise laughed, a sharp crack of joy. "That would be

splendid. I've been rooting for Ingrid Whitfield to get her happily ever after ever since . . ." She paused, flustered. I knew she meant "ever since Ingrid's husband, Arnold, had committed adultery with Jane Porter." But there was no way she'd air that old, dirty laundry in front of one of Ingrid's friends. "Well, never mind that. What matters is that Pearl and I would be honored to share the day with her."

"I'm so relieved. Harvey and Ingrid are so anxious to get married, I was afraid that if I couldn't get them hitched properly this weekend, they'd go down to the courthouse. Nothing wrong with that, of course, but I think Ingrid actually wants to be a bride again."

"Heavens, yes. Don't let that tough old bird fool you. She's got a soft underbelly. She rarely shows it, but it's there. I know she's been looking forward to being the belle of the ball for quite a while now."

All of a sudden, Daisy let out a yip. Then another. Then a full-fledged bark.

She'd been so quiet for the last couple of days that I'd practically forgotten that she could bark when she wanted to.

I followed her line of sight and she was still staring at the TV. There was a commercial for the *Merryville Gazette*, touting its local focus, and Ama Olmstead was doing a sound bite about her coverage of last year's Fourth of July parade.

As soon as the ad returned to the announcer's voice, Daisy stopped barking.

"Well, I'll be damned," Jack said, his smile creeping into his voice. "I think Daisy here has a crush."

"That's funny. She barked at Ama when we ran into her at the dog park the other day. I'd thought it was just a general 'hey, look at me' sort of bark, but I think you must be right. A doggy crush.

"Listen, I ought to get her home and get out of your hair."

"You're fine, dear," Louise said. "It sounds like you have everything in hand, and I can't wait for this Saturday."

As I rose to leave, Jack followed me. He handed me Daisy's leash as we stood in the foyer, but he blocked the door.

"I got a call today from Hal Olson," he said.

"Oh."

"'Oh' is right. The man says you accused him of murder. Twice. For this murder. Not to mention the accusation from six months ago. What do you have against that man?"

"I don't have anything against him. He just always looks guilty to me. You know?"

Jack paused, then nodded. "Yes, actually I do know what you mean. There's something shady about that guy. But still, you need to be a little more circumspect, especially with the man who will likely be our next mayor."

"You're right."

"You're right, I'm right. And I thought I told you to leave this investigation alone. Now you've graduated from snooping to accusing. That's not the direction I wanted to see you take."

Something in his tone rubbed me exactly the wrong way. "Have I done anything illegal?"

"No. Just foolish."

My blood began to simmer. "Foolish, huh? Well, I think it's foolish that you aren't following up on the leads I've been handing you. Hal had motive and opportunity to kill Daniel Colona. Have you even considered the possibility that he might be guilty? And if I haven't done anything illegal, I don't see where you come off telling me to stop."

"First of all, I am not at liberty to share the details of an ongoing investigation. Whether we're taking your so-called leads seriously or not, I can't tell you. Second, when I tell you to mind your own business, I'm not doing it as a cop. I'm doing it as your friend. Is it so hard to believe that I just want to keep you safe?"

Had he not called me foolish, I probably would have melted at his sweet sentiment. As it was, I felt completely patronized. "I don't need you to keep me safe, Jack. I'm a grown woman and I can run my own life just fine."

He stepped aside and opened the door to let me escape, but not before he offered something close to an apology. "Believe me, I know you're a grown woman. But I can't help worrying about you. You're trusting and friendly and maybe just a little naive, qualities I find charming, but qualities that make you vulnerable. It's my nature to protect."

I slipped out the door, Daisy May right behind me.

"We're just going to have to agree to disagree on this, Jack. I won't rest—I *can't* rest—until Aunt Dolly's name has been cleared."

CHAPTER
Sixteen

As a thank-you for all of our sleuthing, Aunt Dolly invited Rena and me to the Thistle and Ivy, Merryville's answer to the classic Irish pub. The restaurant boasted half timbers on the plaster walls, coats of arms on banners hanging from the rafters, a huge map of Ireland, and—oddly—a kilt and sporran mounted in a shadow box frame. The food was good, solid comfort food, though Rena and I had only limited meat-free choices. The chef and owner, Danielle Phipps, played canasta with my mother and Ingrid, though, and she took care of us: every time we came in, she'd make a special vegetarian shepherd's pie with mushroom gravy, root vegetables, and cashews all cloaked in a mound of fluffy white mashed potatoes. Rena had tried to re-create the mushroom gravy on many occasions, but she couldn't quite replicate the balance of salty, earthy, and just a touch of sweet.

The hostess led us to a tall table with equally tall chairs. I had no problem with the chairs, as the McHale sisters are all strapping women, but both Dolly and Rena had to jump into the seat. Dolly actually had a few false starts, and by the time she got situated, her skimpy leather skirt was riding so high I was afraid some poor waiter would see something he could never unsee.

After we'd placed our orders, Rena and Dolly returned to a friendly argument over whether Miley Cyrus was a misunderstood artist who was ahead of her time or a musical hack who would do anything for a little publicity. I'm not saying a word about who was on which side. Their familiar prattle gave me an opportunity to dash to the ladies' room before the food arrived.

As I made my way toward the back of the restaurant, I spotted Steve and Ama Olmstead. They'd managed to snag a coveted booth. Steve wore a tie and a button-up shirt, and Ama looked killer in a clingy red dress with ruching at the side, which really defined her curves. A pair of golden hoops dangled from her ears, and her lipstick matched her dress to a T.

"Hi guys. No Jordan tonight?" I asked.

Steve gave me a big grin. "Nope. Tonight's date night."

"Oh jeez," I said, backing away from their table. "I don't want to intrude."

"No, not at all," Steve said. Ama shot him an annoyed glance. Whether it was me in particular or company in general, it was clear she wanted to be left alone with her husband.

"My sister mentioned she'd had a chat with you out at the lakeside development," Steve said. His tone was casual, but my hackles went up immediately.

"Yep."

"I was a little surprised you were out there. It's quite a hike from town and I didn't take you for the out-doorsy type. And Dee Dee doesn't get many visitors. I can't imagine what you all wanted from her."

I detected an edge to Steve's voice. He must have been used to protecting his quirky sister from being manipulated and teased by other people. I had to say something, but for the life of me I couldn't come up with any explanation other than the truth.

"We went out there because of Daniel Colona. It's just coincidence that we ran into Dee Dee."

"I don't get it," Steve said.

"Well, Richard Greene said he'd seen Daniel up there several times, and your sister confirmed that he was hanging around a lot. We just wondered why." I don't know what devil got into me, but I decided to push him a bit. "We thought maybe there was something going on out there. You know, something a reporter might be interested in."

Steve visibly relaxed. In fact he laughed. "There's nothing going on out there at the moment. Certainly nothing that would interest a reporter."

"That's right," I said. "Pris mentioned that there was a little cash flow issue with the development."

It was crass to bring up money like that, but Steve didn't seem to mind. "Yeah, my workers talk with some of the guys from Brainerd. All of them have beers at the Silent Woman, you know. My guys tell me that Hal hit a bump in the road. I guess I should just count my lucky stars that he didn't grant me the contract. If he had, I'd have been up there with my crew, all of us just sitting on our hands and wondering if we'd get paid."

Ama cleared her throat, a clear girl-to-girl signal that I should leave.

I took a step away, but then stopped and pivoted back to the table. "I almost forgot. Ama, you've got a big fan."

"Really." She smiled. "Who?"

"Daisy May."

She looked puzzled. Because, of course, not everyone remembered the names of other people's pets.

"Daniel's Weimaraner. She's usually really quiet, but when she hears that TV ad for the *Gazette*, she starts barking the moment you start talking. I think she has a crush on you."

For an instant, Ama looked truly horrified.

"Oh, I mean not like a boy-girl crush. Just a doggy crush. She'd never, like, try to . . ." I managed to put the brakes on my mouth. *Stop talking, Izzy. Just stop talking and walk away.*

"Anyway, you two have a good night."

I slunk to the ladies' and managed to avoid eye contact with the Olmsteads as I headed back to our table, where I was surprised to see Jack Collins.

"Look who we found," Dolly crowed. She leaned over a little to rest her bony hand on his. I don't know whether it was intentional, but she flashed a little cleavage. Who was I kidding? Of course it was intentional. Leave it to Aunt Dolly to flirt with the cop who'd arrested her just a few days before.

I slid back into my seat as Jack explained. "I swung by to have a beer with Cliff Johnson. It's his birthday."

I glanced toward the bar and saw half a dozen men I recognized as local police officers leaning against the rail and buying rounds for the short, balding man in the middle.

"I saw him and waved him over," Rena said. She looked at me with a little cock of her head, a challenge in her gaze.

I looked back at Jack and he smiled at me, a slow devilish smile, like we shared a secret.

"Well. Um, yeah. Good to see you."

"Well. Um, yeah. Good to see you, too," he teased.

Rena piped up. "Was that the Olmsteads you were talking to?"

"Yes."

"You were chatting with them a long time. Learn anything interesting?"

"Nothing at all. Just made a little small talk about the Badger Lake development. If Steve has any inside scoop from his sister, he's not sharing."

Out of the corner of my eye, I could see Jack's smile melting into a frown of deep displeasure.

"It's gotta be those owls," Rena said. "I mean we basically ruled out the mob—unless, of course, Hal was lying to you two—but the owls would make a huge story, and Hal's alibi is as flimsy as that house wrap he's using."

"I don't think we should rule out the mob," Dolly said. "We only have Hal's word that the new investor is Japanese, and Hal lies. Besides, there's a Japanese mob, you know. The yakuza. I heard about them on *Byline Crime*. They're apparently every bit as dangerous as the regular mob."

"Enough!" Jack's hand sliced through the air as though he were dropping a NASCAR flag.

"What have you been up to? The mob? What the heck does the mob have to do with anything?"

"It's really just a theory," I said. "Pris Olson said that Hal had found some investors to save the development out by the lake and that they wanted to be silent partners. 'Very silent,' she said. Rena thinks that means the mob, and she makes a pretty compelling case."

Rena held up a hand, and we high-fived.

"Hal Olson the RV King and the mob? That's the most cockamamy story I've ever heard."

"Why?" I asked. I'd played the devil's advocate to Rena's theory, but it was starting to make more sense to me. "You know the mob works with some of those out-state loners."

"Yes, buying meth. Not investing in condos."

"But Rena's right. Investing in the condo development could be a way for them to launder money."

"Do you have any idea how laundering money actually works?" Jack asked.

"Not exactly," I said. "That's why we're giving all our information to you—the mob, the owls, the hole in Hal's alibi. We're not trying to do your job. We're just helping."

Jack crossed his arms on the table and rested his head on them, like a kid catching a nap.

Dolly, Rena, and I just watched him.

Finally, he lifted his head. "First of all, I can't comment on an ongoing investigation, especially in front of an accused suspect, but since you three are operating in some sort of fantasyland, I think it's safe to tell you that there is absolutely no indication of the mob operating in Merryville."

"But have you actually looked?" I asked.

He closed his eyes. "No."

"So then—"

"Unh. Stop. I'm still talking. Once again, the bigger issue is not how crazy you all sound but the fact that you're putting yourself in harm's way. Let's just imagine for one insane moment that you're right. That Daniel Colona was investigating mob activity in Merryville, Minnesota, and it got him killed. What's to stop those same mobsters from killing you?"

Rena, Dolly, and I exchanged sheepish glances.

"Exactly. Now, please, for the love of all that's holy, stay out of this investigation." Jack stood up then, and with a small salute made his way back to the cluster of cops standing by the bar.

Okay, I'll admit he made a good point. I wasn't about to stop trying to find the killer, but I could be a little more discreet in my inquiries.

Later in the evening, I left Dolly and Rena sharing a chocolate molten lava cake with dulce de leche ice cream, and moved to the bar to find Jack.

I caught him pulling on his jacket, ready to leave.

"Can I walk you out?" I asked.

"Sure."

We made our way through the late evening crowd. Jack held open the door as we stepped into the clear night. Spring had come early to Merryville, and the air had a softness to it. It was perfectly neutral in temperature, and the gentle breeze bore no chill. A glance up revealed a sky full of steady stars.

"We okay?" I asked.

"Are you asking if I'm okay with you snooping around Daniel's murder? Because the answer is no."

"I'm asking if you can still tolerate me despite the fact that I have every intention of snooping around Daniel's murder. Slightly different question."

He laughed softly, little more than a vibration deep in his chest.

"Yes, if you don't get yourself killed, I will get past your crazy insistence on asking questions that are none of your business. I understand that it comes from a place of love, and I respect that. I don't condone it, but I respect it."

"Good. Because I forgot to tell you something."

He sighed.

"The other morning, we found one of Daniel's journals."

"You were in his apartment?" I could practically feel him starting to stiffen.

"No, it was on the main floor. Honest, we didn't go looking for it. We just found it. Anyway, it's mostly gibberish. But it did have what we think is a picture of a burrowing owl next to the letters 'DNR,' which we think is the Department of Natural Resources. And the date June tenth, which we haven't figured out. And Dee Dee Lahti's and Ama Olmstead's phone numbers."

I paused to find him staring at me with an expression of mingled astonishment and frustration.

"What?"

"Did it have a map to where his killer lives?"

It was my turn to sigh. "Of course not. Look, we've given you most of the information that's in the journal. We told you about the owls and the Badger Lake development, and that's what the picture and Dee Dee's number was about; he was calling her to reach Kevin, to ask Kevin to take him out looking for the owls. Ama's number makes sense. He was a reporter and he'd obviously want to have some connection in town. Ama swears he never actually called her. And that just leaves the date. We don't know what the date means."

"Are you going to give me the journal?"

"Of course. We just forgot is all. Like I said, we're just trying to help."

"You sure are a stubborn woman."

"Am I?" I'd never thought of myself as stubborn.

He placed both his palms on his forehead and shook his head slowly. "You're kidding me, right? I think I've told you to mind your own business and stay out of this murder investigation two times already—"

"Three, if you count tonight."

He laughed. "Thank you. I've asked you to leave the policing to the police *three* times in as many days, and yet you're telling me about going through Daniel Colona's personal effects."

I drew myself up and planted my hands on my hips. "Look, it's not like we went through his personal effects tonight. It was a couple of days ago, and I'm telling you now because I want to be up-front with you. It's not like Rena and I went looking for this." Okay, we'd gone looking for plenty, but not for *this*. "Val stole it. Hard to say when, but Daniel didn't ask us if we'd found it, so probably the night of the murder."

"Val the ferret?"

"Oh yes, she's a total kleptomaniac. We're always returning wallets and lipsticks and the occasional bottle of Xanax. For all I know, Val managed to finagle Daniel's journal out of his pocket while the EMTs were working on him. She's fast. And crafty."

He narrowed his eyes. "You live a strange life, Izzy McHale."

"Do I?" I teased, flashing him a quick smile.

He laughed in response. "Minx.

"But seriously, even if the ferret dumped Colona's journal in your lap, your number one move should have been to call the police—call *me*—not go snooping through its contents."

"Fair enough. But we did help."

Jack threw his arms wide, tipped his head back, and groaned to the heavens above. "I give up. You helped. Just please, for all that's holy, stop helping."

As he lowered his head and arms, I noticed how the mellow light of the streetlamp picked out streaks of gold in his dark blond hair. It was cut to such military precision, the short strands stood out like sparks around his head. I also noticed how big he was. I mean,

I'd always known he was a big guy, dominating both the football field and the hockey rink in high school, but I'd never thought about how much bigger he was than me. The McHale girls are not petite, but I suddenly felt dainty in his presence.

"Listen," he added. "You have to leave Hal Olson alone. I know you think he doesn't have an alibi, but I assure you he does."

"But he didn't meet Kevin until an hour and a half after the murder," I insisted.

"For crying out loud. Look, I shouldn't be telling you this. I mean I really should not be telling you this—"

"Right, ongoing investigation and all."

"Exactly. But if it will get you off Hal's back, it's worth bending the rules a little. Hal told us his real alibi: he was pulled over for speeding in Round Earth County."

I frowned. "Well, why didn't he just say so?"

"First, let me remind you it was none of your business. Second . . ." He took a deep breath, weighing whether to go on. "Second, he got caught with a joint."

Good heavens, Hal had quite a night planned for himself last Friday. Pot and hookers. Definitely the sort of guy Merryville needed at the helm.

"They hauled him into the police station and he spent a solid hour talking them out of booking him," Jack continued. "Man could sell corn to Iowa. Bottom line, there's no official record of the drugs, and it would kill his political career if anyone found out. I only know because I've got a buddy in Round Earth. And now you know . . . but you won't say a word."

"Of course not. I would never betray your confidence like that. Thank you for trusting me."

For an instant, the mood between us grew fraught yet still. We were in the eye of the hurricane and could smell the ozone of the storm about to wash over us.

Jack scuffed one shoe across the pavement, then looked me straight in the eye. "Izzy, would you go to dinner with me?"

"Dinner." I uttered the word as a statement, because I knew exactly what he said, but I needed to hear the syllables again.

"Yes, dinner." He flashed me that cocky smile. "Or dancing. I'd like to watch you dance."

"No, you wouldn't," I muttered. "It's a horrible sight."

"Well, then, let's start with dinner."

"Jack, are you asking me on a date?"

He laughed. "I'm sure trying to. Must be doing something wrong, though, because you haven't said yes."

I'd never gone on a real date with anyone other than my ex-fiancé, Casey. We'd been a couple since my sophomore year in high school, and when he left me, I hadn't really been in a dating sort of mood. Now, confronted with a yes or no question, I felt paralyzed by fear. But then I heard a voice in my head that sounded suspiciously like Aunt Dolly: *You only get one ride in life. Make the most of it.*

"Jack Collins, I will have dinner with you."

He laughed again. "You make it sound like a momentous decision. It's just a date, not a blood oath."

I felt heat licking up my cheeks. "I know it's just a date. But I've never been on a date with anyone but Casey."

Jack sobered instantly. "Really?" I nodded. "Well, then, Izzy McHale, I am honored. And I'll pick you up tomorrow night at seven, if that's okay with you."

I cleared my throat and tried to get a grip. "Seven it is."

And then he did the most wondrous thing. He leaned forward, rested a hand on my shoulder, and kissed me. Just on the cheek, and only for an instant, but he kissed me. When he pulled back, my hand flew to my face, as though I needed to be sure it was still there.

I looked up to find him smiling like he'd just scored a winning touchdown. Then he spun on his heel and headed down the street whistling a tuneless ditty as he went.

CHAPTER
Seventeen

Thursday morning, I crawled out of bed feeling like I'd been hit by a train. I'd only had two glasses of red wine at dinner the night before, but I rarely drank and I was feeling the aftereffects.

I managed to get Trendy Tails unlocked and Rena set up to start the workday, but then I hobbled down the street to the Happy Leaf for one of Taffy's herbal remedies. And maybe a scone.

"Wow. You look like you had way too much fun last night," Taffy teased.

"Two glasses. Just two glasses of wine, I swear."

"Uh-huh."

I collapsed at one of the chintz-covered tables.

"You have a hangover cure, right? I mean you have a tea for every occasion."

"I absolutely do. Peppermint and ginger for your tummy and a little fennel for your liver. Between a pot of that blend and a few more glasses of water, you should be feeling fine in no time."

"Bless you," I muttered as I rested my head on the table.

I heard Taffy puttering around, the domestic sounds as comforting as her earth mother presence. I heard Taffy squeal before I heard the skittering of tiny feet across one of the shelves behind the counter.

I sprang to my feet—a little too quickly, making my head spin—ran over to the counter, and scanned the shelf of apothecary jars filled with tea leaves and dried herbs. My eyes danced right over him, and then back.

There he was. Gandhi the rogue guinea pig. He sat between two jars, looking me square in the eyes. He definitely was a cute fella, a beautiful fringe of his auburn hair ringing his shiny black eyes. As a pet, he was adorable. However, as an unwelcome visitor, first in Richard Greene's shop and now in Taffy's, he was a royal pain.

"Can you get him?" Taffy whispered to me.

I shrugged, a small movement so I wouldn't scare him away.

Slowly, step by painstaking step, I made my way behind the counter and toward his spot on the shelf. He kept his eyes on me the whole time, casually chewing on some tidbit he'd found.

Now I was close enough that I barely moved an inch at a time. Slowly I lifted my hands to grab him. I swear I could feel his gentle breath against my fingers. I closed my hands together . . . and held nothing but air. In the time it took me to clutch his little body, he'd disappeared back behind the jars. I could hear him running, but the sound grew softer as he made his way through some hidey-hole and out of my reach.

"Oh, Taffy. I'm so sorry."

She shrugged, resigned. "It's okay. Maybe we can lay down one of those humane traps?"

"I think that's a great idea." I made my way back to the table I'd been occupying and gingerly sank into the seat, trying not to wobble or fall before I got myself situated.

After just a few more minutes passed, Taffy brought over a steaming pot of tea that smelled a bit like Christmas and a plate with two plain cream scones. She poured my first cup.

"Drink up," she urged.

"So what kind of shenanigans got you into this state?" she asked after I'd downed the cup of tea in a single slug.

"Dolly and Rena and I went out for a couple of post-sleuthing bottles of wine. I wasn't kidding. I only had two glasses, but they were generous glasses, and I'm a lightweight."

Taffy poured me another cup of her elixir.

"Did you all have fun?"

I allowed a little smile to slide across my face. "I did, indeed."

I took another swig of Taffy's tea. Between the ginger, peppermint, and fennel, it had a real bite. Not delicious, but not horrible, either, and it was already working its magic. I could feel my head clearing a little more with every sip.

"Thank you again. You're saving my life here. I've got a long day ahead of me, and I need to shake off last night ASAP."

"What do you have going on?"

"Hmmm. Well, I have to sit down with Ingrid and Harvey and figure out how to weave their wedding into Romeo and Pearl's ceremony; I have to finish making the bow tie pet favors and the Jordan almond bundles for Ingrid and Harvey; I have to figure out what I'm going to wear on Saturday and do a load of laundry so I have some clean undies; and then, uh"—I ducked my head to take a sip of my tea—"tonight I have a date."

"You have a what?" Taffy asked, leaning forward in her chair.

"A date," I repeated, shrugging sheepishly.

"Oh my. Who with? I want to know everything."

"There's not much to tell. Jack Collins asked me out for dinner last night. It's definitely a date, but it's just the first one."

"You have to have a first date before you can have a second and a third and then fall in love and get married and have babies," Taffy said.

"Whoa. One step at a time. Just a date."

"But with Jack Collins. He's a good-looking man."

He really was, I thought. Casey had been tall and slender and bookish, similar in build to Sean but with blond hair instead of sable. Jack was totally different. He was tall and broad shouldered, with powerful arms and a military straightness to his stance. He looked like he could have stepped out of a G.I. Joe comic. But he had these gorgeous blue eyes that crinkled when he smiled. Oh, yes, indeed, he was a good-looking man.

"I've got news, too," Taffy said, blushing softly.

"Oh really," I said with a smile. "Spill it."

"I'm going on a date tonight, too."

"With Ken?"

"Yes. A real date this time. Not just hanging out."

Interesting.

"What changed?"

"I'm not sure. He said he's not worried about the investor anymore. In fact, his exact words were that it was 'safe' to take me out on the town."

It all sounded very sketchy to me, but Taffy looked ready to float away on a cloud of happiness.

"You're really into him, aren't you?"

She beamed. "I'm completely smitten." Her smile faded just a bit. "I know you're not exactly Ken's number one fan, but I hope you can be happy for me. Since I've moved to Merryville, I haven't had much luck on the dating scene. You know, everyone's dating someone they went to kindergarten with. Ken's been so good to me. Says I'm the center of his galaxy. He's such a romantic, I can't resist him."

I reached across the table and captured one of Taffy's hands in my own. "Of course I'm happy for you. I don't need to love Ken. You do. That's all that matters."

She gave my hand a squeeze.

"Here's hoping our luck has finally turned a corner."

I returned from the Happy Leaf feeling a million times better, both physically and emotionally, and because I was feeling generous, I brought back baked goods for Rena, Ingrid, and Harvey.

We all gorged ourselves on apple turnovers, scones, and cream cheese Danish, while we talked about how the ceremony would unfold on Saturday.

"For the most part, everything will run like it did last Friday—"

"Minus the body," Ingrid said.

"Yes, minus the body. We also have to make a few accommodations for the animals. First, Ingrid, I think you should come down the back stairs and through the kitchen. You'll be walking to the altar holding Pearl's leash. She's not a rambunctious dog, but I don't want her tripping you coming down the stairs in your heels."

Ingrid laughed. "Good idea. I can barely get myself down those stairs in heels, let alone with a beagle toddling along at my side."

"Harvey, you'll be standing at the altar waiting for Ingrid. Romeo will be at your side. Don't worry. He's a pretty chill dog, so I don't think he'll make a run for it."

Harvey looked mildly alarmed at the notion of the dog pulling him along on a mad dash out the door, but he simply nodded. What a good sport.

"We've had to make some compromises with the music. Hetty and Louise are set on 'Puppy Love,' so Pris and I were thinking that would make a good song for you and Pearl to come in on. But if you're really tied to Pachelbel's Canon, we can work something out."

Ingrid waved off my concern. "He's no Johnny Mathis, but I love Paul Anka as much as the next woman."

"Great! Then we'll finish up the ceremony with the two of you dancing to Johnny Mathis's 'Wonderful, Wonderful.'"

Ingrid grinned, and Harvey reached over to catch hold of her hand. "It sounds perfect," Ingrid said.

"Any questions?"

"None. It sounds like the perfect day."

I started collecting the plates and napkins from our morning feast.

"What are you two up to today?" Rena asked. Ingrid had spent the week touring poor Harvey around Merryville so they could relive the memories of their high school romance. Harvey looked like he'd rather just spend some time sipping beers at the VFW, but he indulged Ingrid.

"Today, we're going down to the bluffs where the Perry River splits off from the Mighty Mississippi. You know there are caverns down there. Bootleggers used to use them to hide their hooch back in Prohibition days. When we were in school, the kids would go down there to neck. Isn't that right, Harvey?" she asked, giving him a gentle shove on the shoulder.

Harvey flushed bright red, but he nodded.

Rena laughed. "Kids used those caverns for more than necking when we were in school. Isn't that right, Izzy?"

I shared a commiserating look with Harvey and nodded.

Ingrid and Rena both busted up until tears of mirth were running down their faces. I had a sneaking suspicion they were laughing at Harvey and me.

Ingrid stood, pausing for a moment to get her sea legs. "Are you ready to go, Harvey? I want to see if we can still see the place where you carved our initials into the rock."

Rena clasped a hand to her heart. We were in agreement that Harvey and Ingrid were the cutest couple in the whole wide world.

When they left, Rena helped me finish up both the dog and human wedding favors. My hands were cramping from all the close work of tying little bows and stitching tiny stitches.

"Are you excited for your date tonight?" Rena asked.

"Yes, I suppose so. More anxious than excited."

"Why anxious? Jack's a nice guy."

"I'm sure he is. But this whole murder investigation thing is going to sit in the booth with us. We don't precisely see eye to eye on that score. Plus, this will be my first post-Casey date. And since there never was a pre-Casey date . . ."

Rena stopped what she was doing. "Wow. I guess I hadn't thought about that before. Well, it's time you got back in the ring, and I think Jack's a great partner to do it with. He's generally easy to talk to, laid-back, a gentleman. You don't have to worry about him judging you."

"Oh, no. He's *already* judged me."

"And then he asked you on a date. You must have passed muster with him somehow."

I finished the last stitch on the last black bow tie and tossed it into a box. Next step was to label the boxes with the names of all the four-legged RSVPs so everyone got the right size. I wandered over to the counter to retrieve the guest list.

"I'm not the only one with a big date tonight," I said.

"Oh? Who else?"

"Taffy," I said as I sat back down at the table.

"With Ken?" Rena made a face. Rena was sort of an all-or-nothing kind of person. If she didn't like you, she really didn't like you. And she really didn't like Ken.

"Yes. But we have to be supportive of Taffy. She's really taken with him. Says he's a romantic, told her she was the center of his galaxy."

Rena froze. "Wait. What?"

"I know. It's kind of cheesy, but it made Taffy go all gooey."

"No, I mean that phrase is ringing a bell." Rena tapped her front teeth with her fingernail. Then her face lit up. "I've got it! That story that Daniel wrote about the personal chef who slept with all those women. He reported that that was his pickup line."

It took me a minute to catch on, to remember the article I'd read online and tell Sean and Rena. But then it did, and pieces started falling into place.

Before Rena and I could get down to brass tacks, the doorbell jingled and Sean stepped into the store.

"Hi, girls. Just got done talking to the DA. I don't suppose Dolly is here, is she?"

"No. She went shopping with my mom at the mall in Brainerd."

"Too bad. I really need to go over her options with her." Sean wandered over to the table, absently picked up one of the doggy bow ties, and twirled it on his finger.

Rena was practically jumping out of her skin. "Options shmoptions. The best option is for us to clear her name, and we may have done it."

"Good Lord. What has Hal Olson done this time?"

"Not Hal," I said. "Ken West."

Sean pulled back in surprise, then sank into one of the multicolored chairs that surrounded the folk art table. The blue one. He always chose the blue one.

"Walk me through it," he said.

We explained about Taffy and the phrase Ken had used that pegged him as the Madison "Mystery Chef."

"But surely Daniel didn't come all the way out here for a full month because of Ken West."

I waved my hand. "No, based on everything we've learned so far, I think it's a safe bet that Daniel came here for the story about the owls. But Ken might have been afraid of being identified. Can you imagine what that kind of reputation would do to his business? In a big city, it might make him seem glamorous or intriguing. But in Merryville, it would make him plain old slutty."

"Especially for someone who isn't a native son," Rena added. "Folks around here will forgive our neighbors for a lot, but Ken's an outsider."

"Still, how was Daniel going to recognize him when no one in Madison would identify him?"

"Who knows?" I said. "Maybe one of the women did tell him the name? Maybe he learned enough about the chef's reputation to recognize Ken's food? Put that together with a Madison chef who moves to the middle of nowhere for no obvious reason, and a good reporter might dig deeper."

Rena jumped in. "Ken had access to the upstairs that no one else at the party had. He could have gotten up there and killed Daniel and slipped right back into the kitchen. No one would have known a thing."

"And he's been seeing Taffy Nielson for a few weeks, but he wouldn't take her out for real until this week. I thought he was just trying to keep their relationship a secret. But what if he was trying to keep a low profile more generally? Trying to hide out from Daniel."

"Oooh! And then he couldn't hide from him anymore the night of Ingrid and Harvey's first wedding. Maybe Daniel came down the back stairs to avoid the party and ran into Ken in the kitchen. One thing led to another and—boom!—Daniel ends up dead."

Sean shook his head. "I counted an awful lot of maybes in there. And I thought Ken had an alibi."

"His alibi was a lie," I said. "He said he'd gone out to have a smoke with Steve Olmstead, but Steve doesn't smoke. What's more, Ama said he's rabidly antitobacco. Apparently he's told strangers to snuff out their butts. I can't imagine he'd keep Ken company while he smoked."

"As theories go," Sean said, "I still think it's pretty weak."

I leaned in, trying to make him understand. "At this point, I'll take a weak theory over no theory at all."

CHAPTER
Eighteen

One consequence of the weakness of our theory was that I didn't feel I could call Jack about it. More important, I didn't feel I *had* to call Jack about it. It wasn't enough for him to act on, probably, and it would just earn me another lecture. I could keep this theory to myself for a while. I decided I'd have a talk with Ken, see if I could get anything more solid, and then tell Jack about everything that evening on our date.

At my insistence, Sean accompanied me around the block to the storefront that used to be the Grateful Grape. Ken had made serious progress on revamping the space for his new restaurant. The name—Red, White & Bleu—had been stenciled in classic gold on the front window. Inside, he'd kept the Grape's beautiful bar, but lightened the space with cream walls, amber sconces, and simple wooden tables.

Ken (or, rather, Steve and his crew) had removed all

the dark paneling, set the ceiling fans higher in the vaulted ceiling, and generally stripped away all the architectural clutter that had made the Grape cute. Red, White & Bleu wasn't cute. It was elegant.

We found Ken sitting at the bar taking notes.

"Hi, Ken," I called as we opened the door and stepped inside.

Ken turned to us with a puzzled look. "Hi. This is unexpected."

"Just wanted to make sure we were all set for Saturday," I said.

"Of course. We essentially had a dress rehearsal last weekend, and it went smoothly. Until the dead guy crashed the party. I've repeated my food order for Saturday and I've been in touch with Ollie Forde to be certain there are enough Norwegian meatballs on hand."

Sean stood at my side, hands shoved in his pockets, rocking forward on the balls of his feet, restless as a pent-up tiger. "Place looks good," he said.

"Thanks. Still working on the kitchen, but I'm aiming for a launch in June."

"Sounds great," I said.

Ken cocked his head. "I'm getting the feeling there's something you want to say to me. I'll be honest—I have some work to do. I'm working on the launch menu right now, and I'm going to be going over it with Hal and Pris Olson in just a couple of hours."

I shot Sean a look, and he shrugged, indicating that I could start.

"I might as well just come out and ask. Are you the Madison Mystery Chef?"

"What?"

"Come on, you have to at least know about the story. You lived in Madison when it happened and it involved the culinary world. Are you the personal chef who slept with all his clients?"

Ken stared at us for a solid minute, lower teeth biting his upper lip. Finally, his stance relaxed a little.

"I only slept with the women."

"So you admit it?" I asked, stunned that it had been so easy.

"There's not much point in denying it. With a little digging, anyone could figure it out. I'm just hoping you won't go telling everyone in Merryville. It would ruin me, and I don't see how it helps you at all."

Sean held up a hand. "Don't worry. We're not interested in airing your dirty laundry."

"Then why did you ask?"

Sean held out his hand, palm up, in my direction, offering me the chance to explain.

"Well, if Daniel Colona knew who you were—"

"Oh, he knew."

"—then you might . . . Wait. He knew?"

"Yes. The very first week he was in town, Hal and Pris had a little dinner party. They invited George and Tonya Cooperson, Ted Lang from the *Gazette*, and Daniel. I was hired to cater the party. Daniel enjoyed the filet with truffle compound butter and introduced himself. We made some light chitchat, and before long he'd put the pieces together. Smart man."

"Weren't you worried he would spill your secret?"

"Absolutely."

Sean rocked up on the balls of his feet. "I don't think you understand where this is going. If you were afraid that Daniel was going to write a follow-up piece and ruin your career, then you had a motive to kill him."

Ken laughed. "I wasn't worried Daniel would write another article about the scandalous mystery chef. His career had moved well beyond that sensationalist nonsense. He was doing real reporting and actual news, not tabloid riffs about who was sleeping with whom."

It sounded good, but I wasn't sure I believed him.

"Then why were you afraid he'd expose you?" I asked.

"I wasn't worried he'd tell the world. I was worried he'd tell *Taffy*. That sort of information, so early in a relationship, would surely kill it. Especially with someone as pure of heart as Taffy Nielson."

Pure of heart? Holy cow. Taffy was right. Ken really did care for her.

"Is that why you haven't been taking her on real dates?"

Ken's lips twisted in a wry smile. "Yes. I kept expecting an ultimatum from her, that I had to take her out on the town or she would dump me. But she never complained. I was terrified that the two of us might run into Daniel and he might say something about the old scandal. But now that Daniel's gone, I can take Taffy out and show her off like I want to."

I was still reeling, trying to reconcile this romantic Ken West with the slightly unctuous cynic I knew.

"And before you ask, I had no motive to kill Daniel. He wasn't going to stay in town forever, so I just had to keep Taffy and Daniel away from each other for a few more days. I could swing that with just a little effort on my part. I'm not a monster, you know.

"Now, if you don't mind," Ken said. "I'd really like to get back to my menu so I'm not late for my very first real date with Taffy."

Sean and I cut through the alley and grabbed Packer and his leash so we could take him on an early walk.

"That was something else," Sean said.

"I know. He sounded like he's totally gaga for Taffy. Not that it's surprising someone should care for Taffy, but it's surprising that Ken cares for anyone other than Ken."

"Maybe he's a changed man."

Packer tugged on the leash. He was particularly fired up that day, anxious to get out and be a part of the world. I took a couple of hopping steps to keep up with him.

"You gonna let that little dog push you around?" Sean teased.

"Ha! I'd like to see you do better." I offered the leash to him.

He held up both hands, declining the leash. "I know when I'm licked. Blackstone and Romeo are both way more relaxed than your fella. He's quite a handful."

"You know," I said, "he's not technically my dog."

"Really."

"Really. Casey is the one who wanted a dog and brought Packer home from the pound. That's why he's named after a football team. But then Casey got Rachel the nutritionist, and I got the dog."

"I think you got the better end of the deal."

"Absolutely. What would I have done with a perky little nutritionist?"

Sean tipped his head back and laughed. It was a beautiful sound, both clear and rich. I hadn't heard it nearly enough in the past fifteen years.

"Izzy, I swear I always forget how funny you are. You've been so much more reserved since we hung out in high school."

I smirked. "I don't consider making four murder accusations in a week 'reserved.'"

"Ha! No, you're braver than you used to be, more fearless, but your spirit has grown more quiet. You don't joke around and laugh and goof off like you used to."

I pulled gently on Packer's leash to slow him down. "Mostly that's because I became an adult."

He sighed. "I miss the teenage Izzy."

"And I miss the teenage Sean, the one I could talk to about everything. But that's the problem, Sean. We all grow up."

"Point taken." Sean stepped away from me to get around a fire hydrant and then moved back to my side as though I were his gravity.

"For what it's worth, I like the grown-up Izzy a lot, too. Frankly, I wish I knew her a little better."

I felt my breath catch.

"Don't tease, Sean."

"I'm not teasing, Izzy. I'd like for us to get re-acquainted. If only so we can be better friends again."

He wasn't making any promises, of course. But I

was willing to take whatever he had to offer. If we only became better friends, that might be okay. I hadn't lied when I said I missed being able to tell him anything. If I could start to tear down this sterile wall that separated us, it would feel like a win.

"How about we grab dinner tonight?" he said. "No Rena or Lucy or Xander—just the two of us."

I stopped dead in my tracks, and Packer fell back when the slack went out of the leash.

Sean stopped and turned to me, a quizzical look on his face. "Not hungry?"

"No, it's not that. I would love to have dinner with you. But not tonight."

"What do you have going on tonight?"

I stood silent, debating what I should say. He'd thrown me a line, and I didn't want him to pull it back. But, on the other hand, we couldn't have any kind of relationship at all if we weren't honest with each other. No point in a friend you had to lie to.

"I've got a date."

His expression fell perfectly flat for an instant before he mustered a smile. "Good for you. Who with?"

I knelt down and snapped my fingers for Packer to heel. I scratched his velvety dog ears, and they gave me courage.

"Jack Collins."

"Really? You and Jack Collins?"

I squinted up at Sean. "Why not me and Jack Collins?"

"He's just so . . . thick."

"Thick as in stupid? I don't think so."

"No, he's not stupid. He just lacks subtlety. He's a hammer and everything around him is a nail."

I cocked my head. "I'm not sure there's anything wrong with that. Sometimes simple and uncomplicated is good. You know where you stand with a man like that."

Sean frowned and blew out a breath of air. "I didn't know you were looking for simple."

I stood back up and gave Packer his head.

"I'm not necessarily. Look, he asked, and I said yes. I didn't see the harm in it. When he asked, I didn't see any reason it would matter."

He shoved his hands in his pockets in that familiar rebel high school boy pose. "Fair enough. And I guess I'm not really in a position to offer you an alternative."

"Not now," I allowed.

"Just promise me you won't jump into anything. Can you at least give us a little time?"

"I can't wait forever, Sean. But I can wait for now."

CHAPTER
Nineteen

As promised, Jack picked me up at seven. He stood at the front door of Trendy Tails in a jacket and tie, a single red rose in his hand. He looked as nervous and uncomfortable as a fourteen-year-old going to his first dance.

"Hi, Jack," I said.

He looked into my eyes and then gave me the once-over. "Holy . . . You're gorgeous."

I laughed as I took both the rose and his arm.

"You've seen me every day this week. I'm the same me."

"You know what I mean," he said, leading me down the front steps. "You're always gorgeous, but tonight you are breathtaking. Extra-gorgeous. Smokin'."

I laughed. I had taken a lot of time getting ready for this date. I'd traded in my usual jeans and Trendy Tails golf shirt for a pair of black leggings, knee-high black boots, a black lace cami, and a billowing scarlet silk shirt. My black hair usually fell in irregular waves around my face, but I'd taken the time to blow it out straight and use a serum to make it shine. I'd donned a pair of Jolly Nielson's pussy willow earrings and done my makeup like a proper girl. It was nice to be rewarded for all that effort.

We strolled down the quiet streets of Merryville, the slowly sinking sun casting a golden glow over everything. It was like a natural soft focus, making every brick, every curl of ironwork, every fence post, look flawless.

I watched Jack out of the corner of my eye. He, too, appeared flawless in the evening light. His dark blond hair usually looked like it had been buzzed by a military barber, but that evening the longer pieces on top fell forward over his brow, framing his violet blue eyes. His jaw was strong, but not square, and his lips had a sultry quality that made me feel a little light-headed.

I'd spent all week seeing this man, but I hadn't really noticed how gorgeous he was until that evening. I guess that made us even.

We turned the corner onto Laurel Street and climbed the steps to the Koi Pond, a shockingly authentic Chinese restaurant.

The host led us to a curved banquette separated from the rest of the restaurant by a fish tank filled with waving kelp and brilliant orange koi fish.

"Wow."

Jack shrugged. "Roger Choi and I go way back. He always gets me the best table in the house." He was trying to pass it off like it was no big deal, but I could see the small smile and the look of pride in his eyes. He'd done good and he knew it.

We got settled and the waiter brought us water and menus.

"So," Jack said, "I know we're not going to make it through the evening without talking about Daniel Colona's murder, so let's just get it over with now." He glanced at his watch. "Ten minutes tops, and then the topic is taboo for the rest of the evening. Fair?"

"Fair."

"I have no doubt that you have completely ignored my pleas that you leave the policing to the police, so why don't you tell me what trouble you've gotten into today?"

"Well, I spent part of today pretty sure Ken West was the murderer."

He smiled at me resignedly. "Only part of the day and only pretty sure?"

I explained to him about the Madison Mystery Chef and how we'd figured out that Ken was the guy. I was fair, though, and I explained Ken's insistence that he had no motive for murder.

"Besides," Jack added, "Ken has an alibi."

"Uh-uh. That alibi's no good. Steve doesn't smoke."

"Well, maybe Steve just went out in the alley to keep him company. The two are doing business together after all."

"I just can't see it. From what Ama said, Steve is just too darned antismoking to hang out with Ken while he gets his fix."

Jack shrugged. "Whatever the reason, the alibi checks out. Steve corroborated Ken's story. He says he was outside with Ken having a smoke."

"But—"

"But maybe both Ama and Steve are each hiding their smoking from the other. Sort of like 'The Gift of the Magi' but with tobacco products."

I giggled.

No lie. I didn't laugh or chuckle; I giggled like a little girl. Something—my conversation with Sean, Jack's masculine presence, the mystical ambience of the restaurant—something made me giddy that night.

"How about this?" Jack said, opening his menu. "I promise I'll look into this angle further. I'll talk to Ken, get him down to the station, even. If there's anything there, I'll find it."

"What about the journal I turned over? Did you guys get any more clues out of it?"

"Repeat after me: I cannot talk about an ongoing investigation."

"Oh, I know. But I told you about the calls to Dee Dee and the owls."

"I know. The calls to Dee Dee, the dratted owls, the calls to Ama . . . You were very forthcoming."

I turned my head to give him a sidelong squint. "Calls to Ama?"

Jack slapped his forehead with the palm of his hand.

"You've bewitched me, Izzy McHale. Forget I ever said that."

"But it was calls, plural?"

He drew his fingers across his lips, twisted them,

and made a tossing motion. He'd thrown away the key and would not answer my question. But it was an interesting tidbit. Why hadn't Ama admitted that she'd talked to Daniel?

"Okay," I said. "Our ten minutes are up, right? So we can just talk like normal people?"

He grinned. "I thought it would never end. Let's talk like completely normal people."

"Do you like being a cop?" I asked.

He looked past my shoulder, a thoughtful expression on his face. "Yes and no."

"Why yes?"

"Because I like order. Because I like the idea of people doing the right thing. Because I'm damned good at it."

"And why no?"

"The law's a blunt instrument. People are complex and their lives are complex, but the law—at least the way cops have to follow it—is so black-and-white. Sometimes I appreciate those clear guidelines, but sometimes I feel like I can't really do the right thing, the thing that's going to make everyone whole. I just have to haul someone off to jail.

"You should ask your friend Sean sometime if it feels that way for lawyers, too."

He'd raised Sean's name nonchalantly, but I detected a note of questioning there. I imagined that everyone in town had picked up on the tension between Sean and me by that point. It was only fair that he should be curious.

"You know," I said, "you're one of the big reasons Sean and I became friends in the first place."

"Really?"

"You don't remember?"

He shook his head. "Tell me."

"Fourth grade, Mrs. Adams's class. It must have been November because I know it was before Christmas but I remember wearing my parka. You bet me a cream-filled cupcake that I couldn't spin around sixty times with my eyes closed. I got to something like twenty-four before I stopped in my tracks and upchucked all over Sean Tucker. My mom and I went to his house after we'd gotten his parka cleaned, and I ended up staying over to help him build a snow fort. The rest is history."

"I have no recollection of that."

"Oh no? Well, I remember you being quite a pill in grade school."

He grinned a wolfish grin. "I liked to tease the girls."

"I'll say."

"Well, if I teased you, it only meant that I liked you. My way with the ladies has improved considerably since then."

"Has it really?"

"I guess we'll just have to see."

I'd expected dinner to pass in a wave of small talk, but Jack turned out to be more complex and sensitive than I'd given him credit for. He was a far cry from the blunt-force hammer Sean had labeled him. But over plates of Szechuan eggplant and spicy prawns, our conversation turned personal quickly.

Jack told me about his mother, and his concern that

she wouldn't be able to live independently much longer. I told him about my effort to buy 801 Maple from Ingrid. Jack told me about a girl he'd proposed to in college, about how they got to within a week of the wedding before she got cold feet and canceled it all. I told him about the heartbreak of Casey leaving me stranded, with no way to pursue my half of our grand dream.

"Maybe it's fate," Jack mused.

"What?"

"That we both got dumped before we actually married our fiancés. Jenny was a great girl—before she dumped me, that is—but she was a girl. She was pretty, not beautiful. She laughed a lot, but she wasn't funny. I saw her last year at our tenth reunion, and she hadn't changed a whit since college. Heck, she was still doing Jell-O shots.

"You're more interesting than she could ever be. Big heart, big spirit."

"I thought I drove you crazy with my snooping."

He laughed. "You do. But that's just it. Jenny would never have had the curiosity to go looking for a murderer. You are irrepressible. Crazy-making, but in an exciting sort of way."

I saw his chopsticks creeping toward my eggplant, and I used my own to block them.

"I just wanted a taste. Big spirit, right?"

"All you have to do is ask."

"Please."

"Of course."

He managed to pick up a piece of the slick eggplant

and get it all the way to his mouth without dropping it or even dribbling its rich sauce onto the white table-cloth.

"Good, huh?"

He smiled a wicked smile. "Delicious."

I could have gotten lost in his deep blue eyes right at that moment, but instead I took a bracing sip of water.

"So, I'm starting to see what you get out of this deal. You're right that I am far superior to this Jenny person."

He laughed. "Did I mention modest?"

"But," I continued, "how do I know that you're a better catch than Casey?"

"You forget, I went to school with Casey, too. He was a nice enough guy if you didn't mind a little arrogance."

Point well-taken.

"But he isn't what you need," he said with a slow shake of his head.

"And what exactly do I need?" I murmured.

He rested his chin in his hand and squinted his eyes like he could see some part of me beneath my skin.

"You need someone whose spirit is as strong as yours. Someone who will take delight in your successes and give you comfort when you fall."

By that point, my heart was ringing in my ears.

He grinned. "But most of all, you need someone who can save your bacon the next time you accuse the wrong person of murder."

This last teasing remark broke the tension between us, but my heart was still beating a million miles a minute.

I mustered a smile. "Yes, I can see where an armed bodyguard might come in handy."

He cleared his throat. "I hope you enjoyed dinner."

"It was delicious," I said. That was it, the date was over. I found myself surprisingly sad to see the evening come to an end.

He tucked a handful of bills into the folder the waiter had left behind, stood, and held my chair for me. Once again, I felt the need to write his mother a thank-you note for raising such a polite son.

He walked me home, and we teased each other as we strolled hand in hand. Our steps slowed as we approached 801 Maple. But despite our foot-dragging, we were eventually on my front porch.

I tucked my hands behind my back, and Jack tipped back on the heels of his shoes.

He cleared his throat. "This was a proper date, Izzy."

Though he said it with such force, I took it as a question.

"Yes."

He nodded. "Then it should end properly."

"Yes," I said, my voice barely audible.

He raised his large hands and cupped my face with them. The tips of his fingers crept into my hair, tickled the edges of my ears. Slowly, he leaned down—giving me every opportunity to pull away—and rested his lips on mine. After a breath, he deepened the pressure and I felt his lips part just enough to nibble my bottom lip. It was a gentle kiss, but with the promise of passion simmering right beneath the surface.

When he pulled back, I stumbled back a step. He

grabbed my arms to stop my fall, and a smile of pure, masculine self-satisfaction lifted his lips.

He let me go, tipped an imaginary hat. "Good night, Izzy McHale."

I couldn't find my words. All I could do was unlock the front door and dart inside. I didn't turn on the light, so I could see him standing on the porch. He stood there for a full minute, that smile never fading. When he spun on his heel, shoved his hands deep in his pockets, and started the trek to his car, I could hear his off-key whistling.

I couldn't make out the tune, but something told me that one day soon we'd be dancing to it.

CHAPTER
Twenty

My sisters, Dru and Lucy, stopped by the shop on their lunch hour, with my mother and Aunt Dolly in tow. Mom carried a covered dish, the luscious scent of her ratatouille already making its way across the showroom, and Dolly had a loaf of bread in one hand and a bottle of wine in the other. At the smell of food, Packer and Daisy May came thundering down the steps. Dru and Lucy blocked the dogs until Mom got the ratatouille safely to the table.

Both of my sisters worked strictly nine-to-five jobs. Dru was a CPA who worked for a firm that handled both private clients and audits of the city treasury, and Lucy was a court reporter. The irony of Lucy working as an officer of the court was not lost on anyone. My baby sister broke every rule in the book, and still managed not to get caught. That ability to get away with everything shy of murder had earned her the nickname Lucky Lucy.

She insisted there was no luck to it at all; she just knew how to manipulate people. When she announced that at the dining room table, my mother nearly passed out.

I got along just fine with both of my sisters. I was Switzerland. But proper, rule-following, i-dotting and t-crossing Dru found Lucy's wanton ways infuriating. And Lucy thought Dru was just a prude, the cloud over everyone's party. They often had words with each other, Dru trying to keep her temper in check while Lucy taunted her every which way from Sunday.

Today, though, my night and day sisters appeared to be in cahoots. And they'd brought lunch.

"Guess what we have." Dru crooned.

"You'll never guess," Lucy added.

"Okay, then I'll skip the pointless guessing and just ask you what you have."

"Party pooper," Lucy said before sticking her tongue out at me.

"We," Dru said with a flourish, "have Daniel Colona's obituary from the *Madison Standard*." She pulled a folded piece of printer paper from her purse and handed it to me.

Sure enough, it was Daniel's obituary, shockingly short considering he'd actually worked for the paper.

"What's it say?" Rena asked impatiently.

I read aloud:

Reporter Daniel Colona died on Friday, April 4, in the town of Merryville, Minnesota. Police assert that Daniel was a victim of foul play.

The deceased was an active member of a local

animal rights organization and a deacon in his church. He frequently gave back to the journalism community by speaking at conferences and organizing Shot Heard Round the World, a workshop held every year on September 17—the anniversary of the signing of the U.S. Constitution—for small-town reporters on how to find wire-worthy stories in their communities. Colleagues remember him as a quiet but generous man who always had the time to help young reporters.

He is survived by his parents, Tony and Margaret Colona, and a sister, Marilyn. In lieu of flowers, please send donations to the Madison Paws for a Cause Foundation.

"Wow," Rena said. "Can you imagine? A whole life boiled down to three simple paragraphs."

My mom, Dolly, and Dru began the age-old dance of putting a meal on a table. Mom set the covered dish on the hot pads she'd used to carry it, a sort of makeshift trivet. Dolly laid out the bread and wine and fetched salt and pepper off a shelf behind the barkery display case.

"And he sounds like a nice guy," I said. Something about the obituary was tugging at the corner of my mind, but I couldn't quite place it.

"I know, right?" Lucy said.

"He even loved animals," Dru added as she returned from the kitchen with a stack of plates and silverware.

"No kids," Lucy said. "I don't know if that's a good

thing or a bad thing. On the one hand, he didn't have a chance to have a child. On the other, there's no kid out there crying for his daddy."

"This is really a bummer," Rena said. "I know it's silly, because no one deserves to be murdered, but I'd sorta hoped he was a sleaze."

"Well," Dru pointed out, "they usually only put the good stuff in the obituary. They don't mention that you had chronic road rage or you were cheating on your wife."

Cheating. The pieces didn't so much fall into place as drift into place, the conversation around me morphing into a brand-new theory.

"Ama lied," I said.

"What?" Rena sounded like she had mental whiplash.

"I said, Ama lied. She said she'd never met Daniel. But when I was in her office, I saw a certificate on the wall that said she'd participated in a workshop called Shot Heard Round the World four years ago. She had to have met Daniel then."

Dru jerked back her head and thinned her lips. "Not necessarily. I go to workshops and conferences all the time, and on average I bet I only know ten percent of the people there."

"Okay," I conceded, "she didn't have to meet Daniel then, but I think she did."

Surprisingly, my mom perked up. "I bet she *really* met him."

Lucy blew a lock of midnight hair from her creamy

forehead. "Stop talking in riddles. What do you mean, Mom?"

"Well, I just remember Ama talking about getting pregnant with Jordan. It was right around Halloween, and she was with a bunch of us putting together decorations for the annual Halloween Howl. Ama cracked a joke that pretty soon she'd look like a jack-o'-lantern. It was the first any of us had heard she was pregnant. We all started clucking like a bunch of brood hens. She made another joke about the timing being perfect because she was due in early June and wouldn't be all huge during the height of summer."

"How on earth do you remember that?" I asked.

Mom shrugged. "I remember thinking she was a lucky lady. With the three of you girls, I only avoided a pregnant summer once."

"With me," Dru crowed.

Mom nodded. "Dru's a June baby." Mom started passing the ratatouille and the bread, in opposite directions.

"June fourth," Dolly said, as she cracked open the bottle of wine.

"Right. Your dad had taken a sabbatical the fall before Dru was born, spent three months studying the history of the Vikings in Oslo. I did the math, and the only time Dru could have possibly been conceived was Labor Day weekend, right before your dad left for Norway."

"Ewwww," Dru, Lucy, and I all groaned together.

"Oh, grow up, girls. I'm sure you all know plenty about the birds and the bees by now," Mom said.

Of course I knew my mother had had sex. And I'd lived with Casey for years, so she obviously knew I had had sex. But actually acknowledging the fact that we both knew that about each other felt . . . wrong. Just plain wrong.

"Why are you torturing us with this information?" Dru said. "What does dad's, uh, sabbatical have to do with Ama's baby?"

"June babies and September conceptions," Mom nudged.

"That doesn't necessarily mean anything," Rena chimed in. "She was only at the conference for a few days. She could have easily gotten pregnant before she left or after she returned."

Mom shook her head. "She could have, but I don't think she did. You said that Daniel had written the date June tenth in his notebook. I bet if you do the math there, you'll find that a baby conceived on September seventeenth—the date of that annual conference—would be due right around June tenth. Just about the time little Jordan is having his third birthday party. I don't know that Daniel was Jordan's father, but I'd bet cash money that Daniel thought he was."

"Mom, you're brilliant! And Dolly said that the stack of pictures she found in Daniel's apartment included a whole bunch of pictures of a cute little boy with *dark hair*. Jordan Olmstead is a cute little boy with dark hair, supposedly the child of two very blond parents."

Lucy looked thoughtful. "So you're saying that Ama cheated on Steve with Daniel and got pregnant during the fling?"

"That's exactly what I'm saying."

"That's a pretty major accusation," Dru said.

"It is," I agreed, "but it's not as major as murder."

"It's also all circumstantial. It could just be a coincidence. There are lots of boys with dark hair who play in Dakota Park. We have no idea if those pictures were of Jordan or not."

I was glad to have Dru there to give me pushback, challenge my reasoning.

"I'm right there with you. But if it's all just a bunch of coincidences, why did Ama lie?" Dru opened her mouth to argue, but I raised my hand to cut her off. "Not just about not knowing Daniel, but about her never receiving a call from him. We found her phone number in the back of his journal, but she told us that she'd never spoken with him. Jack slipped up the other night and said that Daniel had placed three calls to Ama's cell phone."

"Whoa," Lucy said.

"Wait right there. 'Jack slipped up the other night.' What other night? What were you doing with Jack Collins?"

"Honestly, now is not the time, Mom."

"Actually," Lucy started.

"It's as good a time as any," Dru finished.

"Oh, all right. If you must know, Jack and I went on a date last night. It was no big deal."

"Details," Lucy insisted. "Was there kissing?"

I felt the heat rushing up my face. I didn't want to be having this conversation at all, let alone in front of my mother. "Yes, there was kissing. That's all I'm going to say on the subject." I slapped my hand down on the table. "Let's get back to the fact that Daniel might have been the father of Ama's child."

Dru hummed softly. "And he was in town. Calling her. Taking pictures of Jordan. He must have known."

"Man, if she thought he was going to drag that secret out into the light . . . ," Rena said.

"Exactly," I said. "It would be a big motive for murder."

As luck would have it, Ama was scheduled to stop by the store after lunch to do some light checks for the photographs she'd be taking of the wedding ceremony the next day. She'd done the same for Ingrid and Harvey's first wedding, but that had been in the evening with the primary light sources coming from the chandeliers that hung in the store. Tomorrow, the ceremony was set for the afternoon, and Ama needed to see what the afternoon sun coming through Trendy Tails' large front window would do to the light.

Packer and Daisy had been enjoying a moment of camaraderie, stretched out in a beam of molten sunlight, both snoring softly. Ama's entrance didn't faze Packer at all. He opened one eye, then grumbled before falling right back to sleep. But Daisy got up, gave a little yip, and then pushed her head into Ama's hand.

Ama pulled back like she'd been burned. I guessed she wasn't much of a dog person.

"Sorry about that," I said, tugging Daisy's collar to pull her away from Ama. "I still think she has a little crush on you."

Ama's eyes grew round with surprise, but she didn't comment. I dragged a reluctant Daisy by her collar and shut her up in my apartment. She whined, and I could see her nose pressing at the gap below my door before I headed back downstairs.

Ama got set up while I assisted a customer who was buying a pair of fleece boots for his border collie. He didn't have the dog with him, so we spent a fair amount of time having him guess the size of his collie's feet and sketch them out on a piece of paper so I could pick the correct size of booties.

"Thank you, sir. And if you get home and find those boots don't fit Loki, you can bring both the boots and the dog back, and we'll get him the right size."

He smiled and waved his thanks as he walked out.

I walked toward the back of the store, where Ama was working. I caught sight of Rena in the barkery, pretending to dust the case but actually keeping a suspicious eye on Ama.

"Ama," I said.

"Huh," she muttered as she stared into the viewer of her camera and slowly turned the dial of an external lens.

"Ama, would you like a cookie?"

She looked up at me, bemused.

"I wasn't craving them, but I wouldn't say no to a cookie. What's the occasion?"

"No occasion, really."

I led her to the red folk art table, where Rena was quickly setting out a plate of human cookies—her oatmeal toffee chocolate chunks—and a pot of tea she'd brewed in advance.

"No, really, what's going on?" she asked as she slowly sank into a chair. "You're both so serious, I get the feeling you're about to give me bad news." There was a hint of panic in her voice. "Is it Steve? Did he get hurt working on Ken's restaurant?"

"No," I soothed as I took a seat across from her. "We just . . . we know about your secret."

Her demeanor shifted from worried to completely closed in the blink of an eye. "What secret?"

"We know that Daniel was Jordan's father."

The words just hung in the room like a pall. All the bright colors of Trendy Tails seemed to fade to sepia as I watched the play of emotions on Ama's face: belligerence, fear, resignation, and just a hint of hope . . . perhaps hope that she could talk us out of our conclusion.

"I don't know what you're talking about." She'd opted for hope.

"We know you were at the Shot Heard Round the World workshop that Daniel ran at about the time that you conceived Jordan."

"So?"

"We also know that Daniel was interested in Jordan's due date, had been taking pictures of him, and had been calling you."

"I told you—"

"Don't bother to deny it, Ama. I'd rather not name our source, but we have it on good authority that he called you several times."

"Again, so what?"

"What is it they say? 'The cover-up is always worse than the crime'? We wouldn't have thought twice about those calls except you were so adamant about denying they happened."

"All right. I should have been more truthful, but I swear he just called to ask about using the archive at the *Gazette*. Completely innocent. Jordan is Steve's boy."

"No, he's not," I prodded. "Jordan looks just like Daniel. I understand why you would go to any lengths to protect that secret."

"Wait. You're not suggesting that I killed Daniel, are you?"

"You have one whale of a motive," Rena said.

"And then there's Daisy," I said. "We all thought she had a crush on you because she'd bark at the sound of your voice, both in the park and on TV and just now. But it isn't random. She knows you. You must have been in Daniel's apartment when she was. And you must have made quite an impression on her."

"She's a dog. You're accusing me because of a dog?"

"Well, first of all, dogs are highly sensitive and they remember negative experiences. And second, it's not just Daisy. It's all of these little things that pile up to a lot of evidence."

Ama sat still for a moment. She even picked up a cookie, took a bite, and chewed thoughtfully. But her hands were trembling the whole time.

Finally she broke her silence. "If I tell you the truth, will you keep it to yourselves?"

"We can't make any promises," I said. "I promised Jack Collins that I won't withhold evidence."

Her eyes were pooling with tears. "But that's just it.

None of it is evidence of anything. You're right—Jordan is Daniel's child. And I never told Daniel that I'd gotten pregnant. It would have killed Steve, and I was so in love with him. I *am* so in love with him. With Daniel, it was all physical."

In my mind, the fact that Casey had cheated on me was a sign that he'd probably never loved me at all. Was it possible for love and infidelity to coexist?

"Why did you sleep with Daniel if you loved Steve so much?"

She shrugged, and wiped away a tear with a French-tipped finger. "See, we'd been trying to get pregnant for a long time, and we just couldn't seem to get there. It was putting an amazing amount of stress on our relationship. Every time we had sex, it felt like we were gearing up to march into battle. I just wanted one completely uncomplicated night with someone. And Daniel Colona was a very tempting man."

She uttered a sharp sound, somewhere between laughter and pain. "Wouldn't you know it? I work for years to have a child with my husband, and no dice. One night of infidelity and suddenly I'm Fertile Myrtle."

"But you never told Daniel? Then how did he figure it out?"

"Oh, he didn't until he got to town. He came to investigate those ridiculous owls and whether their habitat would be destroyed. He apparently saw me with Jordan in the park and quickly put two and two together."

"Did you talk to him about the child?"

"Yes." She nodded, tears now streaming down her face. "We spoke three times. The first devolved quickly into an argument, but during the course of the shouting, I admitted Jordan was his. The other two times we spoke, he called and we met in his apartment."

I frowned. "I never saw you."

"Daniel let me in through the kitchen and up the back stairs. That's when Daisy probably latched on to my voice. I brought pictures and footprints and macaroni art . . . all the things Daniel had missed."

"Did you fight? Is that why Daisy gets so agitated when you're around?"

Ama flushed. "Honestly, you can't let this get out. It wouldn't help anyone with anything. But both times I visited his apartment, we were, uh, intimate."

"Holy cow," Rena gasped.

I shot her a quelling look and reached out to take Ama's hand. "It's okay, Ama. We all make mistakes."

She squeezed my hand. "It was just so sentimental, looking through Jordan's baby things with the man who had given him to me. I shouldn't have done it. I broke my vows again. But I got caught up in the moment."

"Did Daniel want visitation or custody?"

"Yes." She nodded miserably. "And he deserved it. It wasn't right of me to keep Jordan a secret for so long. I was trying to figure out how to tell Steve, but then Daniel died, and suddenly the problem was gone."

Rena cleared her throat. "That's precisely the problem, Ama. Daniel's death solved a huge problem for you. That's what we call 'motive.'"

Ama became animated again. "But I'm telling you, I didn't kill him. He was the father of my child. Besides, I couldn't have killed him. I was taking pictures of the wedding the whole time."

I remembered that she'd been quick to get to the front of the room to take pictures of Daniel's body. Her distress at the time made more sense since she knew the victim. But she was out of breath when she started taking those crime scene photos.

"You were panting," I said. "When you got up to the altar to take pictures of Daniel's body, you were breathing hard like you'd just run down a flight of stairs."

"I was breathing hard because I had to force my way through the crowd with all my equipment. Steve had gone out for some air just before Daniel tumbled down the stairs. He'd left me with all of my camera gear, which is a lot of weight for someone my size to carry.

"Look, here are the photos I took. You can see I didn't miss a moment."

She pulled a tablet computer out of a pocket in one of her bags, opened up a file labeled "Ing_Harv_Wedding," and began scrolling through the photos. There was Harvey standing by the altar, one of me talking with Pris, a photo of my sisters whispering to each other, one of Hetty and Sean Tucker sitting next to Louise and Jack Collins, the two men exchanging hard glares. Finally, there was a string of pictures that ran from Ingrid's taupe pumps appearing on the staircase to the chaos and confusion when the body fell down the stairs. There was a short break, when, presumably, Ama was forcing her way to the front of the crowd, and then pictures of me and Jack kneeling by Daniel's dead body.

It was pretty compelling evidence. Ama couldn't have done it.

CHAPTER
Twenty-one

When Ama left, both Rena and I sank into a funk. Not only had we once again failed to find the real killer, but we'd made poor Ama cry for nothing. When Dolly had told us about Ingrid and her first husband, Arnold's, problem, when he'd cheated on her with Jane Porter, I thought that must have been the most horrible burden to bear through their long marriage. But at least the truth was out between the two of them. Ama carried her secret on her own, hiding something so big from the man she loved. I couldn't help but feel for her.

The door had barely closed behind Ama when Richard Greene made his way into the store. I stopped midway through the process of moving a rack of spangled leashes to the back of the barkery, where they'd be out of the way for the next day's ceremony. I stifled a sigh, just waiting for the next gambit to close down Trendy Tails.

"Miss McHale. Miss Hamilton." He nodded his gentlemanly greeting.

"Hi, Richard. What can I do for you today?"

He thrust his chin out as though steeling himself for a blow.

"I am here to . . ." He coughed and shuffled his feet. "I am here to apologize."

"Apologize? Whatever for?"

"For being so hard on you ladies when it comes to your business here. I was speaking with Dorothy the other night, while we had a bite to eat. . . ."

For a moment, I completely tuned out what he was saying, trying to wrap my brain around the fact that Aunt Dolly had gone on a date with Richard Greene. And that she'd managed to keep it a secret from the rest of us. When I finally processed that little bit of information, Richard was halfway through his speech.

". . . I have to admit she was correct. I've been too hard on you young women. At least you're trying to bring business to the community, and you're not just sitting around waiting for someone to take care of you."

"Thank you, Richard," I said.

"Yeah," Rena mumbled, clearly in shock, "thank you."

"I still insist on you obeying the law, but Dorothy says you've already been in touch with the Department of Agriculture and are working on coming up to code. I expect you to have your food properly licensed and labeled by July, but I won't report you before then."

Not the warmest apology I'd ever received, but definitely one of the most unexpected.

"We promise we'll work with the MDA until everything is resolved. I think July is completely fair," I said.

I couldn't resist a little teasing. "So you and Aunt Dolly, huh?"

Richard coughed and glared at me.

"Don't get any ideas, young lady. Dorothy is a fine woman, and it is sometimes nice to share the companionship of one of your peers."

Didn't I know the truth of that? I caught a glimpse of Rena grinning out of the corner of my eye, and I was worried she'd push it further. No sense poking a sleeping bear.

"I'm glad you and Dolly had a chance to catch up and get to know one another a little better," I said.

He harrumphed, seemingly placated.

"Richard," I said. "Any chance you have space for another dog? Daisy May needs a home pretty bad, and she's a great dog. Hasn't made a single mess in the house, hasn't chewed anything other than toys, and she's quiet as a mouse."

The dog in question was lying on the floor gnawing on a rawhide toy. As if she knew we were talking about her, she looked up, raised her ears, and tilted her head to the side.

Richard looked her up and down, eyes squinted.

"She looks like a fine dog," he said, "but MacArthur flies solo."

"Oh," I said, genuinely disappointed. Richard Greene might be a pain in my patoot, but there was no question he loved his dog. It would have felt good entrusting Daisy to such a solid person.

Richard cleared his throat. "I have to get back to the shop. Left MacArthur in charge."

Without further ado, he left.

I glanced down at Packer, who was chewing on his own spitty rawhide toy. "Listen, little guy, I am *never* leaving you in charge of the store."

Rena whistled low. "Holy cow, that is a relief. I've spent at least an hour on the phone with the MDA ever since Richard brought up the problem, and they still can't figure out which forms I do and do not have to fill out. Richard giving us until July gives us some serious breathing room."

"I'm still trying to get past the fact that Aunt Dolly went on a date with the man and managed to sweet-talk him into apologizing."

Rena shook her head, clicking her tongue. "Don't underestimate the power of Dolly's raw feminine energy. That woman has got it going on."

We both collapsed into a heap of giggles.

When we straightened up, I continued pulling the rack of leashes into the corner. I sobered quickly. Aunt Dolly had done us yet another favor. I felt so deeply in her debt both for the money she'd loaned me to start my business and for her confidence in me, and now she'd run interference between Richard and me twice. It seemed the least I could do was deliver one legitimate murder suspect to the police so my aunt wouldn't be convicted for a crime she didn't commit.

"What are you two up to? All that laughter makes me very nervous." Ingrid made her way carefully down the stairs, a stack of glass dessert plates rattling in her hands.

"We were talking about Dolly," Rena said.

"Well, that is a humorous subject," Ingrid dead-panned.

"What's with the plates?" Rena asked.

"Oh, these old things were up in the attic, and I thought they would be nice to use for the cake at the wedding."

"The attic?" I gasped.

"Yes. Harvey went up to get them."

I gasped. The thought of frail Harvey climbing a rickety folding ladder up into the must and debris of that attic truly terrified me. The words "broken hip" were flashing like neon in my brain.

Ingrid tutted softly. "Give us some credit, Izzy. We may be old, but we do have our wits about us. I held the ladder, and I knew exactly where to find the boxes of plates. He handed them down with great care." She paused. "And I had nine-one-one punched into my phone, ready to hit 'send.'"

I rushed over to take the plates from Ingrid's hands and then nearly dropped them when the bell over our front door jingled. We all turned to find Jane Porter standing just inside the doorway.

Rena and I exchanged nervous glances.

"Hello, Ingrid. Girls."

"Hello, Jane," Ingrid replied. "What brings you to our doorstep today? I didn't know you had a furry friend to pamper."

"I don't. I came to see you. Girls, would you mind giving us a minute?"

Rena and I started beating a hasty retreat to the back kitchen.

"No," Ingrid stated.

We stopped walking midstride.

"Whatever you have to say to me you can say in front of these two. In fact, I'd prefer they stay." Ingrid's words froze hard in the air between us all.

Jane sighed. "I wanted to talk to you about the picture."

"Right. The picture. If you meant to hurt me, you did a fine job of it."

"Ingrid. That wasn't my intent at all. Look, this thing between us has been festering for almost thirty-five years. Knute Hammer isn't just my arm candy."

I coughed to cover a laugh. Knute was a far sight from arm candy.

"We talk," Jane continued. "We've been talking about the need to put things in the past right before you can move forward with a clean slate. That's what I'm trying to do."

"By reminding me of your affair with my husband," Ingrid snapped.

"No." Jane sighed again and her shoulders sagged. "I should have insisted on giving you that picture myself so I could have explained. I took that picture of Arnold one day during our affair. We were picnicking down by Badger Lake, and the light was just perfect. And he looked so terribly happy."

"I noticed," Ingrid said, her voice tight with emotion.

"You know what we'd been talking about? What made him so happy? You. He'd told me a story about you trying to refinish the wood floors in this very room, and he laughed." Jane raised a hand, fending off comment. "Not at you, but with joy. That memory of you gave him joy.

"See, I wasn't happy in my marriage, and I harbored hopes that the affair might turn into something real. But that was the day when I knew it would never be more than a fling. That was the day that I knew that Arnold was with me because he was lonely, but that he loved you deeply."

I glanced at Ingrid, and I'll be darned if I didn't see the reflection of tears in her eyes.

"Your marriage was real, Ingrid. Your love was real."

Rena fixed Ingrid a cup of tea, and sent her upstairs. She was clearly overwrought and needed the time to decompress.

Late afternoon brought a steady flow of customers, all of whom flocked immediately to the center island display that Ingrid and I had festooned in bright springtime colors. She'd made the right choice going for bold rather than pastel. Rena's barkery was hopping, too, with all the customers lured to her baked goods by the luscious scent of carrot-carob cupcakes wafting from the kitchen.

I had just finished wrapping a sparkling pink tutu and a matching pink hair bow for a woman leading a Lhasa apso on a rhinestone-studded leash, when Pamela Rawlins walked through the front door.

I put on my biggest, most welcoming smile, and was happy to see her return it.

"How's Tonga?" I asked.

"Doing well. Thank you for asking. She's been wearing the collar I bought from you, and I must say the craftsmanship is superb."

"I try to make as much in-house as I can, but I have a supplier for my leather goods. She's a genius with dying and stitching."

"Well," Pamela said, "as you can tell by Tonga's absence, I'm not here to shop. I bring you good news."

I felt my heart skip a beat. *Please, please, please . . .*

"I've spoken with our director, Philip Denford, and the rest of the board, and we're in agreement that Merryville will make a perfect venue for our summer spectacular in July, our biggest event of the year."

"Oh, wow. That's excellent news."

"Yes. We were a bit concerned that the town was too small, that there wouldn't be a building big enough to host the main event. After all, we'll be awarding the Denford Prize, a bejeweled collar dangle worth well over a hundred thousand dollars. We couldn't very well just use pop-up tents."

"So, uh, what did you find?" I didn't want to jinx anything, but I really couldn't imagine anyplace bigger than the high school gymnasium.

"We spoke with Hal Olson, Pris's husband. . . . Do you know him?"

Only too well, I thought. I confined my spoken answer to "Yes."

"Well, he has some development he's working on, and he's decided to build a convention center on the site. He assures us it will be done by the end of June, and our July event will be the first held in the new center."

My mind was spinning. Hal was scrapping the half-built condos in favor of a convention center that couldn't be more than a thought in his head? He'd promised it by July? And he somehow thought all this would work out despite the burrowing owls?

It sounded crazy. But like a good small-town girl, I opted to keep crazy in the family.

"Sounds perfect," I said.

"Well, Tonga and I are hitting the road for Fargo first thing in the morning, and I want to take a few last pictures to share with the board. But I thought you'd want to know about the decision."

I reached my hand across the counter to shake hers. "I'm so glad you stopped by. This made my day."

She smiled, an expression that appeared awkward on her face. "I'm sure we'll be in touch before July. But for now . . ."

As soon as the door closed behind her, I rushed to find Rena. "Guess what. That cat show? It's coming to Merryville!"

She squealed in delight. The chains she was wearing

around her neck jangled as she hopped around in exuberant joy.

I grabbed her arms and we hopped together in pure glee. Still, at the back of my mind, I felt that we'd just had too much good news. Part of me was waiting for the other shoe to drop.

CHAPTER
Twenty-two

Rena had left for home to bake the doggy cake, and I had just about finished clearing the showroom for the next day's festivities when our doorbell tinkled again. This time, we found Taffy Nielson and Ken West making their way across the now-empty floor.

"Izzy," Taffy said, "I have some news."

Lord love a duck, this was a day for news. I crossed my fingers that this news, too, was good.

"Ken here was working at his restaurant this morning, and he popped across the alley to have lunch with me. When he opened the door, Gandhi made a run for it."

"No!"

"Yes. Just a little auburn bolt of lightning." Taffy looked sheepish. "I have to admit it's good for me that he's gone. But I know you worry about him."

Once again, the pig was in the wind.

"I tried to grab him for you, Izzy," Ken said.

"It's true. Ken nearly impaled himself on a cut end of lumber sticking out of the construction Dumpster. He really tried."

"Oh. Well, thank you for trying. Hopefully he'll turn up again soon. That pig is as willful as a spoiled toddler."

"I also wanted to thank you," Ken said.

Heavens, I'd just accused the man of murder. Why would he want to thank me?

"After our little conversation the other day," he continued, "I realized that I wasn't being fair to Taffy. I shouldn't have tried to keep our relationship secret for so long, especially in an effort to hide my past from her. A relationship has to be built on trust, so I decided to tell Taffy about being the Madison Mystery Chef. I expected her to run away screaming, but she seems to have found it in her heart to forgive me."

He swung their clasped hands up and planted a kiss on her knuckles.

Taffy colored, that blush a sure barometer of her soul. "I didn't really have to forgive him for anything. I kind of like him having a dark and dangerous past."

I wasn't sure being a lecherous chef constituted "dark and dangerous," but I wasn't about to rain on Taffy's parade.

I picked up the last rack of kitty couture to move it back to the barkery, but I hit my finger against the wood a little too hard, and my splinter wound sent a shot up my arm. I hissed air between my teeth trying to hold the pain at bay, but it was tough. Even with the bandage around my finger, the spot where the splinter had gone in was incredibly tender.

"Besides," Taffy added, apparently oblivious to my moment of crisis, "it was all a long time before he met me. We all have our secrets."

"We also wanted to put to rest any lingering thoughts you might have about my involvement in Daniel's death. I can give you my real alibi now."

Taffy looked down at the floor and leaned into Ken's side. "He was with me."

Ken held up a hand. "I know. As a professional I shouldn't have left the kitchen, but during the actual ceremony I didn't figure I'd be missed. So I scooted down the alley to have a little quality time with my sweetie."

"Then why did you say you'd been having a smoke with Steve Olmstead?"

"I was, at the time, trying to keep our romance under wraps. And I didn't know what had happened, how high the stakes were, so I blurted out the first thing that came to me. Steve had just come into the kitchen to get a glass of water when I decided to leave, so I figured he'd be my cover."

"But you didn't *ask* him to cover for you?"

Ken frowned. "No. I didn't know I'd need a cover when I left, and by the time I got back and said I'd gone out for a cigarette, the place was practically crawling with cops. I just kept my mouth shut."

I leaned forward to give Ken a hard stare. "And you never thought to tell the police you'd lied?"

Ken shook his head, perplexed. "Why would I? Until you came knocking on my door, no one was acting like I was a suspect. And if I wasn't a suspect, why would anyone care about my alibi?"

Because, I thought, *alibis run two ways.*

As soon as Taffy and Ken left, I grabbed my phone and dialed Jack Collins.

I got his voice mail.

"Jack, this is Izzy. Look, I'm like ninety-nine percent certain I know who the real murderer is. But I've had pretty bad luck confronting my suspects over the last week, so I'm going to let you do the confronting on this one. Just come over soon so I can explain everything."

By the time I'd hung up, I'd missed a call from Sean. In his message, he said he was planning to swing by around five to drop off some magic bars his mother had decided to make for the wedding ceremony the next day. We were catered up the yin-yang, but no one in her right mind says no to magic bars.

Two minutes later, I got the text from Jack: "How about 5? Dinner?"

I set the phone on the counter and pressed my temples. Between Ama, Richard, Jane, and Ken, and now a potential showdown between Sean and Jack, my head might literally explode. And I still had a killer to catch.

Later that afternoon, I was enjoying a moment of peace. Rena had brought the doggy cake in, and it was adorable: two bone-shaped tiers of carob applesauce cake with a peanut butter frosting. She'd decorated it with creamed banana piping. Once she'd gotten adequate praise from me for her amazing effort, she had taken both Packer and Daisy for a walk. Daisy's strength and Packer's general grumpiness over sharing the spotlight gave me pause, but Rena was convinced she could handle it. And Jinx, who was often underfoot when the shop was dog free, had decided to curl up with Val on top of the oak armoire for a catnap. A ferret nap? Whatever, they were quiet.

At ten to five, I was draping the front cabinet with the purple velvet cover we'd used the week before, when the bell over my front door jingled, announcing a new guest. I looked up expecting either Sean or Jack.

I was shocked instead to see Steve Olmstead. He looked like he was about to clock me.

"What did you say to Ama? What did you say to make her cry?"

That was a tricky question. I was pretty sure Steve already knew Ama's secret, but on the off chance I was wrong, I didn't want to spill it for her. And I had a lousy track record with lying, especially on the fly.

I settled for a noncommittal shrug.

"Tell me now!" he screamed, his eyes opened to the point that I could see a ring of white around his arctic blue irises, veins visible beneath his ruddy skin.

"We were talking about Jordan."

That's when I saw the outline of the gun Steve had in his pocket. I knew the jig was up. There was no way to stall him until Jack arrived, and I knew Steve had already committed the ultimate sin to save his family once.

Carefully, I reached over to the high stool where my bag and phone lay, and I slowly dragged the phone into my hand.

Steve was looking around frantically, taking in his surroundings, so I risked a quick glance down at the phone so I could hit redial. This time, faintly, I heard Jack answer with a cheery hello. Quickly, I depressed the button on the side of the phone that lowered the speaker volume, so Jack could hear what we were saying but we couldn't hear him.

"Steve," I said loudly, to make sure Jack caught that I was still present, that I was talking to someone else. "What's going on here?"

"Why would talking about Jordan make Ama cry? She loves him."

"I think you know why, Steve."

He pinned me with his glare. "He's. My. Son."

"I think you're wrong," I said. "I think Daniel Colona's his father, and I think you know that." The words dropped like stones from my mouth, heavy words that could not be taken back.

Steve uttered a sound of disgust. "I'm not stupid. I know Jordan isn't my biological son." He closed his eyes, expression intent as he looked hard at the past. "Ama and I tried to get pregnant for so long. She wept every month when we knew we'd missed another opportunity. I was her husband. I loved her. I wanted to start a family with her. . . . Her tears were like daggers in my heart. We finally started seeking medical help, and I learned that I have a low sperm count. I never told Ama, because I couldn't bear to be the one to destroy her dreams, but I knew we would probably never have a child."

He laughed, his expression softening. "Then Ama got pregnant. At first I thought we'd just gotten lucky, that the stars had aligned and we'd gotten pregnant together. I suppose I knew somewhere in the back of my head that I was lying to myself, that it was another man and not luck that gave us our child. But I didn't care. Seeing the joy on Ama's face when the baby kicked, working side by side to create a nursery for our baby. I chose to believe the child was mine."

I could empathize. Looking back, I should have known Casey was cheating on me for months before he finally left. But I wanted so much to believe in the dream of our life together, couldn't bear the thought of it not coming to fruition, that I chose to believe all was well in our relationship. The heart's desire can blind us to so many ugly realities.

"What made you stop believing?" I asked.

He sighed and opened his eyes, but he didn't meet my gaze. "When Jordan was born. Ama and I have blue eyes and Jordan's are brown. I only took biology when I was in high school, but I seem to recall that's a genetic impossibility. Even if it weren't, he doesn't look a thing like me or his mother. I just knew."

"That must have been hard, to realize you weren't his father."

Steve sucked in a lungful of air through his nose, like you do before the doctor sticks a needle in your arm, anticipating the pain to come.

"It was hard. I'm not his father. But I *am* his *dad*. I'm the one who held him as he took his first breath, the one who rocked him through the night when he was sick, the one whose fingers he grasped as he took his first steps. He's mine in a way he could never be Daniel Colona's."

"Did you blame Ama?"

"Sometimes. But I knew in my gut that she'd just had a fling, and I'll never forget the way she cried for a child. It changed our marriage, but I never hated her for it."

"Did you ever confront her?"

He laughed a short, grim laugh. "Absolutely not. She knew what she'd done, and she felt remorse. Sometimes she'd look at me like she was trying to crawl right inside my head, and she'd say, 'I love you. You know that, right?' She wouldn't break the gaze until I acknowledged her love. What good would it have done to say that I knew about her fling? It would have only made her feel worse."

Or, I thought, it might have lifted a terrible weight from her shoulders. Whether he realized it or not, I suspected that Steve held his tongue so his wife had to suffer in silence.

"Why kill Daniel?"

"What makes you think I killed Daniel?" he asked, his voice growing dangerously quiet.

Under normal circumstances, I wouldn't have let on that I knew Steve was the murderer, but I was hoping Jack was listening to every word and trying to get to Trendy Tails as fast as he could. For the same reason—buying time—I figured I ought to explain my thinking.

"Two things, really. First, there was your splinter. I saw the bandage that morning in the park. I recently did the same thing, probably in the exact same spot on the handrail in my back staircase. My first instinct was to stick the splintered finger in my mouth. It didn't hit me until later, but you were sucking your finger right after Daniel's death. You stopped the second you saw me, but I caught it.

"And then there was the alibi. You and Ken both lied about your alibi, saying you'd been having a cigarette with each other in the alley. Ken had a reason to lie, so he could cover up his relationship with Taffy and the extended amount of time he spent with her when he should have been working. But you backed him up. And that made me wonder why you would lie for Ken. The answer, of course, is that you wouldn't. You weren't giving Ken an alibi; he had inadvertently given you one."

Steve cocked his head. "Clever cookie."

"Thanks? But I still don't understand why you had to murder Daniel."

"He was nosing around, taking pictures of Jordan. He'd called her at the house a couple of times. Not that Ama told me. But a few times she'd gotten calls that upset her. I could tell by the way she gripped the phone and the way her lips flattened against her teeth. Then one day her phone rang when she wasn't around. I picked it up. When I answered, I only got silence. But then I hit redial and I got Daniel Colona's voice mail.

"Dee Dee seemed to know who Daniel Colona was and claimed he'd been out by the Badger Lake construction site. So I hoofed it out there a couple of times until I finally saw him for myself. One look and I knew he was Jordan's father."

He laughed, a half-desperate sound.

"He'd figured out he had a kid, and his interest in Jordan could only mean one thing: that he was planning to try to take my boy away from me."

"The courts never would have granted him full custody. Just visitation," I said. "He'd still be your boy."

"But everyone would know. They'd know that I'd been a patsy, they'd know that Ama had had an affair, and they'd know that Jordan was illegitimate. It would have haunted all three of us, completely changed the way the people in this community viewed us. My business would suffer, and Ama might even lose her job."

It seemed to me that Steve was overestimating the extent to which people in Merryville would care about their marriage. Sure, there'd be all sorts of speculation and gossip for the first few weeks, maybe even months. But then things would die down. People wouldn't necessarily forget, but there wouldn't be anything new to say about the subject. Why, look at Jane Porter's torrid fling with Ingrid's first husband. I'd managed to spend over thirty years in the orbit of Ingrid and my gossipy aunt Dolly before I heard even a peep about that affair.

On the other hand, I suppose when you live with a secret the way Steve had been living with this, it just keeps growing in your mind until it's this massive rock dangling by a thread over you. The merest whisper of the secret and you'll be destroyed.

"I didn't plan to kill him. I wasn't even sure if he

was in his apartment the night of the wedding. I went
to get a glass of water, saw Ken leaving, and thought
I'd take a chance that maybe he was at home. I just
wanted to ask him to leave us alone. He hadn't even
met Jordan, so why would he care if he got a chance to?
Why not just pretend it had never happened?"

That seemed to be Steve's MO. He saw the imperfec-
tions in his life, like his wife's infidelity. He wasn't
blind to it, but he chose to pretend it wasn't there. He
must have imagined that Daniel could do the same.

I glanced over Steve's shoulder. By now both Sean
and Jack were late for their five o'clock drop-ins.

"So what happened?"

Steve shook his head as though he were settling
down a bit, giving up, but then he slipped the gun from
his pocket.

"We were just talking, you know? I told him that if
he'd just leave town, I'd be able to come to terms with
Ama, repair our marriage, and that I still loved Jordan
like my own. He laughed at me. Laughed! He said that
he and Ama had met a couple of times since the conference. I thought she was in the Twin Cities to attend
workshops at the U, but she was meeting him. Sleeping
with him. He said our marriage was obviously pretty
shaky.

"I could have let that slide, but then he said that now
that he knew about Jordan, he would sue for visitation.
I said something about how I'd kill him before I let him
destroy my family, and he must have thought I meant
right then and there. He's the one who grabbed the gun

safe and opened it. He's the one who pulled the gun. I told him to stop, lunged for it, and it went off."

"See, it was just an accident," I soothed. "You didn't mean to hurt him."

"But I did. And I meant what I said. At that moment it was an accident, but I would have killed him before I let him take my boy away. I was dead serious about that."

The gun was out now, hanging loose at his side. I didn't know what he was planning, whether he was even aware that the weapon was in his hand.

I was paying so much attention to the gun in Steve's hand that I hadn't noticed anyone approach the door. I was as startled as Steve when Sean stepped into the room.

Steve spun around, raising the gun as he did so. I gasped, but managed to hold back my scream, as Sean threw up one hand in surrender while the other held the pan of magic bars.

"What the . . . ?" Steve yelled.

"Easy, man. I didn't mean to startle you. I'm just here to drop off some cookies."

He glanced in my direction, meeting my eyes, and I could see the question in them. I nodded that I was okay.

"I don't know what to do," Steve said, his voice filled with panic now. He raised the gun, and both Sean and I froze. His hands trembling, Steve swung the gun toward me, then toward Sean, and finally he raised it to his own head.

"Steve," I said softly. "You don't want to make Ama cry, do you? If you hurt yourself, she'll never stop crying."

Tears began to slip down the big man's face. I could read the confusion in his eyes. He couldn't see a way out.

Just as he started to lower the gun at me again, I heard the cock of a gun somewhere just behind me. Jack. He must have heard the conversation through the phone and come in through the back door.

"Put the gun down, Steve," Jack said, his voice steady but commanding.

"I . . . I can't."

"Yes, you can, Steve," Jack continued, putting special emphasis on Steve's name. "We can work this out, Steve, but if you don't put the gun down now, someone will get hurt. And I know you don't want that, Steve."

Steve choked back a sob and jerked, and for an instant I thought all was lost. Either he would pull the trigger himself or Jack would shoot him. But, instead, Sean, standing behind Steve at that point, lobbed the pan of magic bars at Steve and the gun went flying out of his hands and skittering across the floor.

That's when I began to shake. In a matter of breaths, Sean had rushed to my side and pulled me into a rough embrace, trying to calm me with whispered nonsense words. Over his shoulder, I watched Jack grab Steve in a lock grip and quickly pin him to the floor. He was Mirandizing Steve and slapping cuffs on him before I fully comprehended that we were all still alive.

I looked up at Sean and then at Jack, two men who were each trying to protect me in their own way. And then I looked at Steve. He, too, was a protector, but it had led him down a far darker path. Despite his best efforts, I knew Ama would be crying tonight.

CHAPTER
Twenty-three

Ingrid and Harvey offered to put off their wedding yet again, thinking I needed some time to collect myself, but I assured them that keeping busy and reaffirming life and love were exactly what I needed.

Saturday morning broke bright and brilliant, a perfect Minnesota spring day with skies such a piercing blue you could barely stand to look at them. I was already enjoying a quiet cup of coffee at my dining table—Packer across my feet, Jinx across my lap, and Daisy taking up the entire sofa—when Ingrid came out to join me.

"Are you ready?" I asked.

"More than ever," she replied as she took a chair opposite me and poured her own cup of coffee. Packer wiggled off my feet and made his way to her side. She did not disappoint: Packer let slip a whimper, and Ingrid immediately dropped her hand to begin stroking his silky ears.

I shook my head. "Your faith in love is astounding. This week has been incredible. We've seen what love can lead to: betrayal, lies, even murder. Under the circumstances, I'm not sure I'm ready to jump right into a romance."

Ingrid chuckled, the sound like gravel shaken in a tin can. "It has, indeed, been an incredible week. But not just because of Daniel's murder and the fallout from all that. Jane reminded me of something Steve Olmstead should have known. Love may open you to betrayal, but, if it's deep enough, love can survive betrayal. And then *you*—"

"Me?"

"Yes, you. This week you've reminded me of love's payoff. You made me so proud when you gave me that down payment on this building. You went on and on about how much I did for you, but all I really did was love you. And now you've given me such joy and pride."

"Oh, Ingrid . . ."

She raised her hand and laughed. "No crying allowed, young lady. You also reminded me that love has to find a way. After all those years mourning for your relationship with Casey, you're finally getting back out there."

I opened my mouth to protest.

"Uh, uh, uh. I've seen the way those two boys look at you."

"Two?" I squeaked.

"Don't play coy. You went on a date with that hunky cop Jack, but Sean . . . he still has feelings for you. I can tell you're both confused about them, but they're there nonetheless."

"I don't—"

"Oh hush. The point of all this is that I've witnessed love in many forms this last week. And while some of it is tragic, most of it is joyous, and I want to be a part of that mad happiness."

"You're quite a woman, Ingrid Whitfield."

"I know. And you might as well get used to calling me Ingrid Nyquist."

I laughed. "Yes, ma'am. Now, if you'll excuse me, soon-to-be Mrs. Nyquist, I need to walk these dogs before the last-minute crush of preparing for the weddings."

Ingrid patted her leg, and Packer stood up on his hind legs, and strained his neck, licking his chops, looking for a little sugar. Ingrid grabbed both of his ears and scratched them vigorously. "You be a good dog for your mama, sweet boy."

I leashed up the dogs and headed downstairs and out toward Dakota Park. Packer still wasn't thrilled about sharing the limelight with gawky Daisy May, but the two had managed to work out a system so they could walk together without entangling their leashes or tripping all over each other. The two dogs seemed to slalom in wide curving S figures, noses to the ground, until we reached the park.

Suddenly, they were both straining at the leash,

wheezing and panting trying to break free. They had a common goal: Jordan Olmstead, playing in the sandbox.

Ama sat on a bench near him, her head tipped up to the blinding sky.

I let out the dogs' leads and joined Ama on the bench. I wasn't sure if she'd be happy to see me, but I figured it was never too early to begin healing.

"Did you know?" I asked.

She shook her head without meeting my eyes. "I suspected, but I didn't know. It only made sense for Steve to kill Daniel if he knew about the affair, but Steve acted perfectly normal at home. So I had my suspicions, but Steve's own behavior made them seem ridiculous. After all, if he was angry enough to kill Daniel, why didn't he kill me? Or at least scream at me?"

"Because he loves you."

"But I betrayed him."

"The mix of love and betrayal is unpredictable. It's potentially explosive, but you never know which way the path of destruction will go."

I thought about Ingrid. The affair between Arnold and Jane had been complicated: Ingrid had been gone for months, Arnold was lonely, Jane was unhappy in her marriage. . . . At a minimum, Arnold should have borne the brunt of some of Ingrid's bitterness. But she'd saved it all for Jane. As the story unfolded to me, she never mentioned Arnold's betrayal, just Jane's. I suppose you have to do that, to avoid your whole life crashing down around your ears.

If Steve had let the full weight of his wife's affair fall where it may, it would have ruined his marriage, put a strain on his relationship with Jordan, and left him a husk of a man. Directing all his anger at Daniel allowed him to have his rage, to express his rage, without giving up the rest of his life.

"It's amazing how people can compartmentalize their feelings. Be angry about a complicated situation, yet turn that anger laserlike against a single person."

"I suppose. I just wish . . ."

I nodded. I imagined Ama was wishing a lot of things at that moment.

"What are we going to do?" she asked, turning to watch her son holding a patient Daisy May in a headlock while Packer licked his ankles.

"You're a wonderful mother, Ama. And Steve is a wonderful father. You'll both figure out how to keep raising a happy child, even under these new circumstances."

"We've got that big house I can't afford. We bought it back when construction was booming, but Steve has been struggling to find contractor jobs for nearly a year. We were barely making ends meet with Steve's income, and I make way less than he does. Did."

"Obviously, our first effort to rent out the second floor of 801 Maple didn't end well, but the idea was strong. You could move your office inside and take in a renter for the mother-in-law apartment. I know it would mean giving up your adult space, but it would be worth it to take some of the pressure off your finances."

Ama sucked in a deep breath. It looked like something settled in her mind, like she had slipped into a new groove with some of the panic dissipating.

"That's a great idea," she said.

"And we're here to help you. This whole community loves you, Ama. You have a soft spot to land, I promise."

"Thank you, Izzy. I can't believe how kind you're being after me and my problems caused you so much pain. I know that I'll get through this, but I'm worried about Jordan. It's going to be hard for such a little boy to understand why Daddy doesn't live with us anymore."

I watched Jordan playing with the dogs.

"Tell you what," I said. "It's a little thing, but maybe it will help. Why don't you and Jordan take Daisy May? She needs a home, and I can't keep her forever. She seems to like you both, and Jordan obviously loves her. She might be a good friend for him in the weeks to come. What do you say?"

Ama watched her son hanging on Daisy May while she bathed his face in doggy kisses. A faint smile spread across her face.

"Deal."

I glanced at my watch. I could afford five more minutes before I had to go back to Trendy Tails to put the finishing touches on the wedding details. I sat quietly at Ama's side, my own head tilted back to enjoy the spring sunshine on my face, and listened to Jordan giggling with the dogs.

There'd been a dark cloud in Merryville for the past week, but it had finally dissipated. The sun was back.

* * *

The afternoon of the marriages of Ingrid and Harvey and Romeo and Pearl, everything went smooth as silk. Well, almost. Romeo managed to shake his collar around so his bow tie was on his back; one of the guests, a terrier of some sort, tried to hump Lucy's Wile E. Collie; and another critter—a cat named Toast— hacked up most of a piece of the reception cake onto Packer's plate . . . though that did not even slow him down as he gobbled up his food.

And, of course, Ama was not there. It was just too soon.

We still got plenty of pictures of the two ceremonies, with Xander Stephens demonstrating yet another talent by taking incredible candid and posed shots with every- one involved. I was particularly fond of one of Aunt Dolly, decked out in a fringed minidress, standing on her toes to whisper something in Richard Greene's ear. In the photo, he's bending down to meet her halfway, and a soft smile graces his lips. Someday, I thought, someday soon, we'd be planning another wedding.

Jane Porter and Knute Hammer attended the second wedding, but this time, Jane looked genuinely happy for Ingrid and Harvey. The fact that Jane and Knute had gone from social companions to hand-holders might have had something to do with that. In any event, Ingrid brought Harvey over to meet Jane, and the two women clutched each other's hands like they were old friends. I knew they'd still bicker over canasta, but the wound from Jane and Arnold's affair seemed to have healed.

All my friends had coupled up for the event. I could

hear Taffy's lilting laughter coming from the kitchen, where Ken was continuing to crank out delicious appetizers, and Jolly Nielson had pitched in to help Rena serve the array of pet treats she had concocted. Xander stood stoically at Lucy's side while she chatted up everyone and his brother.

I shared a glance with my sister Dru. Uncomfortable in social situations, she clung to Lucy's side, even though the two drove each other nuts. Even from across the room, I could see the glint of pain in Dru's eyes.

Poor Dru. She was so smart and so loving (in her own prickly way), but she'd had even less luck at love than I had. A few loser boyfriends who never lasted more than a couple of months, and long stretches of working overtime and helping my mother scrapbook. She deserved to find love, too. I made a mental note to make it a priority to play matchmaker.

All told, with the exception of my lonely sister, it seemed everyone was having a blast at the combo human/doggy wedding.

Pris approached me as Ingrid and Harvey were getting ready to cut the human cake. She wore Kiki—complete with lavender chiffon ruff—draped over her shoulder. At her initial approach, the cat could see me, and she lifted her head, laid her ears back, and began making a threatening *rooing* sound in the back of her throat. Pris sighed, and turned to angle her body so Kiki had a different view. Kiki relaxed immediately.

I swear, I'd broken hearts, broken rules, accused people of killing other people, yet no creature on the planet despised me as much as that fluffball cat.

"This went well," Pris said. "Not a single corpse."

"I agree. Any interest in making it a regular thing?"

Pris smiled. "We're supposed to be rivals, right?"

I smiled back. "I think there's room for a little rivalry between business partners."

She bobbed her head. "Fair enough. I'll start drafting a menu of services and prices so people can choose which of the wedding amenities they want." Pris had clearly been pondering the idea of a collaboration herself.

"Sounds good. Drop it by when you have a draft, and I'll go over it, adding in the services we can provide. And I'll start working on a plan for the cat show in July. We're really going to have to put our heads together to make that show a success."

She nodded.

"By the way, how on earth is Hal going to get the Soaring Eagles site turned into a convention center by July?"

Pris smiled, that sly mischievous smile of hers. "It didn't take much to convince Hal and the Japanese investors that a convention center would bring a better return than some crappy vacation condos. After all, they'd hardly made any progress at all. And I know Hal comes off as an idiot, but he didn't become the RV King without having a little get-up-and-go. If he's got a specific date in mind, he'll get the job done. He's crap as a husband, but a star as a businessman."

"What about the owls?"

She waved off my question. "We'll get those little

suckers moved, someplace farther north. They'll be fine."

I couldn't imagine moving all those tiny birds, but I knew Pris could always get what she wanted. If she wanted tiny birds moved across state, then they would be moved. I had a ridiculous image of little owls carrying little suitcases and getting on a little bus . . . with Pris at the wheel.

"Oh, and Izzy," Pris added, tilting back her head so she could stare down her nose at me, "no more accusing Hal of murder. That does me no good. It means attorney fees and a bad reputation that could slow down our cash flow from the RV lot. It's mistresses I'm looking for. You find me a mistress, and I'll buy you dinner."

She winked at me, and then glided back into the crowd.

Rena walked over and dumped Jinx in my arms. "Take this cat."

"Okay."

"She's big and pushy and won't leave me alone," she complained.

"She loves you," I countered.

"I know. But now that the cakes have been cut, and your sisters have cleared the chairs away, I need to take up my role as DJ and get this party started."

I lifted Jinx up so my shoulder bore most of her weight, and watched Rena scoot through the crowd to the speakers and MP3 player she'd set up on the shelf behind the front display cabinet. It was the same MP3 player she'd given Ingrid at our impromptu shower, so we were definitely in for some golden oldies.

In a moment the sweet whistles and lilting lyrics of "Wonderful, Wonderful" filled the room. All the guests grew silent and moved as one away from the center of the floor. Harvey swept Ingrid into his arms, and they began to glide across the hardwood like a couple of ballroom pros. Finally, in the last refrain, he dipped her gracefully, drawing a gasp from all present, followed by applause when she was once again upright.

The delight in their eyes was contagious. I stood against the back wall, absently stroking Jinx's head as she purred right into my ear. I sought out Sean on one side of the room, smiling as he listened to something his mother had to say. He glanced up and caught my gaze, his eyes haunted, dark, and deep. When he leaned back down to continue his conversation with his mother, my eyes traveled around the room until they landed on Jack Collins. His head was thrown back in laughter, presumably at the bickering between my sisters. He, too, caught me staring, and eyes sparkling with mirth, he winked at me.

Two men, so different from each other: the poet with a protective side, and the warrior with a sense of humor. And they both liked me, at least a little.

I smiled a smile just for myself.

Tonight, I thought, *tonight, I will dance.*

About the Author

Annie Knox doesn't commit—or solve—murders in her real life, but her passion for animals is one hundred percent true. She's also a devotee of eighties music, Asian horror films, and reality TV. While Annie is a native Buckeye and has called a half dozen states home, she and her husband now live a stone's throw from the courthouse square in a north Texas town in their very own crumbling historic house.

RECIPES

Rena's Enchilada Hotdish

Here's what you'll need before you begin assembly. Don't fret. There are lots of pieces, but they're all super-easy.

1 recipe enchilada sauce
1 recipe potato filling
1 recipe pinto bean filling
18 6-in. corn tortillas
12 oz. cheddar or Colby cheese (reduced-fat is fine)

Enchilada Sauce

¼ c. vegetable oil
2 Tbsp. flour
¼ c. chili powder
1½ c. vegetable broth
1 (15 oz.) can tomato sauce
¾ tsp. ground cumin
½ tsp. garlic powder

2 oz. Mexican chocolate*
salt to taste

Heat oil in a skillet over medium-high heat. Stir in flour, reduce heat to medium, and cook until lightly brown, stirring constantly to prevent flour from burning. Stir in chili powder, then slowly mix in veggie broth, getting rid of any lumps. Stir tomato sauce, cumin, and garlic powder into sauce and continue cooking over medium heat approximately 10 minutes, or until thickened slightly. Stir in chocolate to melt. Season to taste with salt.

*Mexican chocolate comes in tablets for making hot chocolate. Abuelita is the brand I get most often, but there are several. Look for them in the Hispanic or international food section of your grocery store. If you cannot find Mexican chocolate, you can use unsweetened chocolate and add a dash of cinnamon.

Potato Filling

   1 bag frozen, steam-in-bag russet or sweet potatoes,
       prepared as directed on the bag*
   10–16 oz. frozen chopped spinach, thawed (what-
       ever size your grocery store carries!)
   1 tsp. cumin
   ½ tsp. garlic powder
   dash of ground chipotle or cayenne

Press as much water out of the spinach as you can (put it in a colander and press with the back of a spoon).

Mash the potatoes with a fork or a potato masher; they don't need to be smooth, just mushed a bit. Stir in the spinach, cumin, garlic powder, and chipotle/cayenne.

*As an alternative, use 2 pounds russet or sweet potatoes, peeled, diced, and boiled in salted water until tender.

Pinto Bean Filling

    1 can pinto beans, drained and rinsed
    ½ c. fat-free refried beans
    1 (14.5 oz.) can diced tomatoes
    1 c. frozen corn
    1 tsp. chili powder
    ½ tsp. cumin
    ½ tsp. garlic powder

Mix all ingredients together in a small saucepan, mashing some of the beans with the back of a fork. Heat over medium-low flame until hot.

Assembly

Preheat oven to 350. Spray a 9" x 13" pan with a little nonstick spray and spread about ½ cup of enchilada sauce in the bottom. Arrange 6 corn tortillas on the bottom, tearing and overlapping so that the whole bottom of the pan is covered.
    Spread half the potato filling on the tortillas.
    Ladle half the pinto filling over the potatoes, and

drizzle about ½ cup of enchilada sauce over the pintos. Top with 4 ounces of shredded cheese.

Repeat with another 6 tortillas, the rest of the potatoes, the rest of the pintos, and another ½ cup of sauce. Top with the last 6 corn tortillas and ladle the rest of the sauce over the tortillas (so they are totally covered). Finally, top with remaining cheese.

Bake, uncovered, 30 minutes.

Read on for a sneak peek at the next novel
in Annie Knox's
Pet Boutique Mystery series,

COLLARED FOR MURDER

Coming from Obsidian in summer 2015.

Dee Dee Lahti stood in the middle of the North Woods Hotel Ballroom Number One, her aqua kaftan billowing in the intermittent wind from an oscillating fan, a patient Maine coon hanging from her hands by his armpits. Dee Dee cocked her frizzy head, scanning the hutches and velvet-draped cages lining the benches, her mouth—generously outlined in mauve—moving softly as she maintained a running conversation with herself.

Without warning, she lurched forward and down as though she were falling and began to shove the cat into a pink-leopard-print PVC hutch.

Pamela Rawlins had been chatting idly with me while I arranged my chiffon ruffs, hand-wrought collar dangles, and delicate clips sporting rhinestones, bows, and small beaded flowers on my vendor's table. When Dee Dee crammed that cat into the hutch, though, Pamela stiffened and sucked in a breath, her patrician nostrils pinching shut. "I swear, that woman has less sense than a box of hair," she muttered.

"Dee Dee, darling," she called. "You really must put the correct cat in the correct enclosure." She bit off her words like a Connecticut blue blood. Or a shark.

Dee Dee looked up, her features scrunched in confusion.

"You can't put Mr. Big in Charleston's hutch."

Dee Dee stared at the cat she had just deposited, then leaned in to look at the picture pinned to the outside of the enclosure. She stood straight and looked back at us, her expressive face slack, blank.

"You just put Mr. Big in Charleston's hutch. Mr. Big should be in his *own* enclosure." Nothing. "The cage with the red velvet drape."

"Are you sure?" Dee Dee said.

Pamela waited a beat. "Of course I'm sure, you . . ." She didn't finish the sentence, but even Dee Dee knew where it was going.

Pamela was correct that Dee Dee Lahti was a few walleye short of a fish fry. Still, the residents of Merryville were one big dysfunctional family. We could harbor grudges against one another, whisper spiteful things behind one another's backs, and, yes, even occasionally call Dee Dee Lahti "dingbat." To her face. But Pamela wasn't part of the family, and I felt a surge of protectiveness when she sniped at poor Dee Dee.

I'd seen Mr. Big and Charleston, both silver-and-white Maine coons. "Pamela," I said, "it's an easy mistake to make. The cats are almost identical."

Pamela angled her body to face me, her small, birdlike eyes utterly flat and emotionless. "*Almost* identical—but not identical. If she can't tell the difference between those silver markings, how will she tell the difference between two white Himalayans?"

I raised my chin a notch.

She allowed herself a tight shake of her head. "This is all highly irregular. I told Marsha Denham that we shouldn't vary from our usual procedures. The Midwestern Cat Fancier Organization's annual retreat has a pristine reputation precisely because we have rules, and we follow them to the letter. Our silver anniversary is not the time to start bending those rules."

I'd heard this argument a good dozen times since the MCFO had decided to host their twenty-fifth annual retreat in our little town. Marsha Denham, wife of the organization's president, Phillip Denham, had taken a shine to Pris Olson, owner of Prissy's Pretty Pets. While the official rules of the organization specified that the cats were not to be handled by anyone other than the owners and the judges, Marsha had arranged for Pris to provide grooming services in one corner of the ballroom. Pris had a crackerjack crew of groomers, but she'd taken pity on Dee Dee Lahti, who was unemployed and in constant misery thanks to her habitual-criminal husband. Dee Dee was not crackerjack.

Apparently sensing tension in the air, Pris ceased supervising her employees and floated our way. "Is there a problem?" she cooed. Pris sported a perfectly painted beauty-pageant smile and a practiced, formal politeness that screamed "privilege."

"Practiced" is the key word here. In public, Pris defined "Minnesota nice." The term refers to the smiling openness and back-bending helpfulness that most Minnesotans seem to exude from birth. Sometimes Minnesota nice is genuine. Sometimes it is not.

I knew firsthand that Pris's brilliant white smile could be a trap—a colorful Amazonian flower that promised sweet nectar before clamping shut around some poor, unsuspecting insect.

No one was safe. We were all insects in Pris's world.

Now Pris and Pamela faced each other like a photograph and its negative: both tall and elegantly slim, with hair pulled back in a sleek knot, clad in figure-skimming suits. But, whereas Pris wore baby pink that matched the soft blush of her porcelain skin, her eyes a pale, Nordic blue, her hair shining the color of fresh butter, Pamela's olive complexion reflected the onyx black of her hair, eyes, and suit.

I took a step back. Like all the McHale sisters, I'm tall and athletic. In theory, I could have snapped either of these model-thin women in half. In a physical fight, I would have had them licked. But this promised to be another round in the women's months-long battle of wills, and I was hopelessly outmatched.

Pamela's crimson lips curved into a smile. "Mrs. Olson—"

"Please, call me Pris."

A heartbeat of silence.

"Pris, your assistant over there"—she waved dismissively in Dee Dee's general direction—"was just returning Mr. Big to Charleston's hutch."

"Oh dear," Pris said. "Well, those two big boys really do look alike. And I did urge Mrs. McCoy to stay with us while we gave Mr. Big his blow-out. It's our policy, you know. But she was far too eager to start getting ready for tonight's festivities. I'm sure she didn't even consider the possibility that her cat would be confused for another, nearly identical cat . . . but that's what policies are for!" Pris concluded, her mouth settling into a wicked little smile.

Harsh red heat spread across Pamela's cheeks. I took another step back. Pamela was about to blow.

Still, when she rallied enough to speak, her voice remained as flat as Iowa. "You're absolutely correct. That's why we have policies. Like the policy of requiring owners to groom their own animals."

Pris raised a single shoulder. "Well. What are you gonna do?"

The phrase was as much a challenge as an expression of commiseration.

I held my breath, waiting for the fireworks, but they never came. The whole situation was defused when my aunt Dolly sashayed up, back from her tour around the ballroom. In typical Dolly style, she wore glittering stack-heeled sandals. Her tunic-length T-shirt, featuring a tropical sunset picked out in sequins, was draped over a pair of neon orange capris. No matter the occasion, Dolly dressed with flare.

"Ladies," she drawled, her head swiveling back and forth between Pris and Pamela as if she were watching a match at Wimbledon.

"Hello, Dolly," Pris responded.

Pamela extended a hand. "I don't think I've had the pleasure."

My aunt took the proffered hand and gave it two vigorous shakes. "My name is Dolly," she said, overenunciating each word. "Just like Pris said," she added helpfully.

The tendons in Pamela's neck stood out. "I'm Pamela Rawlins, co-coordinator of the show."

Dolly grinned. "Well, it's a mighty fine cat show. Not that I've ever been to a cat show before. But this is terrific. I've never seen so much drama packed into a single room.

"That lady over there," she said, turning to me and jerking her thumb in the direction of a heavyset woman in a cobalt blue tracksuit, "said that sometimes people poison other people's cats." She shivered in morbid delight.

I gasped. "Really?" I said, turning to Pamela for verification.

"Once," she Pamela emphatically. "That was six years ago. And the accused insists to this day that she accidentally dropped those acetaminophen tablets into Betsy Blue's bowl of kibble. Besides, she's been permanently banned from participating in our shows."

I was still reeling from the notion of a cat owner poisoning someone else's pet, when Dolly jumped in again. "That guy over in the corner," she said, indicating a balding gentleman wearing an argyle sweater-vest, despite the summer heat, "confided that one of the female judges slipped her room key under Toffee Boy when she returned him to his cage." The man glanced up, almost as though he knew we were talking about him, but then went back to methodically running a brush over the sleek coat of a caramel-colored Burmese.

Pamela appeared stricken. "That doesn't happen anymore."

"Ha! He said it happened last year."

Pamela quirked her head to the side, frowning in confusion. Her eyes scanned the room, pausing on each judging ring. Her lips moved slightly as she counted them off.

"Well," she finally said, "I assure you that I run a tight ship. There will be no such shenanigans under my watch."

Dolly shook her head. "I hate to tell you, Miss Pamela Rawlins, but I have a hunch that this week will be a hotbed of shenanigans. And my hunches are never wrong."

Also available from
Annie Knox

Paws for Murder
A Pet Boutique Mystery

Izzy McHale wants her new Trendy Tails Pet
Boutique in Merryville, Minnesota, to be the
height of canine couture and feline fashions. But
at the store's opening, it turns out it's a human
who's dressed to kill....

**"I'm already panting for the next book in
the series."**
—*New York Times* bestselling author
Miranda James

"Five paws up!"
—**Melissa Bourbon, author of**
A Killing Notion

Available wherever books are sold or at
penguin.com

facebook.com/TheCrimeSceneBooks

OM0139